Scandalous in Huntington Beach

by

Melody DeBlois

Love is a Beach, Book Three

Scandalous in Huntington Beach

Cover Art by *Diana Carlile*

The Wild Rose Press, Inc.
PO Box 708
Adams Basin, NY 14410-0708
Visit us at www.thewildrosepress.com

Publishing History
First Edition, 2025
Trade Paperback ISBN 978-1-5092-5948-9
Digital ISBN 978-1-5092-5949-6

Love is a Beach, Book Three
Published in the United States of America

Dedication

For my children, Craig, Kari, and Nicholas. Each of you is special in your own way, but I love you equally for who you are. Thank you for inspiring me every day and for being the light of my life.

Content Guidance

This novel explores aspects of mental health and suicide.

Chapter 1

Heavy rain allowed Bennett's anonymity as he kept his distance from the mourners beneath the tent at Rachel's graveside service, his emotions a tight ball in his chest. When the service concluded, the mourners dispersed through the soaked cemetery, leaving him alone at the casket with a woman. Her resemblance to Rachel drew him. Was this the older sister he'd heard about? She was shivering, so he edged closer to share his umbrella.

"I'm sorry for your loss," he said and, against his will, found himself intrigued by the face she directed at him—the faint, upward slant of her eyes, the slash of high cheekbones.

"Thank you for coming."

He caught himself then. "I'm Bennett Browning."

"I know," she responded with quiet emphasis. "You're the senate hopeful."

"And you must be Emma?"

She raised her chin, luminous mahogany hair blowing back from her exotic features. "Emma Kuan. Rachel and I had different fathers."

"Emma, like in the Jane Austen novel."

"Right," she said with a trace of sarcasm.

Had she detected his unease? Appalled, he dropped his stare to his wristwatch. "I've got an appointment with Child—"

"Child Protective Services," she finished for him after he'd tactlessly dropped that bombshell. "The judge awarded you Rachel's baby."

"I didn't know—before, I mean." The words came out gruffer than he intended. "I didn't know she was pregnant. She never said." And he believed she had taken precautions.

"If it makes you feel any better, my sister didn't tell me either."

He shrugged to hide his surprise. "Really?"

"I'd been trying to find her for months. She just up and vanished." Emma's eyes narrowed slightly. "You know anything about that?"

"I don't, but I wish I did. Rachel bailed the night I asked her to marry me." The memory tore at his insides. "I never heard from her again. It's been over a year."

Her expression softened as if she guessed how miserable he felt. She couldn't know how humiliated he'd been or how shocked and confused he felt now.

The arrival of the cemetery workers was Bennett's cue to cut the conversation short. "I better get a move on. Good meeting you, Emma."

At the sight of the casket lowering into the ground, she let out a strangled sob, and a sudden protectiveness swept over him. He couldn't desert her. A cold knot formed in his stomach as they perched a safe distance from the grave. The backhoe rolled in, and soon the shrill slice of shovelfuls of damp earth and the dull thuds were enough to make Emma waver as if she were about to faint. He folded his arm around her slender waist. Her scent made him think of the rain and the dark afternoon and how he might not forget this moment. Ever.

The crew finished their job. Emma laid the funeral

flowers on the grave, and he uttered a simple prayer. His doing so seemed somehow right—as right as anything could be after someone as young as Rachel died.

Her fast-paced life made him wonder about the sister he now accompanied under the shelter of his umbrella. They passed the grave markers shimmering in the rain, the palm trees swaying like charcoal question marks against the sky.

He said, "You have a ride?"

"I've got a rental."

"I'll walk you to your car."

And before he knew it, she was opening the door, sitting in the interior, and sliding those long, silky legs inside. "Thank you for being here."

"Well, guess this is goodbye. Have a—"

"A nice life?" She flashed him a bittersweet smile. "You'll soon be getting the baby—Madelynn Grace. That's her name—a pretty name too, don't you think?"

"Yes, I do." *And I'm scared shitless.* He didn't know what to do with an infant. He wasn't even sure what to think, especially about his raising a baby girl. Alone.

Emma was looking at him like she could read his thoughts. "I'm sure you'll be fine."

"Guess so." He'd never imagined fatherhood being a solitary undertaking. His previous plans had included a woman with beliefs that matched his own. A partner who would stand by him and help him when he needed it most. Like now.

"Is something wrong?" she asked.

"I was just thinking." A sense of urgency drove him. "You want to meet the baby?"

"What?"

"After all, you are her aunt."

"I am." She bit her full bottom lip.

"And you're here in town." He experienced a flood of reckless abandonment that was so unlike him. "Tomorrow, you'll most likely be back in San Francisco."

"I will."

He didn't want to take Rachel's sister home with him. But more than that, he wanted to hold her again, lessen her pain and his own—wrong on every level.

Still, he couldn't tear himself away from her.

"You could follow me," he said. "Unless you don't want to see Madelynn."

A sheen glistened in Emma's eyes. "I can't think of anything I'd like more."

****

The penthouse boasted lots of chrome, black leather, framed art, and a panoramic window that looked out on the skyscrapers in downtown Los Angeles. To Emma, the setting reflected a bachelor pad—almost.

Traces of the safety measures told a different story. Unused outlets were covered, cords concealed, and windows reinforced with latches. Bennett had done his best to prepare for his daughter. The only drawback, just one bedroom.

He nodded as if aware of her observation. "The judge rushed the adoption process. I'm happy about that, believe me." He rubbed the back of his neck. "But with the campaign and all, I haven't the time to hunt for more suitable living arrangements."

"I understand." And she did. He'd been born privileged, unlike her. But had a positive paternity test guilted him into taking on such a life-altering responsibility?

He had that do-gooder thing going for him—she'd give him that. His kindness at her sister's burial service wasn't lost on her. She'd noticed, too, that he was handsome, but he seemed unaware of it. His dark hair went all curly in the rain, and his sultry brown eyes were at once sympathetic and then suddenly full of something she couldn't quite name.

She respected him for all he'd done for LA's troubled youth. He'd built a rec center, organized youth sports teams, and for a short time practiced law—working mostly pro bono. Before he became a senatorial nominee, he'd mentored small businesses. True, his accomplishments impressed her. Who wouldn't be? But all this didn't mean he welcomed becoming a single dad.

Then, unexpectedly, he pulled something from a shopping bag.

"Aww," she couldn't help but say at the sight of the snuggly teddy bear.

"I had a moment this morning and saw this in a shop window." A helpless expression spread over his face. "Do you think Madelynn will like it?"

Emma's chest felt as if it would burst. Still, she'd just composed herself when someone knocked at the door. A thick-figured woman introduced herself as Riley Morgan while trying to contain the squirming baby in her arms.

Emma's heart melted at the sight of her niece. Because of their dire living conditions, Emma, now nearing the end of her twenties, had mothered her sister, who'd been four years younger.

She clamped a hand over her mouth. Fingers that reminded Emma of her sister's extended from the sleeves of a ruffly pink dress. Eyes, the same chocolate brown as her daddy's, thickly lashed and alert, took in her new surroundings, her thumb in her mouth.

Bennett made the introductions.

Riley offered condolences while her stare roamed the apartment as if pleased at all she saw. "I heard you passed the inspection with flying colors. I can see why."

"I merely followed the guidelines CPS gave me," Bennett said. "I've raised the kitchen detergents to a top shelf and added safety latches to all the drawers and cabinets. I've gotten the baby food and the formula and have enough diapers to last months. I know my apartment is too small to raise Madelynn, but I'm looking for a better place—bigger, a property with a good-sized yard, maybe a dog or a cat..."

He was rambling. Were his nerves getting the best of him? After all, his life was about to change drastically.

"You were given short notice," Riley said. "Even under the circumstances, you've managed to childproof your residence. Sadly, this isn't always the case. If you only knew the things I witness on a daily basis, you'd add child endangerment to the issues you plan to address if you win the election."

Emma suspected this caseworker saw more than her share of neglect and cruelty. What she witnessed had probably hardened her—and thank God for that. If only she'd been around when Emma and her sister were little, then Rachel might still be alive.

"Would you like to hold your daughter?" Riley asked Bennett.

When he appeared unable to move, Emma stretched her arms toward the baby. "May I take my niece for a few moments? I'll be leaving soon and might not get another chance."

Riley handed over the infant, who cuddled her small, warm body against Emma's chest and gazed up at her. As Emma inhaled the sweet baby scent, she felt a bond as strong as when she'd first held Rach all those years ago.

"Looks like you're a natural." The lines on Bennett's forehead relaxed a little.

"Well." Riley brushed her hands together. "I'll be on my way for now but will return for a follow-up visit in a few days. All of Madelynn's important papers are in the folder inside her diaper bag. If you have any questions, don't hesitate to contact me. You have my number."

After Riley left, Bennett let out an audible breath. "Thank you. I don't know what I would have done if you hadn't covered for me. I—" He appeared to see Madelynn for the first time, and the vulnerability in his expression made him even more appealing.

"Hi there, baby," he cooed. "I'm your daddy."

Emma had to speak up. "Please don't think I'm being pushy—well, maybe I am. But I must ask. Are you planning on taking Madelynn on the campaign trail with you?"

"Of course not."

"Then what will you do with her?"

"I'll hire a live-in nanny." He made a face as though the idea wasn't to his liking.

"You don't have any in mind?"

He crossed over to the desk and held up several resumés. "There's been no time to go through these. I'm at my wit's end here."

He sounded desperate, and any of Emma's previous

reproach dissolved. "Tell you what. I'll care for her until you find someone more qualified to take my place."

"I can't let you do that. You've already got a job—your sister told me."

"They can do without me for a few days."

"I appreciate your offer but—"

"Look, it's plain to see you need help." She laid her cheek over Madelynn's bonneted head. "I'll bet you've never even changed a diaper."

His shamefaced shrug told it all. "I watched an online video."

"Not good enough," she said gently. "Let me be clear. The last thing I want is for my niece to end up in the foster care system."

"I hear you." He paused with a sigh. "All right, I concede. Just know I'll work on getting a replacement for you ASAP. In the meantime, my humble abode is yours. Make yourself comfortable, and I'll help in any way I can."

Emma slipped off Madelynn's bonnet, and burnished copper tendrils popped up around her head. "Would you look at her? What a surprise."

"I'm told my mother's hair was curly," he said wistfully.

Madelynn peeked in the spaces between her spread fingers at her daddy and broke into a gummy grin.

"And those dimples…" He smiled and tapped his cheeks. "See what I mean?"

"You're dimpled too. Will wonders never cease?"

Emma laughed for the first time since learning about her sister's death, and Bennett joined in, their laughter filling the apartment. They were like two people who met at a party and were attracted to each other. Only the opposite was true. She was the nanny. She mustn't forget Bennett had loved her sister. Because of it, he was being amiable to Emma. Allowing her a position she probably otherwise wouldn't have gotten.

Caring for her niece was akin to getting a second chance with Rachel.

Chapter 2

"Sure," Bennett said a few seconds later when Emma asked if he wanted to hold his daughter. He'd always liked children but never held one so young. He looked around for somewhere to sit. Not a stick of furniture was out of place, but before today, he'd been the only resident—a bachelor who'd lived by himself for far too long.

Now it seemed his life was just beginning.

Emma held up the little bundle. "Ready, Mr. Browning?"

He lifted his brows. "Mr. Browning?"

"It's imperative that we keep our relationship on a professional level."

He'd begun to feel a camaraderie for her, which made him think of her on a first-name basis, but she was right, of course. She'd been nice enough to step up to the plate, and he felt lucky to have her.

Conceding, he raised his hands. "Whatever you say."

"Perfect." Emma moistened her full, sexy-as-hell lips. "All set?"

He stripped off his black suit jacket, rolled up his shirt sleeves, and then sat on a hard-back chair, all at once worried. "I won't break her, will I?"

"Just hold your arms out facing upward."

"Whatever works, Ms. Kuan." He repositioned

10

himself on the stiff cushion, feet flat, back as straight as if he were about to rise to a podium. "How's this?"

"Relax." She slanted a critical look at him. "She'll feel your anxiety."

He was having a hard time believing any of this was real. But it was, and his baby girl would depend on him for everything. He leaned against the chair and did what Emma told him. "Better?"

She nodded and handed over the wiggly Madelynn Grace. Bennett tried his hardest to hold on, afraid he'd drop her. With that in mind, he let Emma readjust his position with a nudge of his arms that had been too far apart and a lift of his right elbow to tilt her head a little. He intuitively lowered his face and sweet-talked the baby. In turn, she blew bubbles at him.

"I think she likes me." He allowed her to poke him in the nose.

"Looks that way."

His heart swelled. "I promise to give you the best life I can."

When he glanced up, all smiles, he noted Emma's quivering lower lip. Was she thinking of Rachel? Something in the hunch of her shoulders and lowered chin made him realize he knew so little about her.

She cleared her throat. "I'll just get into your fridge if you don't mind."

"Let's hope there are enough supplies to get us through the night." His words induced second thoughts. What if he had to leave for the market? Would Emma kidnap her niece? Awareness set in that, in a moment of duress, he'd put a woman he didn't know in charge of his daughter. He usually studied every angle before making a decision.

"There's more than enough," she said. "I'm going to warm a bottle."

"Good idea."

He'd let Rachel into his heart, and she hadn't been straight with him. She'd lied about her motives and about loving him. He hadn't been with a woman since. Had he made a hasty mistake by trusting Emma? Because he needed a nanny, not to mention his rapport with her, had he acted out of desperation?

She returned minutes later. "Would you like to do the honors, Mr. Browning?"

"I think I'll sit this one out, Ms. Kuan. But I'll take notes."

He leaned back, sizing up his recent hire and resisting the urge to glance at her legs again. He'd always considered himself a keen judge of character. That was…before Rachel.

Emma tested the temperature of the milk on her wrist. She moved in so near to him that he felt a magnetism he couldn't deny.

"Here you are, little one." She cocooned Madelynn in the small blanket she'd retrieved from the diaper bag and sat in front of the window.

The sun had come out and beamed down from the clouds, glazing the woman and the baby in a soft yellow. Emma's face had a tender look. Madelynn made little sucking noises as she drank, and her eyelids gradually closed.

Bennett's mother had died giving him life, and a succession of nannies followed. He'd always resented them, but now he needed one to care for his daughter.

He had shut off his phone before the burial service and hadn't turned on the ringer again. For the first time, he thought he should check the voicemails and texts from his staff members. But he refrained, unable to take his attention off the scene playing out right before his eyes.

He hadn't felt this calm in…he couldn't remember when. Maybe never. He hadn't witnessed anything as amazing as Emma tending to the baby. His head dizzied, and his eyes blurred with the marvel of it.

When the bottle was empty and Madelynn had fallen asleep, Emma said, "We should put her on your bed."

He sobered. "We need to talk, you and I."

****

Was Emma about to get sacked before she'd begun? The severity of Bennett's tone had shaken her. Perhaps he'd somehow discovered she hadn't been entirely honest with him.

True enough that she'd cared for her little sister, but she hadn't confessed they'd been homeless and on the streets in a part of the city where no one ventured at night—or during the day, for that matter. Emma hadn't said she'd been seven when all the trouble started, and Rachel had only been three.

Her sister had refused to mention their past and urged Emma to keep it secret. To all those who knew her, Rachel was born into wealth. Plus, Bennett couldn't have discovered anything on the internet. Unless. If he had read any of Emma's articles, he might have guessed her crusade against child abuse was personal.

With all this running through her mind, when Bennett started their talk with, "I want you to sleep in my bed," she had to readjust her thoughts.

"Excuse me?"

"For the baby's sake. I'll crash on the couch since you know what you're doing, and I have much to learn."

"I can't take your bed, Mr. Browning."

He was already pulling fresh linens from a closet. She followed him into his bedroom, done in blacks, grays, and shades of brown. Then she noticed something totally out of place.

"A baby crib with pink blankets and frilly lace." And so incredulously feminine among the masculine design that something inside Emma broke. She gulped hard to ward off the flood of emotion.

"You don't like it? Your sister said you were a women's advocate. You think it's too gender specific?"

"Because of the color? I love pink. That's not it." She swallowed. "To me, this crib signifies someone who has rearranged his dreams to include a new reality. That's not easy."

"Thank you." He pulled back the blanket. "I'm trying."

"I can see that." Emma carefully placed Madelynn on her back.

While she napped, Bennett and Emma replaced the sheets on the king-sized mattress. They were doing what they needed to make it through the night—keeping it professional. She could handle whatever came her way with proficiency.

He studied her as if cataloging her with his eyes. "Are you thinking of Rachel?"

"You wanted to talk." Her sister was always on her mind, but she couldn't say this without losing it again. "Was it merely about where I'd lay my head?"

"No." His voice dropped in volume. "Would you care for a drink?"

"Water would be great, thank you."

Minutes later, as they sat at the table in the kitchen,

Bennett's left eyebrow rose a fraction. "I plan to pay you three times what you're making at the magazine."

She wet her lips but couldn't address the subject. Yes, she could negotiate and get Bennett to pay her a considerable salary. Hardly anything pleased her as much as building up her bank account. After all, she'd lived with the deep-seated fear she would somehow lose everything and end up homeless again. But helping out here had been her idea. At the end of the day, no price tag was high enough for being able to sleep with her decisions.

"There's no need to triple my income," she said. "I'll email you my last pay stub."

He shifted his position in the chair. "To show my appreciation, will you allow me to make you dinner?"

"You know how to cook?"

"I grill a mean cheese sandwich, and there's the tomato soup."

"From a can?"

"You've got it. Unless you prefer takeout."

"Whenever I felt sick or down in the dumps, my mother made me tomato soup—a simple remedy that worked wonders." Her mother had been a loving mom until she wasn't. "I'll go along with your menu choice if you allow me to help."

"You're my guest." He pulled ingredients from the fridge.

"No, I'm your employee." She opened a cabinet. "If I am going to work for you, no matter if it's for a few days or a month, I need to know where things are."

"Why? We can't stay here. The apartment's too small, and you heard the ole battleax. She's coming back to 'check' on us."

15

"Riley Morgan's just doing her job." Emma set the table with ivory plates and stainless-steel utensils. "She has to be tough."

He buttered the bread. "Sounds like you've had firsthand experience."

She'd allow some of the truth as she heated the soup on the stove. "I've published several pieces on the subject. If you'd read them, you would know my stand on rotten parenting."

"How could I? Until a few hours ago, I barely knew you existed, Ms. Kuan."

The huskiness in how he said her last name was cynical and sexy.

"Because you were dating my sister, I studied your bio."

His eyes widened with what could pass for amusement. "What did you discover?"

She poured the steaming soup into bowls. "You've been a business advisor and have guided small firms along the way, advising them on everything from leasing or buying a property to arranging tax deductions. Easy for you since you've always had money."

"Do I hear a note of sarcasm?"

"Maybe. But I must admit you've devoted much of your time to organizing neighborhood youth programs, and now you hope to serve as a California senator."

"Right." He sighed, his brow heavy.

"Running for office is your goal, isn't it?"

His upper lip tightened. "Sure."

"Why do I suspect you're not being entirely honest?"

His shoulders sank. "Perceptive, aren't you? Let's just say I don't really know what I'm going to do now."

16

"Maybe you're considering your options."

"Hmm, true enough." Without taking his gaze off her, he sat across from her at the table. "Is there anything I should know about you?"

His question gave her the opening she'd been waiting for since she'd noted that the apartment wasn't conducive to child-rearing.

She hesitated, not for effect but to organize her thoughts. She took a bite of the sandwich and rolled the taste around in her mouth, then savored the tartness of the soup and enjoyed the warmth it created after swallowing. Only then did she feel pacified and confident enough to pursue the touchy subject.

"I have a business proposition, Mr. Browning, that should appeal to you."

"I'm all ears."

"My sister named me as the beneficiary of the assets she'd inherited from her father on his death. Because she, to put it bluntly, blew through her fortune, the only property left is a bed-and-breakfast in Huntington Beach. The Nightingale was where we hung out together."

"So this B&B's very special to you?"

"It is." Emma swallowed some water. "The place has been closed for the past year. I don't know why, but I suspect my sister's problems prevented her from handling its upkeep. I'd planned to look at The Nightingale tomorrow before my flight. I didn't want to sell it but thought I had no choice."

"Tell me more about it."

"It's a house. Six bedrooms. A great big kitchen. And it's oceanfront."

"That means no smog and a calm, pleasant atmosphere." He set his soupspoon down in a

17

contemplative silence. "Ms. Kuan, are you thinking the same thing I am?"

"It would be a great place to raise Madelynn." She met his stare with hesitation. "It's about a forty-five-minute drive to LA. Will that be a problem for you?"

"It'll give me time to conduct business and plan my day."

His positivity was unexpected and accommodating. Emma's skin had turned all goose pimply, so she rose to clear the dishes.

All too soon, he came up behind her. "This business deal—you want me to buy the bed-and-breakfast from you?"

"No, that's not it." She ran her plate under the hot water. "The Nightingale probably needs some work. I imagine it's been a while since the walls have seen a paintbrush."

"I can help with that." He got his phone and clicked on his calendar. "Tomorrow's Sunday. I can catch tonight's church service. That leaves my morning free."

"Good," she said but stopped before adding, "Then it's a date."

Chapter 3

Bennett listened from his position on the couch. Not hearing if the baby was still breathing made him uneasy. What could he do? Charge inside the bedroom? Not an option. But maybe— He almost groaned aloud. His uncertainty was killing him.

Then, suddenly, Madelynn's cries drifted from the bedroom. Before he knew it, Emma streamed past him with the infant in her arms. He darted after them, discovering them in the kitchen, and tried to look as if he'd been asleep. He yawned, rubbing his eyes with his fists so Emma wouldn't guess he'd been sitting there for hours staring at their closed door.

"I tried not to wake you," she said.

He held out his hands, and she passed him the baby. "No problem."

Emma was wearing some white, silk, lacy number. He pictured a women's libber in a cotton number buttoned up to the neck. Stereotypical on his part. He wasn't proud of himself. His only excuse was he'd grown up with a single dad and no women around to speak of.

"Can I help? Maybe give Madelynn her bottle so you can rest?"

"No. You go back to sleep. You must be tired."

The hell if he was. "I'm used to grabbing sleep when I can. Sometimes, my political conventions are all-nighters. You learn pretty quick when to grab a little shut-eye."

"I'll bet." She tested the bottle, and as she drew near to take the baby, her hair still smelled of rainwater. "But ensuring the baby gets fed is part of my job description."

The view from the window had the city lights twinkling in their tall buildings, with the moon and stars smiling down. Emma tending to the baby against that setting brought back the serenity he'd known earlier, but when she began to yawn, he tapped her shoulder.

She looked up at him. "What is it?"

"You go on to bed, and I'll take over. After Madelynn's asleep, I'll put her in her crib."

"I can't let you do that. It wouldn't be right."

"Listen, I'm appealing to you as a father." *A father.* He unexpectedly liked that word for himself, and his change of heart was almost too much to comprehend.

"When you put it that way," she said, yawning, "how can I refuse?"

Emma waited for him to take her place, and then she left him, but by now, he was too busy to have any qualms about his being competent enough to care for his baby. He was already bringing Madelynn to his chest and patting her back. Soon, she let out a big whopper of a burp.

"Whoa." He resumed feeding her the rest of her bottle.

Concern over how to get Madelynn back to sleep worried him. He couldn't remain in the chair. He might conk out and lose his grip on her. The couch wasn't safe. He considered himself an innovative man. If he thought this through, a solution would surface. Eventually, one did. He found a spare comforter in the linen closet and spread it on the rug.

Then he lay on his back and propped the baby on his chest, and she immediately drew in her tiny legs and arms until she formed a little ball. *She feels secure.* He rolled his body back and forth until she fell sound asleep. And so did he.

****

Emma woke to find the baby missing from the crib, and her stomach lurched. Had Bennett experienced second thoughts and taken off with Madelynn? "Stop it," she told herself, shoving her feet into running shoes and dressing in the shorts and blouse from her suitcase. She'd distrusted men since childhood. Early traumas had left her thinking the worst and kicking herself for it. It wasn't fair. Down deep, she knew this, but that hadn't kept her from studying martial arts and learning how to defend herself if needed.

She stormed out of the bedroom with her arms pumping, hair gathered up high on the crown in a scrunchy to get it off her neck. Not till she came to the area carpet in front of the couch did she freeze in her tracks. Madelynn lay curled up in the fetal position on her daddy's chest. A cry of relief broke from Emma's lips.

The baby raised her head and lifted herself onto her forearms.

Emma lowered to a squat. "Hey, lovebug."

Madelynn smiled, kicked, and stretched her legs, her chest bobbing in delight. Bennett's eyelids flew open, and he sat cross-legged with his daughter on his lap.

"Good morning." Emma couldn't help the relief that flooded through her.

His stare seemed to take her in all at once. "Wow,

21

Ms. Kuan, you…" He stalled as if he'd deemed what he'd been about to say inappropriate. "You look…hungry. Are you?"

The two banded together to feed Madelynn her applesauce and rice cereal. The procedure would have been simple if no baby was on board, making it impossible to get even a sip of coffee. They got Madelynn fed, bathed, dressed, and ready to go. Was this the first time Bennett had left his apartment in such utter chaos?

He ducked inside his four-door CUV with Madelynn's new car seat. He struggled to get it secured in the back and hemmed and hawed. While he connected one strap to another with no success, Emma studied the back of him with approval. He had paired an oxford shirt with worn jeans. He kept himself fit. Something about his determination to figure out the car seat impressed her. Although he resurfaced from the inside, scratching his head, she guessed he wouldn't quit until he conquered his goal. She liked that about him.

A bonus was when he admitted, "I need help."

His comment proved he thought of her on an equal ground. Nothing to her could make a man as attractive. "All right. Let me try. It can't be that hard."

She leaned into the back seat, thinking she'd ace the problem in seconds. When that didn't happen, she turned and spied Bennett raking a suggestive gaze over her. Despite everything, her body heated with unfamiliar pleasure.

He lowered his expressive brown eyes, bouncing the baby on his hip while reaching for his phone. "Let's get a video. We're both college graduates. This shouldn't be so difficult."

"No, it shouldn't."

Perhaps their minds just weren't on the task at hand.

Minutes later, with things settled, they were cruising down the Pacific Coast Highway like a family on vacation. While Madelynn babbled from the back seat and Bennett talked on his car phone, she took in the sights—the sunlit ocean after the rain, the aromatic scent of eucalyptus and pine, the pale-blue skies, and glittering mountains on the other side.

Huntington Beach was super laid-back and cozy. Folks came here to relax, catch some rays, and surf. Before this, Emma had always thought of nothing but spending time with her sister. The enormity of what she was doing now hit her. She was moving in with Bennett Browning, who was running for the US Senate while striving to bring up a baby.

Then she noticed his knuckles white on the steering wheel as he worked things out with his staff. His sunglasses hid the shadows she'd spotted this morning under his eyes, and his voice held a slightly manic sound as he said he was taking the day off for personal matters. He was doing the best he could, she realized. She was too. Would it be enough?

****

"Maybe coming here this soon wasn't a good idea," Bennett said when Emma burst into sobs after entering The Nightingale.

She waved a dismissive hand. "Give me a minute, please."

She buried her chin in Madelynn's curls and looked around while Bennett opened windows to rid the house of its musty odor. Soon, beach noises drifted in, waves crashing on the shore while seagulls and other birds

Bennett didn't know the names of serenaded.

"I could get used to this," he said. "The floors could use a sander and the walls a fresh coat of paint, but I'm fond of all the Chinese imports. I'd have thought there'd be a nautical theme like every other lodge on the coast."

"Rachel's father hired a decorator." Her voice steadied as she lowered Madelynn to the couch to change her diaper. "Anything my sister ever wanted, he got her." She said this grudgingly.

Because he still had questions, he asked, "Are you insinuating Rach was a poor little rich girl?"

"She never got what she really wanted from him."

"And what was that?"

"Love—unconditional."

Bennett had found out about Rachel's other side after she disappeared. He'd dodged a bullet, but Emma didn't seem to be functioning well. Had she been close to her sister?

"The view's spectacular, but why the Eastern influence?" he asked, still fishing for answers while picking up his freshly diapered daughter.

"Rachel lived with us in Chinatown until she was in her teens. She was happiest there. Consequently, she was partial to Asian design."

He turned to find Emma in the lobby, unlocking a curio cabinet. She took out a small globe that housed a cherry tree within it. When she shook the glass ball, iridescent glitter flew, dancing like snow. Her sad expression touched him. He longed to comfort her.

"I've had this since I was little," she said as if that explained everything. "Rachel and I used to listen to it whenever we were blue."

His throat had gone tight with an aching soreness.

He didn't have a sister, no brother—just him and his dad. If he had his way, his daughter would grow up with siblings.

Emma was winding the clockwork, and the base tinkled in a tune that brought to mind the cosmic energy in the music he'd heard on his travels to the Far East.

"Has this globe a special meaning?" he asked.

She managed a choked laugh. "Is it that obvious?"

"They say every object tells a story."

"Yes, well, maybe I'll fill you in when we aren't so busy." She quickly returned the translucent sphere to the cabinet. "Do you want to see the house?"

"Sure."

Most of the furniture was the same up the sweeping staircase as below—carved ebony, satin embroidered in gold thread, and rich Oriental rugs. Oversized windows showed off killer views of the Pacific. This structure interested him. He sensed in Emma a passion in her core for The Nightingale, which fascinated him even more.

"I'm with you on this." He thought past the beauty to the commercial aspect.

"Then let's get to it, Mr. Browning."

They were back to business as usual, and he welcomed it. He didn't go for sharing feelings, and between yesterday and today, he'd had his fill of emotional roller coasters.

First thing on the agenda, he phoned the crew delivering Madelynn's furniture and supplies, making sure they would arrive at The Nightingale by late afternoon. Next, they ducked out for groceries to stock the kitchen, then detoured to an open-air market to buy produce.

Emma inhaling a cluster of grapes intrigued him.

For a second, he imagined her feeding him like some earth mother—filling those places inside him that were always hungry. Just then, he longed for her touch...not acceptable thoughts.

To maintain a professional alliance, he'd have to quit deluding himself with intoxicating images of the nanny. Besides, she was only helping out because of her sister and Madelynn. He closed his eyes, and when he opened them, he spied Emma holding a fig in her hand as if to gauge the weight of it.

She sent him a shy smile. "You like figs?"

"You...can...cook?" His tongue, so used to public speaking, stumbled.

"My auntie taught me. Then, too, there was that summer I took off from college to attend culinary classes in Shanghai."

"And I made you a cheese sandwich."

The corners of her mouth turned up. "The best I've ever had."

"Would you mind doing dinner tonight?"

She winked at him, actually winked. "I'm all over it."

No wonder fruit excited her. All Bennett could do was follow behind, Madelynn in tow, his senses heightened. He smelled the aroma of thyme and rosemary from the plant stand and caught sight of water droplets sparkling from the lettuce Emma had chosen.

He was coupled with her as she talked to the farmers about their crops. He'd pored over volumes about the water shortage in Orange County, but this one-on-one contact turned into a true asset. He was enjoying himself—on a holiday and networking with prospective voters. He'd gotten so caught up in the moment he temporarily forgot he'd assumed a brand-new role that might come off as questionable.

Then Emma grabbed his arm and pointed to a guy with a cell-phone camera. "Look."

"Let's get out of here."

How would he present his new lifestyle to the press? Hell, he hadn't thought this through. Twenty applicants hoped to be voted to their party in the primaries come June. Not that far into the campaign, and the dirt had already begun to fly. Did Bennett want to subject his daughter to idle gossip? He studied the baby he had fathered, realizing that, although he'd met her less than twenty-four hours ago, he would do anything to keep her from harm.

Chapter 4

When Bennett told Emma he had to attend a fundraiser in San Francisco the next day, she jumped at the chance to accompany him on the flight. Doing so allowed her to stop at home and bring her family up to date, which she'd been putting off.

After the plane landed, they rented a car. Those deep-throated foghorns moaned, and the bridge lights strung across the Bay Bridge glimmered in the misty dawn. Iron gates across storefronts clanged open, and merchants set out crates of fish and produce, turning sidewalks into vegetable bazaars that would later be crowded with shoppers.

Bennett stopped at a red light. "Would you look at the duck and pork hanging in the meat shop window?"

Emma straightened her shoulders with pride. "Some of the best cuisine in the world comes from here." Her stomach rumbled, and that made her long for home. "You should taste my auntie's cooking."

"Your auntie...you mentioned her before." A curious quality hung in his tone. "Must be your dad's sister. Was she at the graveside?"

"You couldn't miss her." What harm would it be to open up a little? He'd meet her soon anyway. "She's elegant and straightforward. Junie Moon, as my sister calls—called her. The mayor of Chinatown—that's how the locals describe her."

"Why is that?"

"If there's a problem from cleaning up the litter on the streets to finding a lost bicycle, she's your woman. Add to it, she teaches school. This superstar raised me."

"Of course she did," he said with an amused smile. "At what age did she adopt you?"

"Nine, and my sister was five. My auntie took in renters and gave them a place where they belonged. She gave all of us stability."

"She lucked out with you and Rach."

"Don't know about that," Emma said, recalling how rebellious she'd been. "My sister and I didn't fit in because I look more white than Asian, and Rachel was straight-up Caucasian."

"That had to be tough. So your aunt runs a boarding house?"

"She did, but the boarders have lived there so long they've become permanent fixtures."

He glanced down at his lap when they stopped again at another intersection. "I'm sure they think of me as the jerk who knocked up your sister."

"They don't know that Rachel never told you about the baby."

His brows drew together. "I could have been there for her during her pregnancy. Maybe if she'd let me, she wouldn't have felt so alone and desperate. Who knows? Maybe the outcome would have been different."

Emma felt her emotions getting the best of her, so she wasted no time pointing out a house in the middle of the block. "None of this is easy. But I'll clear things up, so come inside when you return."

He nodded and parked at the curb. Then he retrieved his daughter from the back seat and settled her in

Emma's arms. She watched the way his eyes darkened in a frown.

"Don't worry," Emma said, trying to sound confident.

He kissed Madelynn's forehead. "Bye-bye, princess." He nodded to Emma. "Ms. Kuan."

She shoved a key into the lock in an iron gate, then climbed the enclosed steps. Her heart was clamoring so hard against her chest it hurt. What if she couldn't get everyone to understand why she'd moved in with the supposed enemy?

When June opened the door and looked at Madelynn sleeping peacefully, all the blood drained from her face. "You've got the baby."

"Yes," Emma whispered, and those inside crowded at the entrance. Emma lowered the infant in her arms like an offering to the gods.

As if on cue, Madelynn awoke, boxing the air with her teensy fists, the receiving blanket that had encased her loosening. Her chestnut eyes observed the group hovering over her, and she broke into a sob.

June gently plucked the baby from Emma, sat in the rocking chair inside the house, and took the bottle Emma had warmed up in the kitchen.

"There you go, little one," June said. "We're going to take good care of you."

"I want to…" Emma got all choked up.

To her left, Eddie Wong had lowered his baseball cap to his chest so that his short, cropped gray hair shone in the light from a floor lamp. He smiled as he pointed to snapshots of a very young Rachel on the mantel and nodded vigorously. Yes, the baby did resemble her, which didn't surprise Emma, but her throat ached just the same.

To Emma's right, Rai expressed herself with a face full of joy. "Baby's so sweet." Having lost her hearing in her thirties, Rai spoke almost clearly but mostly Cantonese.

The wheels in Alexis Nathan's brain were clearly spinning a poem he'd later recite at the local bookstores. People read his poetry the world over. Madam, as he referred to June, had sponsored him in Tamil Nadu until he could make it on his own.

Emma sank to the chair next to the Buddha statue where, on a table, incense emitted the sweet smokey vapor she associated with home.

"May I present Madelynn Grace," she said to Alexis Nathan.

Emma always felt she had to dress up her talk in the poet's presence. His speech, so formal it just missed being absurd, reflected Britain's long-ago influence in India. His eyes appeared so large and inquisitive that Emma wanted to blindfold him.

"There has been an arranged marriage between you and the politician?" he asked, having arrived only yesterday after being in his native country for three months.

"No." Emma laughed nervously. "Nothing like that."

Eddie angled his head. "You kidnapped the baby?"

"God, no." She couldn't get the words out fast enough.

Rai's hands signed, "The politician gave her to you?"

Swallowing, Emma said, "I'm the nanny."

"Emma, what have you done?" June asked, the

tension in the room immediately mounting. "Tell me you didn't quit your job."

"Not yet. I've got to call my boss. I'm due back tomorrow. I won't be there. I need more time off so that I can help out until Bennett can get someone else."

A vein in June's forehead stood out. "How could you do this? Move in with…"

"A dishonorable man," Eddie finished for her.

And Alexis Nathan added, "Such a dishonorable man, he should be court-martialed."

To which Rai nodded so vigorously that her powder puff of a wig nearly fell off her head.

Emma met everyone's antagonism with a frown. "Rachel didn't tell Bennett she was pregnant. She left and never contacted him, which is what she did to all of us."

They looked glum but nodded.

"I don't know why she did it. She must have had her reasons, but it's not Bennett's fault. He's trying to be a good father but doesn't know what he's doing. I couldn't just stand by when my niece was involved. I'd hoped all of you would understand."

June raised the baby to her shoulder and patted her back. "But you've got your job."

"That's true. Still, I can't be in two places at once." She yanked out her phone. "I should call right now. Would you watch Madelynn for a few minutes?"

Emma could cross off dealing with her family—almost. Not that they'd welcome Bennett with open arms, but they would be civil to him. She went upstairs to her room.

Ava Perez answered on the third ring. "Emma, how you doing? Are you ready to return to work? Bright and early as usual."

Emma had been dreading this conversation. "Well, about that…"

"You're not doubting your ability to take on more responsibility at *Iron Butterfly*?"

The endless hours Emma had dedicated to developing a point of view while remaining true to the magazine's brand flashed before her eyes. She valued her collaboration with her coworkers and her dealings with criticism. She damned well deserved the promotion Ava had offered her on the morning she heard about Rachel's death.

"That's not it," Emma said. Although none of the last several days felt real, she relayed the events to Ava, beginning with hiring a moving company to close up Rachel's New York flat and slowly working her way up to the present, and ending with her decision to stay on until Bennett could get another nanny.

Ava said, "I'm very sorry you had to go through all of this, and I sympathize with your pain. Given the situation, I might have made the same decision, but as the sole owner of *Iron Butterfly*, I must do what's best for the magazine."

"I completely understand." She did, but that didn't prevent the disappointment from rippling down her spine.

"You've got to decide. Either stay with your job and bring your sister's baby here to the city, or—"

"I can't," Emma cut in. She'd gotten Bennett to agree to commute to Huntington Beach, but his moving to San Francisco was out of the question. Plus, Emma would have to find childcare to remain here to work. She'd be back to square one. "I'm sorry."

"So am I." Ava sighed loudly. "You leave me no alternative but to let you go."

Her previous life was going up in smoke, and Emma could do nothing about it. "I know. I want to thank you for all you've taught me."

Silence followed so long that Emma wondered if Ava had ended the call.

"Hear me out," Ava finally said. "Send me an article every so often about your experiences working with Bennett Browning, and I'll allow a leave of absence. You've made a name for yourself here. I'm certain our readers will be interested in what you have to say."

A cry of relief broke from Emma's lips. "I can do that."

A long pause followed. Emma could swear she heard her mentor tapping a pen on her desk as if thinking something over.

"A piece of advice," Ava said at last. "Politicians are slaves to their schedules. Don't let yours use you."

"Oh, Bennett wouldn't—"

"Trust me, he will if you let him. Where does he stand on feminists' issues?"

Emma thought of what little she knew of his intentions. "He seems interested in equality across the genders, though he could use help defining his goals."

"There's where you come in. Working with Bennett and for him may be a rocky road, but it could be good for everyone concerned."

"I couldn't ask for more than that."

"Email me a story when you can," Ava said. "And if you want to run something by me or just need to talk, call me."

When the conversation ended, Emma lost herself in

the sights and sounds from the open window. The streets rolled down to the water where the Bay Bridge shimmered like a mirage. The cable car station, not far off, hummed. Chinatown's squat buildings crowned with pagoda roofs had been her home since June had rescued her and Rach from the uncertainty of foster care. Now Emma had just selected a path that would take her away from the security she'd come to know. No wonder her stomach wouldn't stop its frantic churning.

Chapter 5

Bennett had earned enough donations to make the trip to San Francisco more than worthwhile. Now he had at least a half hour's drive before he arrived back on the other side of town. He'd make use of this time to catch up with his father.

These days, Dad attended almost all of Bennett's fundraisers and other events, lending advice even when not asked. Charles Browning had been at odds ever since he'd retired, and helping his son seemed to give him purpose, which was fine, but lately, Bennett steered clear of any talk about his personal beliefs with Dad.

A discussion quickly turned into a debate—a debate, an argument. Nobody won, leaving both father and son exhausted and not speaking to one another. That's why Bennett hadn't told Dad he was a grandfather. He should, though, even if it meant an ugly scene.

Better now than later when the rest of the world found out first. Bennett didn't even want to think about that. When his phone rang, he had just connected it to the car speakers. When he saw *Liam Archer* flash across the screen, he answered eagerly.

"Where have you been, mate? I've left you a string of voice messages and texts." When Bennett relayed all the news, Liam shouted, "Bloody hell, this is the worst thing that could happen! No disrespect to the dead, but Rachel's a sore subject."

"I know, but Emma's turning out to be a blessing."

"I wouldn't be so sure." Liam's tone was disapproving. "Better get rid of her before it's too late. The bad publicity could end your career, which would be a terrible shame."

"Liam, we're not living in 1960." Bennett needed to believe this statement. "Besides, Emma wants to care for her niece. She's taking time off—"

"Time off from what? Breaking hearts and burning rubber?"

"You've got it all wrong." Bennett wished he'd gotten hold of Dad instead of his friend, but his father would have been just as brutal. "Emma's nothing like her sister. She's doing me a favor. You can't fault her for that."

He understood Liam's concern. The Brit ran a teahouse with his wife where poets recited, but back in London, he'd been a SAS soldier and a spy. His undercover work had led to his discovering all the dirt on Rachel.

Bennett didn't want to recall how thoroughly she'd made a fool out of him. "Could you and Audrey help us paint the interior of the B&B I mentioned?"

"Certainly." Liam didn't hesitate a second. "If you fancy a couple weeks from today for the project, I'll ring Madison and Brandon."

"Terrific. Thanks."

"The least I can do for a bloke who, with a mere four-day notice, booked a flight across the pond to be the best man in my wedding."

Bennett laughed, letting some of the strain roll off his shoulders. Prove to his friends that Emma wasn't a villain, and he'd probably let go of any doubts he still had about her.

"See you then." He ended the call.

The sun splayed among the purple shadows of the buildings, splashing Chinatown in gold. He drove through streets that conjured up the ancient culture he recalled with such fond memories. This part of the city appeared veiled in mystery. Because of her secrecy, Emma Kuan fit right in.

After a lengthy drive in the heavy traffic, he finally came to the tenement houses on Jackson Street, painted in pastel colors, each different, each the same. No yards. Single-car garages. Bay windows. Drawn blinds.

A dark-skinned man answered the door and bowed his head full of thick black hair. "Hello, Mr. Browning," he said in a refined manner. "I am Alexis Nathan."

The name brought the photograph to mind at the back of Bennett's favorite book of poetry. At second glance, he said, "You're the one and only! The rock-star poet." He had unaccustomedly lost his cool. "I'm just such a fan."

Alexis Nathan raised his chin. "And how would a political contender like yourself know about my humble occupation?"

The elegant way he talked impressed Bennett to the hilt. "I'm a poet." *Yeah, sure.* "I'm not gifted like you, of course. Do you live here too?"

"Most gratefully, I do. Please come in."

He led Bennett through a sitting room that was soft and enveloping, lush yet serene—Oriental lampshades, jade-green couches, sacred objects, and paintings that reflected, through the movement of the brush strokes, an awareness of the inner life of things.

They came to a kitchen painted tangerine, where the

food on a crowded table made him salivate—delicacies he hadn't tasted since he was in the Peace Corps and living in China. Then he spotted his baby girl in the arms of the lady who must be the auntie. But where was Emma?

He greeted his daughter and told the rest of the group, "I'm Bennett Browning."

He might as well have said, "I'm the Grim Reaper," with the looks he got from those who had looked up to glare at him.

Alexis Nathan lowered his gaze. "Bless the man who embraces his responsibilities. He is indeed worthy of praise."

Slowly then, the others introduced themselves one by one, and June gestured to an untaken seat. He wasted no time dishing up servings and using his chopsticks to shove a little bit of Heaven into his mouth. He looked around for Emma.

"She's packing," June said as if she knew he'd been searching for her niece. Her black braid threaded with silver fell over a purple turtleneck, and her bare feet in flip-flops poked out from the hems of slacks.

The others stared at him as if waiting for him to speak.

"This is the best food I've had since I left Hong Kong," he said, and he meant it.

Everyone in the room nodded, and Emma, standing in the doorway, said, "June drilled me with her standards of cooking everything the 'right way.' It taught me to take pride in the performance, even if I'd prepared a dish a thousand times. To accomplish this, I had to learn the correct technique and find joy in each small victory."

June said, "I can't tell you how many times Emma

failed before she produced the perfect scrambled egg for Chinese recipes."

"And she told me," Emma added, " 'something as humble as rice noodles prepared with competence proves worthy of praise.' "

"All day, people recall the meal with contentment. They don't forget."

Bennett exhaled a long sigh of envy. "You're lucky to have such a mother—aunt."

June turned her stiff shoji-screen of a back on them, but he'd caught her blushing with what looked like pleasure a moment before.

Emma took the baby from June and went into the other room after he'd finished eating. She handed Madelynn over to Bennett. He held the baby, who clasped her tiny fingers on his tie clip. He was completely at ease as he bounced his daughter on his thighs and played peek-a-boo.

Emma's forehead creased. "I've been thinking. We need help painting the B&B. How would you feel about my family helping out?"

"I—" he started.

"Maybe a couple of weeks from today?"

He tried again. "Okay, but—"

"We've got enough room for them to stay."

Absently, he made funny faces at the baby. "We do, but—"

"You don't feel comfortable around them?"

He'd been trying to tell her about his friends coming to help paint on the same day, but she wasn't giving him a chance. "Quite the contrary. Your family's been welcoming and—"

"Good thing you didn't show up earlier. You

wouldn't have gotten the same reception."

"Thank you for speaking on my behalf. I—"

"You're set in your ways after living alone, so you probably don't want loads of people staying in the B&B."

"Are you kidding? Growing up with my dad meant I had to be flexible. When I was a kid and my father was running for office, we had to change our living arrangements at a moment's notice. Sometimes, we housed staff members and volunteers. We often slept in a motel. We had to be willing to go with the punches and the flow." He lifted Madelynn and pushed her toward Emma. "I think she's wet."

"Uh-oh. I should have changed her." She laid the towel across the sofa and passed him the diaper. "Would you like to do it?"

He shrugged. "I hope it's easier than assembling a car seat."

"Piece of cake, Mr. Browning."

With her help, he changed his daughter and rocked Madelynn until she fell asleep. After getting the baby down, he sat on the sofa and watched Emma pack the stuff to be delivered to her new address.

"I should take some of my things to the storage unit I rented for Rachel's belongings."

Bennett leaned forward when she opened a box containing a stethoscope, plastic gloves, a suction bulb, and other medical supplies. "What's all this?"

"My midwifery kit."

"You know how to deliver a baby?" he asked in amazement.

"Yes, that and perform the Heimlich maneuver, CPR, tie a figure-eight knot, and pitch a tent." She tightened her fists. "I'm prepared for anything life throws at me."

"Hmm…" What had brought about her drastic need for survival?

She gave the box a little shake. "This stays with me. After all, you never know…"

"No, I guess not."

The snapshot on a side table caught his eye. Somehow, that sad-faced young girl made him long to put his arms around the woman and never let her go. Her body, as catlike as it was today in her dark jeans and sweater, made his longing to hold her almost unbearable.

He wished the time spent here could go on indefinitely, but that was not to be. His chest felt heavy. The other world, his world of campaign speeches and election polls, awaited—a world where there could be no dropped balls.

"Thankfully for both of us, we've had this weekend to get to know each other," he said, dread cooling his thoughts. "Because things will be different tomorrow."

Chapter 6

Sixteen hours later, blurry-eyed from the lack of sleep, Emma had just retrieved Madelynn from her crib and had headed down the stairs when the front door swung open. The next thing she knew, Bennett was marching toward them with strings of balloons.

Dressed in his senatorial garb, complete with campaign pin and dark hair gleaming in the morning light, he bowed. "Good morning, ladies."

The look of him—his charm—made her grin. "If I'd known there would be entertainment, I would have brought out the fireworks and bottle rockets."

As she buzzed around the kitchen, she noted the bold way he assessed her in her violet nightshirt. He relayed his schedule, watching her intently, and she ached for the fun they'd had yesterday in Chinatown. Before his staggering comment that things would be different. Different how? She'd carried the word to bed, wondering what was in store when she awoke.

With that in mind, she faked an air of efficiency while she fed the baby and pretended not to be interested in everything Bennett had to do or say, but who couldn't get caught up in his charisma? A person would have to be asleep not to. No wonder her sister had fallen so hard for him.

"So about those balloons…" She had to conquer her involuntary attraction to him. "Do you plan to take them to the children at the school where you are to speak?"

"No. I compiled a list of bike facts to play a quiz game with the kids. The balloons are to get attention when I stand on Sunset Strip during rush-hour traffic this morning—with campaign signs and literature."

"Selling yourself on a street corner?" She shook her head, her mouth twitching. "That's racy, Mr. Browning."

"You bet." He broke two balloons away from the cluster and handed them to her. "Anything to get a vote," he added.

She noted the sarcasm in his tone and wondered why.

Just then, a horn honked from outside, and Bennett tucked his briefcase under his arm, clasping the bagged lunch he'd assembled in his fingertips. "There's my ride."

"You're not driving?"

"I always get more work done if someone else is at the wheel." He headed toward the front of the house. "Besides, you might need the car."

"Thank you." She trailed behind him with Madelynn in her arms.

"I'll get in touch with you in an hour or so. If you have any problems, don't hesitate to call me. I can be back here in a flash." He kissed his daughter's cheek and stalled at the entrance like he didn't want to leave. "Bye-bye, baby girl. Daddy loves his little Madelynn Grace." He sent Emma a smile that never made it to his eyes, then started down the walk but stopped suddenly and turned back, balloons billowing around him. "Oh, I almost forgot. I scheduled a coffee hour for seven."

"Tomorrow morning?"

"I should have given you a heads-up. Sorry, my bad.

It's tonight here at the B&B."

She stiffened as she recalled Ava's warning about his taking advantage of her. "Kind of late for coffee, isn't it?"

"Folks usually arrive at six, so they have time to settle in and grab something to eat or drink. There's no involvement on your part. Just hang out upstairs with Madelynn."

"I can organize things for you."

Surprise crossed his face. "You'd do that for me?"

She should have rallied and been quick to protest. Bennett hadn't told her he was bringing home a crowd— hadn't considered her thoughts on the matter. That said, she knew from the first moment she'd volunteered for this job that things would get crazy. But although being smack-dab in the middle of it was overwhelming, she couldn't complain.

"Is that what you meant yesterday when you said things would be different?" She looked at him dead-on. "Is chaos the new norm?"

"Yep, that about sums it up." He sounded resigned, sad even. "Are you game?"

Meeting his eyes without flinching, she said, "I'm in."

Whenever she thought of him during the day, she recalled that hanging-out-at-the-ocean smell of suntan lotion—a necessary ingredient when christening a dignitary's boat and addressing a schoolyard full of students and a stadium crowded with teamsters.

All she had to do was care for the baby and throw some food together. How hard could it be? It wasn't like she had to write an article for *Iron Butterfly* herself because the original journalist was already a week late.

She didn't have to drown herself in coffee because the makeup artist just pulled out of a location shoot. No online meeting to stress over because the internet failed midway—for the third time in a week.

She had only to deal with Madelynn, who, while in the market, had one of her blowouts, sending Emma scurrying to find the changing table in the restroom.

Bennett emailed her a coffee-hour protocol, asking her to pick up some refreshments at the store, but she volunteered to whip up her own. To take the guesswork out of the process, she texted him. She asked the approximate number of people he expected, then prepared finger food and desserts while Madelynn contentedly rolled around the kitchen in her walker.

The baby had gone to bed when the first bunch of supporters arrived. Some were the parents of kids on a baseball team Bennett managed. Others were business contacts, friends, and social connections. Most were guests, people he didn't know, he'd told her, but she could tell he felt comfortable around strangers.

His congeniality showed when he began speaking beneath the recessed lighting. "I'm so happy all of you came out tonight. I'm grateful too for our hostess, Emma Kuan." He shielded his eyes with a hand. "Where are you, Emma?"

With her face warming, she raised her arm from her position at the front desk. She didn't take well to the limelight, preferring the protection of remaining behind the scenes.

"Ms. Kuan managed this event singlehandedly on short notice," he said. "I couldn't have done it without her."

Although she couldn't fault his praise, he hadn't

mentioned her current occupation or brought up his daughter. His avoidance of such relevant news didn't sit well with her.

She listened as he told everyone where he grew up, a little about his father, nothing about his mother. He mentioned his education and professional experiences. He seemed to connect with his audience, but his voice sounded strained.

Half in anticipation, half dread, Emma nearly blurted. *What about the baby sleeping above us? Isn't she yours? And what about the woman you mentioned? Hasn't she very recently taken up residence here, even if temporarily?*

Her trepidation won out, so she held her tongue. Even when asked to close the meeting, she wrapped things up with a mere "thank you for coming."

Someone volunteered to host the next coffee hour. The helpers gathered up materials. Finally, everyone left, prompting Emma to say, "I think you should address the fact you're now a single father before the reporters get ahold of it."

"I know." He tucked his arms in at the sides. "I just need to find the right time."

A tight knot had formed in her throat. "The trick is to stay on top of any allegations."

"I suppose I should grant an interview," he said with a long, stoic sigh.

"Good idea. Take care of it while you can—show people you've nothing to hide."

"You're right, of course, and I will." He avoided eye contact with her. "But first, I have to tell my father."

"What?" Her astonishment had her reeling. "He doesn't know about Madelynn?"

A look of discomfort formed on his face. "He won't be happy."

****

Bennett had taken a hiatus from guiding small start-up businesses, keeping only a few new clients, but even those he'd given to colleagues when he realized he was too busy to keep up with his responsibilities.

He left his car in the parking garage, never missing a beat in his cell-phone conversation, and headed into the small meeting room. "I get that those smart meters can be wonky, and after I'm elected, I plan to do something to improve their proficiency."

Seeing his team, he removed his earpiece and continued as if he'd been with them the whole time. "Our goal is to get as many people out to vote as possible…"

A hectic day flew by without a break or time for Bennett to do anything but text Emma now and then. But by early evening, he drove along the coast with its whitecaps on dark, choppy waters and a gray whale breaching in the glow of the setting sun. The calm scene helped him switch into son mode.

Put a positive spin on the situation, and his father might not completely come unhinged. Already, Bennett couldn't live without his baby girl. She deserved the moon and the stars, and Emma was part of making that happen. The challenge would be to get his dad to agree.

As he walked inside the restaurant, he aimed to project confidence—a man who would spend every waking moment winning an election and being the perfect son.

His heart thumped against his chest. He had learned to thwart a full-blown panic attack by taking a deep breath from his diaphragm. His doctor had told him shallow breathing exacerbated the affliction. Bennett knew better.

The problem only occurred when he met with his father.

He took a moment to lean against a column, seeing himself on his sailboat drifting in those wind-spun waters with no place he needed to go. Maybe as soon as this weekend, he'd take a day off. A holiday, he decided. Perhaps the nanny would go along. What was he thinking?

He pushed through to the dining room's deep-green mottled walls. Pale gold highlighted and infused the tables with a subtle sheen as soft lights caught the reflective surfaces.

His father stood and motioned Bennett to a booth with a courtyard view. Pushing seventy, Dad looked younger than his years. Oh, his hair had grayed to a silvery white. But his sky-blue eyes hadn't lost any of their keenness. His sporty clothes fit as they had in his youth, rooted in the tradition of simplicity and refinement.

Dad clapped his son on the back, and they hugged. Soon, they fell leisurely into topics relevant to the election.

When the waiter brought their salads, his father dropped his stare and drummed his fingers on the table. "I don't mean to get overly sentimental," he started with an accent reminiscent of his Texas upbringing. "I never told you this, son, but I've always had one regret."

"I never thought of you as someone with regrets." Bennett very seldom heard his father express self-reproach. The discrepancy made Bennett rearrange his silverware as if doing so would prevent Dad from entering territory open to another one of their scathing disputes.

"I wish I would have spent less time working and more time cultivating a relationship with a woman after your mother died. I didn't do both of us any favors. I suppose I put Maura on a pedestal. It wasn't healthy to throw myself into everyone else's problems but my own. I worry I did you a disservice and set a bad example."

"By being noble? Is there such a thing?"

Dad slid a hand across his heart. "I don't express my concern often, but I worry about you. You're thirty, and you've never been married. Have you considered settling down? Being a family man would gain more voters."

Bennett looked away. "As a matter of fact…"

He gave the insane details of the past weeks, starting with Rachel. His father listened. He didn't try to interrupt. Still, Bennett knew from experience his dad was turning the facts over in his head, calculating, and coming up with alternatives. That's why after Bennett had presented the recent events, his father leaned forward, elbows on the table, positioned for a counterattack. Yes, an attack, no matter how diplomatic, and he wouldn't sugarcoat it.

"You've taken a paternity test?" was naturally the first thing out of his mouth.

And because he was his father's son, Bennett was at the ready. "The DNA shows I am the daddy. I've accepted my part in this and have done the right thing."

Dad lowered his voice as if afraid someone would hear. "If the other candidates discover you have a secret baby when you've openly criticized absentee fathers, they'll call you a hypocrite—or worse."

"But I didn't know Rachel was pregnant."

"Doesn't matter." Dad pulled his handkerchief from his breast pocket and wiped his forehead. "We'll give this Emma Kuan enough money to hide out in a foreign country with the baby until after the election."

"She'd never agree to that, and neither will I." Bennett felt sick. "My daughter has just lost her mother. I'm not sending her off to Timbuktu because I have to win a race."

"It won't be forever and will be for the best. I say this because it means you can correct your mistake of hiring Rachel's sister."

"Hold on." Bennett should have seen this coming. "First off, Emma loves the baby as much as I do."

"You care for this woman?"

"We're keeping things on a professional level."

"Really?"

No. I am getting more attracted to Emma by the day, sometimes by the hour.

"Yes." He pushed the lettuce around his plate with his fork. "Last night, Emma helped create a successful coffee hour. She's been an asset to my campaign."

Dad's jawline tightened. "She's wheedling her way into your life like females often do."

Did Bennett notice his father's chauvinism because of Emma's influence? "You're way off base. Ms. Kuan isn't a wheedler."

"This is your modus operandi, son. You always fall for the wrong sort of woman."

Bennett rubbed the back of his neck. "That's how you see me?"

"My fault entirely." His father leaned back as the waiter placed their orders on the table. After taking a bite of roast chicken and a sip of wine, he continued, "As I said earlier, I should have gotten married again when you were growing up."

"We're not in a courtroom, Dad." Bennett slid a knife through his fillet of sole. "There's no verdict of right or wrong here."

"The fact is you'll probably be able to convince the public to accept an illegitimate child. After all, you didn't know about the baby—you took responsibility the moment you found out about her. But live with the sister of the child's mother, who coincidently died far too young, and any cutthroat opposition will have a field day creating a scandal."

"I can't believe that—"

"Believe it." His father had the nerve-wracking habit of talking over Bennett. "Rachel Bellamy was from old money—very classy. You should have done more to keep her."

"Dad, Rachel was a slut."

His father dropped his knife, and it clattered on the plate. "Excuse me?"

Bennett hadn't meant to be so blunt. "Rach was promiscuous, adrenaline addicted, and she probably killed herself. Nobody knows for sure."

"And you know what they say about a bad apple," Dad muttered.

"Emma's a hard worker. She's climbing the ladder at *Iron Butterfly*."

"*Iron Butterfly*?" Dad stopped chewing and scrunched up his nose like he'd tasted something bitter. "Isn't that some feminist rag?"

"It's highly respected, second only to *Ms. Magazine*. Emma's helping me out, but she's returning to her job as soon as I find a replacement." The idea of her leaving caused a surge of regret deep inside him.

"Then yesterday wouldn't be too soon to start interviewing applicants. Count your blessings, son, that you have a way out of this debacle."

That did it. Bennett shot to his feet and threw down his napkin. "I'm done. You don't understand. For you, it's all about impressing others. Don't do anything that would cause folks to talk. There's more to it than that, but you don't want to help me find a solution." He started to leave but added, "You didn't even ask to see a picture of your granddaughter."

His father had risen from his chair and outstretched an arm toward his son. "Don't leave. Not yet. Not without... Please, show me a snapshot."

Bennett rocked back on his heels, then turned on his phone. "Here you go."

His father's eyes grew misty. "She looks like your mother."

"You should see her. She's so young, but when we're at the beach and I sit her on my lap, she throws her little arms open wide like she's holding the entire ocean in her hands. And talk about a right hook. When she gets excited..."

"Okay, you've sold me." He strolled beside his son with an air of solidarity. "When it comes down to it, I want you to be happy. But are your new living conditions worth sacrificing all you've worked so hard to achieve?"

Becoming a senator had always been Bennett's dream. He had wanted to make a difference in people's lives. But right now he needed to step back and help his daughter adjust to her new life.

"I've got a lot to think about," he said, feeling miserable.

Chapter 7

Bennett's face appeared drawn when he entered the foyer after meeting with his father. Emma wanted nothing more than to make him feel better—anything to take that look away.

He collapsed in the kitchen chair, loosened his tie, unbuttoned the top of his shirt, and stared at the darkness out the window. He hadn't moved when, minutes later, Emma placed a cup of steaming tea in front of him at the table.

"Did your dad clobber you?" She purposely kept her voice light and teasing.

He glanced at her with a face full of hurt. "You could say that."

"He didn't take well to having a surprise grandbaby?"

"Not at all unless you count his reaction to Madelynn's picture. He got choked up when he saw it."

Emma was off and running. "That's a start. Maybe we should invite him to dinner."

"Don't think so."

The curtness in his attitude caught her off guard. "What aren't you telling me?"

"Nothing."

"You're holding something back. What did your dad say that's gotten you so upset?"

He removed his suit jacket and flung it back over the

chair. Sweat beaded his upper lip, though the temperature wasn't warm in the room.

"Bennett?"

"Okay." His eyes flared with a resentment she didn't recognize. "He thinks our living together with the baby will create a scandal."

Her stomach dropped. "Why?"

"Right now my favorability rating is high. It could get ugly if any of the candidates decide to use smear tactics, questioning how far you and I go back."

"Are you implying what I think you are?"

"Not bad enough that Madelynn's illegitimate. Some asshat might spread rumors about you and me."

Confused, she shook her head. "Why?"

"When it comes to a spot in the senate? It's dog-eat-dog."

"I'll leave now," she said, ice spreading through her gut, "before I wreck everything."

"No, you can't go." A possessive desperation hung in his tone. "It wouldn't be good for Madelynn. She's gotten used to you."

He didn't add that he'd already gotten used to Emma too, but she saw how he stepped toward her as if to defend her. Or seduce her. His eyes burned into hers. She immediately lowered her lashes, hoping to mask his dangerous effect on her. Although they were inches apart, she was aware of every pore on his face, every whisker. She leaned forward without touching him and rested her head on his shoulder, a gentle and unassertive act but not in the realm of strictly business.

She lifted her head. "It would be easier if you found Madelynn a new nanny." But she could no more walk out on the baby than she could have her sister.

"Let's sleep on it." He dumped his untouched tea down the drain. "We'll tackle things tomorrow."

"That reminds me I made an appointment for Madelynn tomorrow with a doctor at the medical center."

Bennett drew in a sharp breath. "Is she ill?"

"No, no. Riley Morgan showed up unannounced late this afternoon. You were already on your way to see your dad, or I would have texted you. It's good that I'd installed some childproof locks on the cabinets and drawers and had put anything potentially hazardous out of reach. She was okay with it all."

"I'm impressed, but I should have done it."

"Not a big deal. I expected Riley to pay a surprise visit and wanted to be prepared." Emma's throat ached with the memory of what the caseworker had said. "But to warn you, there were no medical records for Madelynn, except for her birth at the hospital."

"Rachel never took her to a doctor?" His shock was evident in the lift of his brows.

"Not that CPS could uncover. They did a quick medical assessment, but Madelynn needs a thorough physical exam and well-baby visits."

"Damn it, Rach," he said thickly, his cheeks flushed. "What the hell?"

Emma's humiliation festered inside her. "If only I'd searched for my sister when I didn't hear from her. I tried to give her space, but I waited too long. If I could only get a do-over, I'd have hired someone to find her."

"Why? You weren't her keeper."

There's where you're wrong, she wanted to say. She'd tried to keep her sister happy and healthy, tried her hardest, and failed.

Emma made pancakes with smiley faces the following morning, wanting to cheer Bennett up. When he entered the kitchen, she could tell he hadn't slept. Dark circles encased his eyes, giving his irises a dull look. The contrast between now and a couple of mornings ago, when she'd found him surrounded by balloons, was shocking.

He met her three hours later at the doctor's office. She'd noted the photos snapped by proud parents tacked on the bulletin board. A growth chart displayed children's heights. In comparison, Madelynn was much smaller than average. That made Emma squirm.

Books, both cloth and paper, stood inside miniature wooden racks. Bennett chose one, and with his daughter on his lap, he read to her until a nurse came in who asked countless questions, some clinical, some uncomfortably personal, and then left.

Soon, with a relaxed smile, Dr. Nguyen entered and introduced herself. She was probably in her forties but seemed younger in her scrubs and daisy-patterned clogs.

She sat on a stool and looked at the nurse's notes from the desktop computer. "I see that you recently got custody of your daughter." Her grin faded as she read more. "I'm sorry for your loss."

"We weren't together," Bennett said, his face flushing. "I didn't know I had a daughter until after Rachel's death."

Feeling awkward, Emma reached out a hand. "I'm Madelynn's nanny," she said, careful not to mention her name.

And when Dr. Nguyen responded with a shake, Bennett quickly added, "I apologize for not making the proper introductions. Guess I'm a little nervous."

As if he'd given the doctor the go-ahead, she started her examination by taking Madelynn's measurements and asking if they had any concerns.

Their discussion proved difficult, with Madelynn wailing at the top of her lungs and lifting her arms for Emma. This motion tore through her, sending alerts through her head. She suffered the urge to whip Madelynn away from the source of her discontent. The back of Emma's neck ached, and she tried to find relief with a bend of her head. It didn't help. Did all mothers go through this torture during a simple doctor's visit?

Bennett brushed the fingers of Emma's hand with his own. "This is hard."

The doctor nodded with compassion. "I won't be on Madelynn's list of friends until she gets to know me better." She checked the baby's eyes, ears, throat, and heart. She talked to Madelynn all the while, trying to relax her. When the howling grew even louder, and Emma didn't think she could take it a second longer, the doctor said, "I need to order a test."

"What for?" Bennett and Emma asked simultaneously.

Dr. Nguyen lowered her stethoscope. "I'm hearing an irregular heartbeat. Nothing to worry over. An electrocardiogram will rule out any serious ailments."

****

Bennett lived through the following days in a stupor. He arrived late for the lobbyer's boxed-chicken luncheon and had to read his speech instead of having it memorized. He nodded off during his meeting with the governor and later forgot to pick up his suits from the cleaners. Consequently, he showed up at an assembly wearing a navy sports jacket spotted with spit-up milk.

The sour smell had him upchucking before noon.

He had to get with the program. Stat. But keeping a smile plastered on his face was almost impossible in light of the result of the EKG. His precious baby had been born with a heart defect. To put it mildly, Bennett was peeved. His father had gotten wind of him shouting at someone who disagreed with his position on a political issue.

Dad wasted no time showing up at The Nightingale. "Going off on people because they don't think like you will cost you votes." He shoved inside without being asked.

Emma picked up Madelynn from their current game of patty-cake and turned away. Dad kept his gaze on her back, but Bennett wouldn't allow animosity on his father's part toward any of them, no disapproval or singular agendas, especially after the bad news they'd received.

He was about to voice this when his father said, "Wait."

Emma stopped in her tracks, her shoulders rigid.

"May I see my granddaughter?"

She pivoted around and stared at his father. Then her expression softened.

Bennett squared his shoulders. "Dad, this is Madelynn Grace—your granddaughter."

"The picture you showed me looked like your mother. Now I see she has your expressions. What am I thinking? Naturally, she takes after you. Maura has been gone for so many years. This baby is a priceless gift."

Any hostility Bennett had felt for his father dissolved. "I know."

Emma cut in. "She has my sister's fingers and toes."

"I'll just bet she has more than that," Dad said with one of his winning smiles.

"When Rachel was a baby, she crumpled up her face and held her breath. Madelynn does the very same thing."

"That's amazing. Please." Dad raised his hands, and Emma handed the baby over. He rocked her back and forth, then got down on the carpet and played with her.

Minutes passed, and Emma went to check on dinner.

Bennett struggled to keep his emotions in check before saying, "About Madelynn…something's wrong. She's—she's sick."

"No." Panic spread over Dad's face. "What is it?"

"In layman's terms, she has a small hole in her heart. The cardiologists think it will most likely close up on its own."

"And if not?"

"She'll need surgery." Bennett swallowed hard to bite back his fear. "Hopefully, given time, the problem will mend itself, but it's too early to know for sure."

"That's why you haven't been in control. I'm so very sorry. Is there anything I can do?"

"For starters, you can let me live my life as I see fit. I welcome your advice, but stop insisting that I share your beliefs. Secondly, Emma's family is here. I'd like you to meet them, stay for dinner, and just enjoy being a papa."

As if his father hadn't heard, he dangled a toy with a series of loops that Madelynn playfully grabbed and shoved in her mouth. A stubborn man, his dad, but as soon as he said in an oddly gentle tone, "I might," Bennett guessed he'd decided to hang around.

But how long would his father's compliance last?

Chapter 8

Emma had weighed the consequences of giving Charles Browning the cold shoulder but, because of Madelynn, opted to keep the peace. Besides, Bennett had been smiling a little since his father's apparent attempt to accept the situation.

Not that she trusted the former senator. She didn't like it much that he'd sat next to her mother at the table in the dining room. Dropping his napkin on his lap, he glanced around at the fragrant Asian food. And when he nudged June with his arm against hers, saying, "A meal fit for an emperor," she thanked him graciously.

"June cooks like an angel," Bennett said, "and so does her daughter."

"I can see that." Charles quit struggling with his chopsticks and picked up a fork. "You girls should open a Chinese restaurant. I'd certainly patronize it."

Pleasure seemed to bubble in June's laugh, but later, when Emma and June were alone in the kitchen, June said, "Hand me the wok so I can hit Charles Browning over the head with it."

"He's a pain, I know," Emma said. "But Bennett needs his father right now."

June placed the pineapple tarts that Rai had made on a platter. "And my niece needs her auntie. It's not like you aren't worried sick."

Emma didn't speak as she turned on the hot water.

She appreciated that June was receptive to her feelings, but if she gave in to them, she might not be able to function afterward. She started to rinse the dishes, but her hands were shaking too much to continue, so she set the plates on the granite countertop.

"I should go back home with you," Emma said, stating the truth. "But now, more than ever, I have to care for Madelynn. If anything happened to her…"

June nodded. "You wouldn't be you if you gave up on the baby."

"I keep asking myself why my sister didn't take Madelynn to the doctor."

"Poor Rachel. I watched you and your sister grow up, and both of you could be difficult, but we know how hard she fought her demons. If she'd quit taking her meds, as she sometimes did, any postpartum depression would have been debilitating."

"You believe she just couldn't cope?"

"I'm not certain what to think." June put the silverware in the dishwasher. "I'm trying to make sense of it."

"All I know is what I hear." Emma slid her cell phone from her pocket. "Rachel's voice is the most valuable thing I have left of her." She thumbed up *Voicemail* and hit play.

"I met a man," Rachel said, jolting Emma anew with its significance. "He's different than the rest, so call me."

June's lips trembled. "Hearing her like that makes me feel like she's in the room with us. I don't understand. Why would she go away without telling anyone?"

"I've asked myself that a hundred times, and this is all I can come up with from all her voicemails."

"I'm off to New York. Don't worry about me like

you always do, and don't try and get in touch—please." Then the kitchen filled with Rachel's laughter, but it sounded forced and unnatural. "I'm ready to party. Love you, Em."

"That was the last time I heard from her."

****

The early morning sun had burned off the fog, and the view of the ocean quieted Emma's nerves as she drove. Last night, Madelynn had awakened more than usual. Emma had tried to fall back asleep but tossed and turned, unable to relax enough to forget her worries.

Without the energy or time to cook for a crowd, she ended up at a donut shop off the highway. If only she had enough painting supplies and walls to warrant inviting so many people. When she'd asked her family to a work party at the B&B, she hadn't known Bennett had arranged for his friends to help out on the same weekend.

Normally, she wouldn't have minded. Bennett probably wished they hadn't scheduled this bash either. Not with their present circumstances. Too late for canceling out, she thought while looking through gritty eyes at the cars in the small parking lot. If she had a choice, she'd turn around and run, not walk, to the beach. Walk, lie in the sun, build a sand castle—anything to forget her niece's prognosis, even if for just a while.

Emma hurried toward the back entrance, the biting wind making her shiver, though it was a perfect day to keep the windows open. *Think positive.* New people meant new beginnings. She wanted that, especially when she'd left all her acquaintances in San Francisco. She entered the kitchen and overheard Bennett talking to someone, their backs to her.

"What about this Emma Kuan?" the man asked with

a British accent. "Did you find out if she's as irresponsible as her slag of a sister?"

"Why don't you see for yourself," she snapped, and when the shit-talker whirled around to face her, she shoved the box of donuts into his gut, forcing him to take them.

He had a head full of sun-bleached hair and a body that looked like he worked out daily. "Sorry," he said, his face crimson. "I didn't know."

"See, that's the problem." She glanced at the open paint can and, eyeing him, considered picking up a paintbrush. "You don't know a damned thing."

Bennett edged between them. "Stop it, please," he said with the diplomacy she had come to expect from him. "It's not like Rach is here to defend herself."

Was he on Emma's side? Of course, he was. After all, he had loved her sister too. He lowered his chin, understanding glittering in his eyes as he observed her. Then he recovered the box from his friend and heaved it on the counter.

"Are we good?" Bennett asked, and when they nodded solemnly, he introduced them. "Liam, I know you're looking out for me. Emma, you've gotten me through some pretty rough times. You're both top-notch in my book, so I want you to like each other."

She would be civil to Liam Archer for Bennett's sake, but her fury caused her to ball up her fists. Nobody talked about Rach that way and got away with it.

Refusing to let her emotions get the best of her, she entered the living room to find two women walking across the plastic drop cloth covering the floor.

The redhead held a baby. "Brandon and I have a playmate for Madelynn." Her voice boomed. She nodded at Emma standing where the furniture and wall hangings had been pushed together and protected with a tarp. "Hi there. I'm Madison, and you should be in pictures." She switched her baby to a hip and lifted Emma's chin. "Those looks of yours are what's selling."

Heat spread to Emma's cheeks, and she lowered her gaze. "Nice to meet you."

The other woman, a modern-day Grace Kelly, was pregnant and told Emma her name was Audrey, adding, "Don't pay Maddie any mind. The girl can't help herself. She's a Hollywood agent through and through."

"Discovering talent along with a face is me hitting the jackpot," Madison said before Emma could respond. "Can you act? Oh, wait. Very hush-hush and all on account of Bennett's political aspirations, but rumor has it you're the nanny."

Another woman, Lucinda, who identified herself as Audrey's twin, said, "You've got guts, girl. I don't know if I'd take in my sister's baby."

Audrey rolled her eyes. "If something happened to me, you'd be the first to nab Jack. You'd do it in a heartbeat, a man at your side or not."

"Who needs a man," Lucinda said, then stopped, her face turned toward the open doorway. "On second thought, retract that last remark. Who the hell is that? And what planet of perfect specimens did he drop out of?"

Emma decided she liked these women when she saw who had just entered, hauling a brand-new ladder and paint paraphernalia. "That's just Alexis Nathan."

Leave it to him to show up late. To her amazement, when she introduced him, everyone gaped at him in a clear state of hero worship.

Bennett said, "He's the poet…in the flesh."

Liam twisted around from the wall he'd started sanding. "Didn't I read something about you living in the States? Lucky for us."

Before Alexis Nathan could answer, Lucinda sauntered close to him, her hips swaying. "Would you grace us with some of your soulful odes while we toil and sweat?"

Alexis Nathan nodded and grinned at her, which was no small feat because he rarely showed any teeth. Emma had asked him why he never smiled, and he'd said he put all his feelings into his writing. Although Emma usually favored female poets, she could identify with his poems about being lost and hungry in the streets of India. He'd been around since she came to live with June, so she considered him a brother, but Lucinda must be feeling something entirely different.

Another male joined them, Brandon Kennedy. He was Madison's husband and bequeathed the table with dishes filled with quiches, strawberry tarts, and a loaf of healthy bread. Emma managed to ditch her donuts in the nearest cabinet.

Once fed, the group separated into the rooms. Eddie Wong wore earbuds, and Emma knew he was plugged into some sports event while June and Rai tended to Madelynn and the Kennedys' baby upstairs. Soon, people talked the way friends did when they'd known each other for years. Alexis Nathan blended in with these fans who adored his poetry. To be accurate, he'd probably never felt so appreciated.

Emma watched Bennett on the other side of the room. The wind blew in from the open windows, messing with his wavy dark hair in the best possible way.

Unlike her, he kept fit by a daily swim in the sea. He was lean in the right places, broad in the shoulders. Yet nothing was glary or shouty about him in his cut-offs and faded T-shirt. His was quiet simplicity at ease in whatever he wore.

He caught her eye. "Hey you," he mouthed.

"Hey yourself," she mouthed back, her head angled in his direction. She had an odd and unforeseen urge to grab his hand and drift outdoors—just the two of them, free of all care. The sand squishing between their toes would feel warm and the ocean's spray invigorating. She stopped her daydreaming, realizing this was the second time the impulse had struck her to escape to the water's edge this morning. Funny, when it wasn't on her list of usual pursuits since she'd never learned how to swim. Maybe she was punchy after her sleepless night.

An hour later, Emma and Bennett had painted their way toward the middle of the wall and each other. The nearer they came, the more she felt uneasy. Her constant reaction to him made no sense. She had always thought of herself as having willpower, but what if she'd inherited a fraction of her mother's recklessness? She didn't want to believe it, but the fact was that she'd taken up with a man she didn't exactly know, gotten herself crazy involved with him. Were those the actions of a stable person?

Yes, when she considered, if she hadn't, Madelynn would most likely be ill without two people to love her. Good thing Emma hadn't allowed that to happen. Madelynn Grace was her essential reason for sticking around. She had to keep this in mind if she wanted things to work out. Coping with a little harmless flirtation would be worth her niece ending up well-adjusted.

"The way you did up your hair suits you," Bennett said just loud enough for her alone to hear.

A hundred nerve endings caught fire inside her. "Thanks, but they're just pigtails."

"With those, uh, pigtails, you look like you'd knock a guy's lights out if he bugged you. I believe you would too, judging by your confrontation with Liam. You were about to smear his face with paint."

"Because he was talking crap about Rachel." And she'd do it again. Did that, too, make her reckless?

"He kind of deserved it if you ask me. In his defense, though, he didn't know you were standing there. I meant what I said about wanting you two to get along."

"I know. I promise to be nice to him." She only hoped she could keep her word. "It's just my sister wasn't irresponsible—well, maybe a little. But she certainly wasn't promiscuous."

"Of course, she wasn't," he agreed in a monotone. "Rach was a saint."

A discrepancy hung between what he said and how he looked—dull eyes and the corners of his mouth turned down. Emma's breath burned in her throat. Rather than react, she went into the kitchen with the women wrapping the pewter and old glass in newsprint.

When they noticed her, she said, "I should have done the prep work here."

Lucinda was stirring a can of paint. "Don't sweat it. From what we've heard, you've had your hands full."

Audrey's violet eyes were sympathetic. "We're sorry about your sister, and how's Madelynn doing?"

"It's a little early to tell." Panic rioted to get the upper hand. *Stay optimistic.* "But she's strong. She's now kicking and scooting when she sees the teddy bear her daddy gave her. And, oh, she gives us these adorable sloppy kisses."

"I can't wait to be a mother," Audrey said.

Lucinda laid the stir stick down on a newspaper. "The time will be here before you know it, Aud, and you'll be hitting me up because you need a break."

Madison said, "Don't forget Auntie Mads. I'll always be good for a timeout when you need it."

"Love you both." With a contented look, Audrey rested a hand atop her belly.

Something about the conversation dragged Emma back to her past and the fact she had never fostered any real friendships, not even at the magazine. She'd worked so hard that she hadn't had enough time to form bonds, but right now she needed someone on her side, someone who would listen and understand.

Just then, she met Madison's gaze, which showed curiosity.

"What exactly did you do before you became..." Madison fashioned her fingers into quotes. "The nanny?"

An instant of wistfulness waved through Emma as she recalled her promotion. "I'd just assumed more of the responsibilities at *Iron Butterfly*, a—"

"*Iron Butterfly*," Lucinda interrupted. "You've got to be jiving us."

"Lucinda's impressed," Audrey said, "because she's the editor-in-chief of a small press called *Powell's Review*."

Emma blinked in surprise. "The publication that features entrepreneurs." She nodded at Audrey. "Didn't you run it initially?"

"I did, but my sister is much better at the managing

part than I am."

"It appears what we have here is another go-getter," Madison said. "Still, you could use some support, Emma."

"We get together a lot," Audrey put in. "Sometimes to go shopping or out for a meal."

"Not to mention, I get free movie tickets to premieres," Madison added.

"Nothing like a night out on the town with the sisterhood." Lucinda wrapped her arms around the two at the table and looked up at Emma. "How would you like to join us?"

Astonishment had Emma breathing in and out to keep her cool. "You have no idea how much your offer means to me." She swallowed. "Thank you."

"Then it's settled." Madison raised a hand, palm out. "Now, let's doll up this kitchen in seafoam green."

As a result, all the women grabbed rollers and began to paint. The morning wore on, her new pals chatting about things important to Emma now that she had a child—*had a child?* This new beginning seemed all she had to cling to. Yes, she was always tired and so worried about Madelynn she daydreamed of running off to silvery shores, but these generous women had welcomed her into their fold. Her mood mellowed with her gratefulness over her good fortune.

Then she spotted Rai warming two bottles of formula. When June found her, Rai had been living alone and excluded in an upstairs tenement house. The walls had been filthy. She'd been abandoned and left to fend for herself, which she had difficulty doing. Not solely because of her deafness but working in a noodle factory in Chinatown had taken its toll on her small frame.

Emma set her paint roller in its tray, went to Rai, and attempted to break through the loneliness of the older woman's unchosen exile.

"Everyone, this is my auntie," she vocalized, using sign language in both Chinese and American. "She's been helping us by taking care of the babies."

The ladies thanked Rai, and Madison went so far as to sign her words. "Would you like to be on TV? There's a spot in a commercial. I've been on the lookout for someone like you."

When Rai looked confused, Audrey explained, "Madison mainly deals with getting parts for people with disabilities."

Emma's jaw dropped. "Talk about impressive."

"There's a need," Madison said with resolve. "Why should someone pretend to be deaf when we have the real deal who can do a much better job? A win-win."

Rai's round face crinkled with a smile. "Win-win."

Emma reveled with admiration for her new friend. Now the fear in her heart lifted a little, and for the first time in days, she could breathe easier.

****

When Bennett heard the baby crying that night, his initial reaction was to jump out of bed and run to her, even though Emma claimed it was part of her job description. Add to it, he'd seen the redness in the nanny's eyes and knew she hadn't been sleeping well. Before she could respond, he bounded into the nursery.

"Hey, sweetie." He scooped his crying daughter into his arms and cuddled her. He brushed the tears from the tiny cheek and rested his own against her smooth head. He then changed her diaper as best he could while she kicked her legs and cooed. Because this was all new to

71

him, he tried putting her back in the crib, but she started to protest with a sob.

"I'll get you your bottle and be right back," he told her anxiously, temporarily placating her with her pacifier and little teddy bear.

As he rushed by Emma's open doorway, he heard her shouting incoherently and dashed inside the room. He switched on the bedside lamp, sat on the mattress, and gently shook her. She stirred, her fists punching the air as she woke, her eyes luminous. Her arms curved around his shoulders as if of their own volition, and she clung to him. Her firm breasts beneath the satiny fabric pushed against him, her body warm and scented with sleep.

"A nightmare?" He groaned, trying to keep control while burning with unsated desire.

She let go of him, her trembling hands straightening her silky gown. "Yeah."

"About Rachel?"

"I see her…she's afraid…and I'm trying to get to her." She tore back the sheets. "I hear Madelynn fussing. I'd better get up."

"I've already got this. You stay put."

Without wanting her to talk him out of it, he took the stairs two at a time. Emma was working his mind as no other woman had done before her. She had revealed how much she loved her sister, not in so many words but in her actions. The fact was that what he'd learned about Rachel had deadened any warm feelings toward her. He couldn't tell Emma the truth. Not yet.

Maybe not ever.

He prepared the bottle and watched Madelynn calm down and drift slowly to sleep in his arms. He laid her back in her crib. Her tiny eyebrow lifted as she slept, and an arm jerked out from the blankets. What went on in her mind? Was she dreaming about Rach?

All these questions triggered emotions he hadn't dealt with through the years. He hadn't known his mother. Yet her death had left a wound that never quite healed.

Wide awake, he decided to give in to that constant call of the ocean from the open window. He padded across the plastic covering the floor and outside with his running shoes. He hopped, slid one shoe on at a time, and headed to the beach.

Jogging allowed him to review data or devise a plan to target potential voters. Bennett did well in the polls but was more recognizable than the other nominees. Father and son had been in the public eye as far back as Bennett could recall. Recently, life had happened, and sadly, he'd begun to rethink his goals. He wanted his daughter to thrive. These days, it was all that mattered.

If something terrible happens... Don't go there.

Back home, he noticed the volunteers had shown up, if not ready to go, willing to get started after eating breakfast, this time prepared by the chief cook of the teahouse.

"Thanks, Liam," Bennett said. "You're a good man."

"No problem." Liam set out a tray of croissants. "Remember when you chartered a plane to fly to Alabama to secure a book for the Beatnik Fest? Nobody does that but a loyal soldier."

This morning, the Archers had brought their Boston terrier, Percy Shelley. The pooch was named after the poet. What else could anyone expect from a couple who ran a teahouse that promoted poetry? Bennett petted the dog, who remained still and alert.

Emma smiled despite any grudges she might have had with Liam. "Who's this?"

"Percy, the lionhearted," Liam told her. "When I first met him, he was such a sissy."

Emma bit her lip. "Percy changed? How?"

When Liam answered, "I taught him to man up," she cringed.

While she knelt to scratch Percy behind his ears, Liam took Bennett to a far corner where they could talk privately. "What is it with your lady? It's like she has a stick up her arse."

"She's not my lady," Bennett said. "And you—"

"Right, mate. Who'd want to be saddled with her, eh?"

He respected Emma, who had brought his unconscious bigotry and the bigotry of others to his attention. "She's one in a million."

"That's what I mean. I don't see you two together. Thank your lucky stars that she'll soon go back to where she came from. It's high time to make that happen."

Emma's return to San Francisco was the last thing Bennett wanted, but he wouldn't make waves, not here. "We'll talk about this at another time."

Until Emma, Bennett hadn't paid any attention to gender discrimination. Why hadn't he ever noticed? She'd already brought so many changes into his life he couldn't suppress his awe.

By mid-afternoon, The Nightingale had that clean look only fresh paint could produce. Bennett's friends— Emma's now too—were heading out the door. Even Percy sat straight and as tall as he could get, grinning, head cocked, saying his goodbyes, while Madelynn jabbered away on Emma's hip.

Bennett decided he wanted a puppy someday, a roly-poly breed with big feet and floppy ears, one that his daughter could grow up with, one that would make Emma laugh. Wait, what was he thinking? His somedays with Emma were numbered. Someday, the nanny would leave and reclaim her real job. He would be alone—without her. He didn't want to think about it.

A few hours later, he had showered and slipped into his campaigning duds. He'd already sent out thank-you notes and gift cards to everyone who'd helped this weekend and was rewriting his speech when Emma approached him in their upstairs office.

He drew in his breath at the sight of her wearing a shade of midnight blue that complemented her wintery looks. He tried not to be affected by that bolt of lightning that always struck whenever he laid eyes on her.

"There you are," she said with a sensuous smile.

He rose as she approached the desk, because her dressing up warranted his good manners. Plus, he didn't want her to see his project. Not yet. Not until he'd added the finishing touches—the part about Emma. He had not referenced her name, but she was his template, his guiding light while composing this speech.

She straightened the campaign pin on his lapel, and his eyes rolled back in his head because of the newly added fragrance. If he'd created it, he'd call it Temptation since, whenever she came near, her scent affected him with the longing to take her to bed.

"Wow," he said languidly. "You look stunning."

"Thank you." She tilted her head to the side. "And you look like the once and future king—or senator. Take your pick."

Not touching her and not brushing his mouth over hers was almost impossible, so he went along with the myth. "Do you wish to accompany me, fair lady, to the Isle of Avalon?"

"If this is your way of asking me to attend the convention tonight..." She flicked two fingers against his sleeve. "I can't be seen with you. Therefore, I'll travel there incognito."

"How can I resist? There's nothing like a little danger to get the blood pumping."

She leaned around him to glance at the computer screen. "Can I take a peek at tonight's speech?"

"Not if you value your life."

"Spoilsport." She returned to her position, hands in her pockets. "My family leaves tomorrow, so they want Madelynn to themselves. As for me, even though I might feel like throwing tomatoes after your spiel, I'm interested in hearing what you have to say. After all, it's been a while since the coffee hour. I know I should keep up with my employer's mindset."

"Your employer approves." He hit the computer's printout key and straightened his tie. "You take my car. I'll hitch a ride."

"No, your CUV is too recognizable with that bumper sticker that says *Future Senator On Board*." With an amused smile, she pulled the phone from her pocket. "I'll get a ride."

"Fantastic." He opened the office door for her. "I'll see you there."

"All right. Don't act like you know me."

"I won't," he said with a wicked grin. "That'll be our dirty little secret."

Chapter 9

No one seemed able to soothe Madelynn but Emma. Her caring for the baby and the arising storm caused her to arrive late. The community center, situated in the heart of a ghetto, held a crowd. She ended up slipping into a seat near the back. As luck would have it, Bennett stood at the lectern. He had moved into what seemed the final part of his speech.

He mentioned the sexist terms people used without thinking. "All that should be eliminated in today's world," he said, speaking of humanity and the need for every living being to matter.

Her heart caught in her throat. She'd had an impact on him without knowing it.

She glanced up to discover he had spotted her. In those moments, they were the only two people in the multipurpose room. A warmth flowed through her, and feeling fully alive, she gasped. She heard the burst of applause and noticed that the audience had stood—all but her. She stumbled to her feet and applauded.

Afterward, keeping her distance, she watched him talking with people. But just then, Charles Browning nodded in her direction and gave his son a look of disapproval. That was enough for Emma's face to heat. She took off like a jackrabbit to the restroom down a corridor to hide out for a while. Her smartphone beeped.

Bennett had texted her. —*What did you think?*—

She typed back. —*I'm proud to know…*—

A woman was tapping her arm. "Your turn."

Emma absently forced her mobile into her jam-packed purse and entered the stall. When she shrugged off her shoulder strap to hang it on the door hook, her phone flew out and landed in the toilet just as the sensor activated the flush mechanism. Her only link to Bennett or any other transportation had gotten stuck in the hole that led down the sewer line. *Argh!* She fished the phone from the bowl and, gagging a little, wiped it with toilet paper.

Her finger tapped against the screen—nothing. She pressed the button on the side to no avail. She kept trying—and trying. Still no success.

While washing her hands with the hottest water tolerable, she peered through the steam at her deathly pallor in the mirror. She'd read something about rice. Good to know if she were at home. She held her phone under the dryer not just once but several times. When she finally gave up, no one else remained in the bathroom. Every swallow she took met with a cottony dryness in her mouth. The lights suddenly went out. If only she could find help, but everyone had left.

Emma made her way in the dark, searching for a security guard. When she couldn't find one, she slipped outside and heard the metallic click of the door shutting behind her.

Rain pelted the awning where she huddled, hugging herself to keep warm. She squinted to see in the dimness of streetlamps. A man with soaked dreadlocks clattered past her, the wind blowing flattened boxes from his shopping cart. At mid-distance, three children, their father, and a massive dog were piling into a broken-down car with personal belongings inside—blankets, pillows, and food wrappers. Shivering, Emma remembered when she and Rachel had lived in similar conditions.

And just like that, Emma was back in that alley where she and her sister had taken refuge. Mom hadn't been around, and Emma had been out begging for scraps from the food trucks and rummaging through garbage cans. Usually, she alerted Rachel when she returned, but approaching, she heard a gravelly male voice.

"Yo sure as shit a pretty little girl."

Emma eased a hand inside her pocket. "Rachel, come here."

Sobbing, her sister obeyed fast enough, but the creeper followed on her heels.

"Y'all is being rude to your elders," he said in a slur.

Emma raised a gleaming shard of broken glass. "Come. One. Step. Closer. I'll. Cut. Your. Belly. Open." Her voice left her mouth like spitting seeds.

Acting badass was all she had, and it caught the drunk off guard. They had to use his muddled state to get away. She grabbed Rachel's hand and dashed off as fast as she could, dragging her sister along. Later, the beat cops stopped the girls and put them in their car.

That had been then. Madelynn existed in the present. Rachel did not. The baby needed Emma. And Bennett… She tried to conjure up images of him, remembering him in the spotlight, his eyes brightening when he saw her, capturing her where she sat when the world had been theirs—an hour ago?

The wheels of a vehicle sliced toward her through the greasy puddles. She automatically stepped into the shadows to see if the car would stop. It passed her by. But a short distance down the street, the brakes squealed.

Bennett burst from the interior, ran down the sidewalk, and pulled her into his arms. "I kept texting and calling you." He sounded frantic.

She could hardly get the words out. "My phone died."

They held on to each other while the storm raged outside the awning.

"Let's get out of here," he whispered in her ear.

He led her across the sidewalk, past a skeletal woman selling her body, to his car. The heater toasted Emma back to life. The hooker beckoned them through the window, a zombielike creature who could have been Emma's mother—if she'd still been alive.

"Are you okay?" Bennett asked, his own vulnerability laid bare.

She nodded, wanting to say something clever, make things as lighthearted as they'd been earlier in the office at The Nightingale. But all she could think of was how much she longed to fill herself up with him, with the hardness she had felt when he'd held her. Never had she experienced such a surge of unadulterated need.

Their gazes lingered on each other in the pale light. After a moment's hesitation, they were leaning into each other. Bennett's lips met hers with so much pent-up passion that she saw stars through the rain. She closed her fluttering eyelids. His muscular chest pushed against her breasts, and her nipples tightened and ached in response. She heard the moan, his or hers. She wasn't sure. His mouth against her flesh was red-hot as he trailed kisses down her neck to her pulse beating wildly.

He threaded his fingers through her wet hair, and she rested her head on his shoulder. It had been so long since she'd kissed a man, so long since—had she ever allowed herself to feel?

Then he grabbed her shoulders. "I can't do this anymore, Emma."

While their intimacy screeched to a shattering halt, burning sobs harbored in her throat, making it impossible for her to comment.

"I nearly went out of my mind when I couldn't find you," he said. "I blamed myself for letting you go to the convention alone and not meeting up. I'm tired of hiding you and Madelynn."

Her relief knew no bounds, but she had to ask, "What do you plan to do about it?"

"I don't know, but I have to change things."

"What will your father say?"

"He'll fight me on it, but I can't let that control my decision. He'll probably refuse to speak to me."

"I'm sorry."

Bennett looked sensual in the light from the intersection, his shirt wrinkled and unbuttoned, hair curly and damp. "It's not your fault."

She had to stop tingling at the sight of him. "When I first started at *Iron Butterfly*, my job included promoting the magazine," she managed to say. "I designed the web page that's still used today and built us a sound media presence."

"Why are you mentioning this?"

"Madelynn doesn't need me every single second. I've been thinking about opening The Nightingale for business. Maybe since you're the pro when it comes to mentoring small start-ups, you could help. If you have time, that is."

"I do," he said without hesitation.

She'd gotten caught up in the moment. "We'd use

most of what we make renting out the rooms in the lodge to make money for your campaign."

"I'm honored, but that's out of the question."

She almost asked why, but something in his tone told her to keep still—for now.

****

The following morning, Bennett drank coffee and called his father. "How about breakfast, say, at the Pancake Parade on Wilshire? Ten o'clock?"

By the time he rushed into the country-style diner an hour later, he was starving. He hugged his father, slid into the booth, and ordered. One of his earliest memories was of coming here with his dad. The color scheme and style might have changed a few times through the years, but the aroma of pancakes always made him hungry.

Today was no exception, save for the sharp pain in his stomach over what he needed to say. In the meantime, he allowed Dad to counsel him on publicity-based fundraisers.

Listening, Bennett took a bite of his pancakes, relishing the taste and the burst of blueberries. But when his father turned the conversation to Emma, Bennett put down his fork.

Dad sipped his coffee. "Did you think it a good idea for her to be there last night? Especially when you're still in the beginnings of the campaign."

"I did, and I still want her in my life."

"If the wrong person were to find out—"

"I'm tired of the drama, Dad. I'm withdrawing from the election."

"But why?"

"Madelynn's dealing with her mother's absence and living with a health challenge. I can't be off crusading for votes all day and night when my daughter's so helpless—I just can't."

His father opened his mouth to say something but didn't speak.

Bennett had to fill the ensuing silence. "There will be other elections. I—"

Dad held up his hand and sighed. "After your mother died, I threw myself into my work. I wasn't around for you. Consequently, you were alone a good deal of the time. I can't help concluding my neglect is part of your need to do the opposite."

He was probably right, but it didn't matter. "I got by," Bennett lied. "No harm done."

"Look on the bright side." Dad shrugged. "Now you can let Emma go."

"No," Bennett choked out. "Madelynn needs her."

"Son, why are you so enamored with this woman?"

Unable to answer his father's question, he picked up his fork and speared another bite of his pancakes. Dad chewed on a strip of bacon as if this action bonded them, and Bennett remembered again coming here when he was young and needing his father's presence.

"Dad, now that I'm stepping away from politics, maybe it's time for you to discover another way of being useful."

"By doing what?"

"Emma and I could use some help with Madelynn. We're considering opening The Nightingale to guests, which would bring in a steady income and allow me to stay home in good conscience."

Dad drummed his fingers on the table. "That's a big responsibility with the baby."

"It is. That's why we need you to watch your

granddaughter when you can."

"Hmm, I see where you're going with this, and I…"
Dad nodded with a slight grin as if even he was surprised
at his own reaction. "Have to admit I'm interested."

Bennett paid the bill and put on his sunglasses. "All
right, then. I'm not going to worry about anything from
now on."

He only wished that were true.

Chapter 10

June had gotten up with the baby during the night so that Emma could get some much-needed sleep. Bennett had left this morning before Emma could talk to him, and she'd gone a little bonkers. She couldn't stop thinking about their being together last night and how it changed the way she thought of him, perhaps irrevocably. Plus, he'd mentioned bringing his daughter out into the open.

"How could anyone not fall in love with you?" Emma asked the baby sitting in the stroller and looking up at her with eyes a polished golden brown in the sunshine. "You know where you're going, don't you, lovebug?"

She had gotten into the habit of adding a floppy little hat to Madelynn's outfits and taking the sandy path down to the water. After all, what could be better for her niece's health than the fresh ocean air?

It was only midmorning, and the beach had already been filled with vacationers out to enjoy the benefits of Huntington. Families were unpacking coolers while young adults played volleyball, and in the distance, boats sailed like targets in an amusement park arcade.

Emma carried Madelynn to the fizzy foam as it swept ashore and spread across the sand. The baby gasped when her bare feet skimmed the surface. She giggled at the kids leaving their half-built fort behind to gather around her. The smell of sunscreen filled the air as the children romped, and a delighted Madelynn pumped her arms at her sides and chattered in her indecipherable baby talk.

Emma seated herself with her back to a rock warmed by the sun. She held Madelynn on her lap while the cattails nodded softly in the breeze. Some unaccustomed part of her had reared its head this morning. She rubbed her lips with the back of her hand, recalling the feel of Bennett's mouth on hers the night before. Her instincts were to fight these new feelings rising inside her by swearing what she shared with him was still nothing but business.

But her heart betrayed her in return. *Not so.*

Lunchtime came, and the drone of the beach people grew fainter as Emma carted Madelynn back to The Nightingale. Once inside the entrance, she called out for Bennett. He didn't answer. His absence didn't stop the deluge of mental images—the kisses and the protectiveness of his arms. The tenderness they'd shared last night returned to taunt her.

After Madelynn ate, Emma rocked her and sang a lullaby. Her niece's head grew heavy on Emma's shoulder, so she snuggled the infant into the crib and rubbed her back until she fell asleep. Emma grabbed the baby monitor from the nursery before proceeding down the hall.

Without the commotion of the past weekend, the house had grown quiet. It offered the perfect time for Emma to document her experience with the prospective senator, introducing his daughter to others. She felt up to the task, with her previous exhaustion dulled by a good night's rest.

She loved being in their office. All the trade books

Bennett had brought with him, her classics. The white noise of the sea outside the open windows, the cozy leather chairs inside.

She started by creating storyboards, listing her research about him, and printing up his photos at various events. She couldn't mention her relationship with him yet. But she would only do so after he gave her the official go-ahead.

Her boss and mentor, Ava, expected Emma to use her real name as an endorsement. But that wasn't possible without Bennett's okay. Because of this, thoroughly engrossed, she multitasked, wanting to complete more than one goal by the time Madelynn woke from her nap.

Footsteps approached from the hall, and within seconds, Bennett plopped a cell phone on the desk. His open jacket, the lopsided pen in his pocket, the blueberry stain on his shirt, and his hair rumpled as if he'd been driving with all the windows open. All of this unusual disarray was, to her, endearingly sexy.

"I hope you're okay with lavender," he said.

"This is the latest model." How had she gotten so preoccupied she'd forgotten about her phone dying? "Thank you for this. I'll set it up in a bit."

He laid his hands flat on the desk and leaned toward her. "Didn't you get enough of me last night?" He nodded toward the photos. "I see my mug everywhere I look."

"Maybe I wanted a few dartboards." She bit back a grin. "Seriously, I won't mention the baby or me in the article I'm doing till you approve."

He stiffened but didn't respond. Instead, he unwrapped the box and opened it, exposing the cell phone. "Now you can recover your sister's voicemails."

"How do you know about them?"

"I heard her—Rachel, I mean, from your phone. It freaked me out a little at first. It was like being in earshot of her ghost. But guess her voicemails bring you comfort, huh?"

Dark emotion pushed through to blur Emma's thoughts. She recognized the feelings rolling inside her, not as jealousy but as remorse. "I should have turned down the volume. Listening to Rach must have been tough on you—sorry."

"I…" he started, glancing above her shoulder, his face unreadable. "So I had breakfast with my dad this morning."

"You did?" The pitch of her voice rose an octave at the mention of his father. "How did it go?"

He shrugged. "Let's just say he's working for us now."

She about came off the chair. "What did you do?"

"Well, I fired him. Now he's in charge of helping us out."

"Seriously?" Could this be what it felt like to drown, sinking into the cold, dark water? She hadn't ever worked with a father figure and hadn't a clue how to behave. "I don't think that's a good idea. You and I will get things under control."

"I know we will, but he'll watch Madelynn when needed. He'll be an asset. You'll see."

She crossed to the books on their shelves so he wouldn't see her rolling her eyes. "And his helping out will give you more time to campaign—right?"

"Hardly." He paused. "I told my father, and now I'm telling you. I am getting out of the race."

"Why? Because of Madelynn? Because of me? Because if it's me..." She'd seen his disillusionment in the past weeks and hoped it had nothing to do with her.

"All of the above. Frankly, it's a relief to have made a decision."

"I see, I think."

He edged around to face the computer screen. "May I read what you've written?"

"It's a story about you—well, you and your daughter—for *Iron Butterfly*."

Bennett's expression soured. "Hold off on that, would you?"

Heat crept up Emma's neck. "You aren't ready to bring us out into the open yet, are you?"

His jawline hardened like stone. "No."

"Are you ashamed to be seen with me?"

"It's not that," he said, but his manner wasn't convincing. "I want to keep my life private."

Emma seethed inside. If she weren't so attached to Madelynn, she would disregard her attraction for him and book a flight back to the Golden Gate City.

****

The ache had settled in Bennett's chest, the pain put there by the wounded look on Emma's face. After all his encouraging her, now he'd just taken away her incentive. Nothing was more gut-wrenching than hurting her, but he had to make her understand.

He dragged up a chair. "Listen, Emma, we should give it time before we're seen together. Your sister—she hasn't been gone all that long. And I—I—"

"You love her more than ever."

No, he didn't, but how could he burst Emma's bubble with the awful facts? Rachel had done him so wrong he couldn't give his heart to another this soon. Even though he cared about Emma, cared deeply, he still hadn't recovered. Therefore, he couldn't speak, let alone deny her statement.

He sat in the chair, ready to level with her. "I just need a while to adjust to being a father. I'm still new at all this."

"Ah, so that's it." She hunched over the desk, then lifted her head as if spurred on by a sudden thought. "You wouldn't have to worry about fatherhood if you give up your parental rights to Madelynn and let me raise her."

"Damn! I can't believe you'd say that." Her threat had sucker punched him. "Don't you know my daughter is the most important thing in the world to me, along with…" He'd almost said, *along with you*. He was falling from a great height. "Last night—"

"Last night should never have happened." A tear caught in the corner of her eye, and she swiped it away with a brush of a finger. "We made a mistake."

"You're wrong. We've been through so much together. I've gotten closer to you these past few weeks, especially after thinking I lost you. You can't imagine how worried… And then I saw you standing under that awning in the rain and the dark. You looked so upset, and I didn't blame you. Anybody would be scared, abandoned in that part of town. I should have given you my car. I will from now on, believe me."

"Stop it right now." She raised her chin. "I can take care of myself, have been for most of my life."

He took her by the shoulders. "Let me in, Emma. Don't push me away."

"You and I share a desire to make a go of The

Nightingale, but collaborators are all we can ever be. I'll work like the devil to prepare the inn for customers, but that's as far as it goes. No more fooling around. Any chance of there being an 'us' is off the table. Got it?"

"You think we can go back to business as usual?"

Though she didn't answer, the coldness in her manner spoke for her. The silence in the office had just become toxic when a loud cry from the baby monitor told him Madelynn was up and most likely wet and wanting a bottle. Emma started for the stairs with that fear on her face he also experienced whenever Madelynn fussed more than usual, a dread that the baby's medication wasn't doing its job.

Bennett streamed past her. Moments later, he was opening the nursery door. "Hey, sweet girl."

Madelynn stood with her hands clasping the crib rail. "Da," she sang out in a glorious welcome.

He nearly fell over. "Oh, my freakin'… Did you hear what she said?" His eyes stung with moisture that, under ordinary circumstances, he would have hidden.

"Da," Madelynn repeated as if she knew he was leaping hurdles inside. "Da!"

He lifted the baby in the air and studied her speculatively. "Who's your daddy?"

"Da," she said again as if it was the only word she knew, and maybe it was. Her first, anyway. How did he get so damned lucky?

Emma's eyes widened with evident wonder. "She's so clever."

And thank God for that. Emma would abandon him as her sister had if it weren't for the talented baby. The same as every woman he'd ever cared about, beginning with his mother.

Chapter 11

On a positive note, to Bennett's surprise, Emma took well to plotting the "Grand Opening" of The Nightingale. She took to it as if no off switch existed in her head. As a result, any other topic, except for the baby, gave way to her latest idea.

As for his father babysitting, that road had been uphill and rocky. Emma behaved toward him like she'd never taken orders from a man. He kept pushing for complete authority. Their arguing resulted in long wallowing silences. The fact that they worked things out seemed nothing short of a miracle, but his stubborn father had met his match and gradually yielded.

The months flew by. When the pair were halfway decent to one another, Bennett tried unsuccessfully to win his way back into Emma's good graces. No matter what he did, she didn't warm toward him. They talked and even laughed occasionally, but after he dissed her, she'd regressed to treating him like no more than a business acquaintance again.

Now he sat at the dining room table with a bottle of scotch after the baby had been tucked into bed and his father had gone home. Emma came in, her face flushed a becoming shade of pink from her shower. Her beautiful body in those bare midriff PJs made him take such a hearty pull from his glass that he coughed and choked.

She sat across from him. "Is there a problem?"

"Huh?" The tightness in his chest made it hard to breathe. "I'm tired of being left out of your and Madelynn's lives. My father sees more of you than I do."

"That's your doing." She massaged her forehead. "The way you wanted things."

"Yeah, I get it," he said. *And I'm fricking sorry.*

"We're all doing the best we can. Madelynn seems to be thriving. Your dad's coming around. It pains me to admit this, but he's a big help. He's given us time to work on the operations for the B&B—the finances and networking."

"Yeah, everything's good." But it wasn't. "I'd like a day to hang out with you and my daughter, just the three of us."

She furrowed her brow. "I don't know if that's a good idea."

"Why the hell not?"

She shrugged, but her face had brightened. "How would you like to go on a quest?"

"A quest?"

She nodded her pretty head. "To find the real Huntington Beach. Tomorrow. Early."

He wouldn't dare protest—not the man who hadn't had sex for over a year and was living with a woman who wore short shorts and drove him wild by showing off her awesomely firmed legs. "I would love to go."

"Under wraps so that you can keep your precious privacy?"

"You bet." A little humor usually won out over wrath.

The following day, he appeared downstairs, clothed like someone hoping for a seat on a city bus. He wore raggedy cut-offs, a faded T-shirt, a day-old beard, dark shades, and a beachcomber hat pulled down over tousled hair.

"Wow," Emma said with an amused wink. "You dress down well."

"Ready to roll." He flipped open a treasure map he'd drawn that included the places to shop, good food to eat, and attractions to see.

Tramping from beach to beach, they stumbled upon a crowd of residents mixed with a priest, a minister, and a rabbi. The scene turned out to be the "Blessing of the Waves." This celebration brought together all faiths. The clergy wore wetsuits, and their disciples carried surfboards. Where else but in a town where the waves were considered sacred was such a thing possible?

Forgetting himself, Bennett blew into a conch shell to produce an eerie alien-like sound while Emma moved her hips in a way that made him stagger. She didn't even swim, yet she was caught up in the surf—from a safe distance of sand.

Watching her, he thought he'd die of neglect. All those nights of her disappearing into her bedroom while he scurried off to his own had been eating away at him.

Now she was taking notes that he thought of as "hen scratches"—a gender slip of the tongue he dared not voice. But a surfing padre and a congregation waving palm fronds deserved a place on Emma's list of "Fun Things to do in Surf City."

While out and about, they discovered one of the reasons why Huntington was also sometimes referred to as "Dog Town." Between Goldenwest Street and Seapoint, an entire stretch of beach existed for canines. These four-legged critters played tag in the waves, and every human counterpart wore a goofy smile.

For an instant, Bennett entertained the thought that they should get their own little tail-wagger. There wasn't a chance of that happening since Emma already had her hands full taking care of his daughter and working at getting the B&B ready with his dad.

But Emma swept a glance brimming with evident puppy love his way. "We never owned a dog."

He'd never seen that expression on her face. A craving, he'd call it. She wrapped her arms around her torso as if protecting herself from getting hurt, and that caught him with a surprise thump between the ribs. And right then, he'd do anything to strip whatever had happened to her away and make her feel secure and loved.

They meandered by the pet owners and the frolicking menagerie of purebreds and mixed breeds. In his arms, Madelynn kicked her feet and straightened her body. Her cue that meant she'd had enough of his restraint—thank you very much. It was time to get down and boogie. He gripped her hands as she toddled, kicking her high-tops in the sand. They'd just come around a trash can when he noticed a little furball cowering.

Before Bennett could prevent it, his daughter had lunged, cooing at the mutt who licked her chin. For crying out loud! He jerked Madelynn back into his clutches like some creepy kidnapper while she shrieked.

Emma knelt to inspect the shaking rat dog. "There, there," she soothed the little fellow. "No one's going to hurt you. Looks like you've been through the wringer, poor girl."

He zeroed in to protect his family. "Don't touch him. He's dirty and probably full of fleas. Who knows where he's been?"

"Look at her adorable face," she added, using baby talk he'd never associate with her from as little as ten minutes ago. "How can you insult her?"

"Well, I don't know." He suddenly suffered a pang in his solar plexus as if he'd kicked a down-and-out tramp. "He's obviously a stray. We can't be certain of his temperament. Watch it. He could have rabies. Don't get too close to him."

"She's all alone in the world." Of all the wrong moves, Emma patted the mutt's head of matted black hair, and he raised his white snout to lick her hand. "Aww, she's such a dear."

Bennett frowned as he considered the teensy beast. "With the way his fur sticks out from the sides of his face, he looks like a mad Scotsman."

As if the dang dog could understand, he puffed out his chest and uttered an offended yip.

"He's a she," Emma insisted with a lift of her chin. "Come on, how could you be so unfeeling? If we don't take her off the street, she'll starve."

"You can't be serious."

"Do you want her death on your conscience?"

"That's a low blow, even for you. If I were a good public servant, I'd take this hairball to the shelter."

"And break your daughter's heart?"

Madelynn voiced her opinion by slugging his chest with her fists. "Da...Da..."

"You two really know how to gang up on a guy." He resorted to adding begrudgingly, "If this adoption fails, don't come to me to bail you out."

Emma tugged off her denim jacket and draped it around the dog. Bennett fell in behind her, enchanted by how her muscles tightened like a dancer's as she moved.

The turquoise sundress paid homage to her figure—the leanness and curves in all the right places.

She opened the CUV's door, and while he buckled Madelynn into her car seat, Emma slid into the passenger side with the whimpering pup.

"What should we call her?" she asked.

"How about Lunacy?" he muttered.

She held the pathetic mutt up for inspection, rewarded with a kiss on her nose. "Doesn't she look like a Rosie? What do you think?"

"Rosie. Fine." He scowled. "Everything's coming up roses."

That was a lie. Things had gone to the dogs. He was being swallowed up by doubt, mainly by a mind-blowing chorus of *What the hell am I doing?* Following this, the confidence boosters. *Things will turn out okay. But why am I bringing home a mutt? Why am I even on a dog beach? On the plus side, Rosie will complete our family. What the hell am I thinking?*

Now that "you and me and baby makes three" had changed to "the dog makes four," they had to readjust their ads. Fess up. "Make sure the public knows that the B&B on Palm Tree Way is featured as pet friendly."

Emma had become acquainted with the people scheduled to stay at The Nightingale by exchanging several emails. She found out what each guest was interested in and how many days they planned to stay, advising them on making their itinerary fit their needs.

Who'd have guessed, with Emma's history in the foggy city by the bay, she'd brag about nine-point-three miles of beaches glittering in the sand? Or that she'd tread out to the length of the pier—"The fifth largest in California," she boasted—forgetting her fear of the water. If asked about a dress code on the beach, she'd respond, "A mix of wetsuits, bikinis, and sandals accessorized by volleyballs, surfboards, and beach towels."

Bennett didn't know how she talked him into exploring the Boho boutiques on Main Street and Beach Boulevard—"All in the pursuit of research," she told him. But, frankly, he enjoyed their outings. Hanging out with his daughter and the nanny made him thankful for the females in his life.

One afternoon, his heart flipped at the sight of Emma and Madelynn in the matching ruffled hats Emma had bought.

He'd forgotten to think before saying, "I spy two girly girls."

Ordinarily, that would go over like a sudden blackout. Still, Bennett couldn't be sure why—maybe because of the day, the sunshine, and their exuberance—she let his faulty male wiring slide.

"Let's get ice cream," she said as if to take the attention away from his folly.

"Sounds good to me."

The evening before the "Grand Opening," Emma peered at him over her laptop. "I feel like I'd know each guest if I saw them on the street."

"And they'd probably know you," he said, conscious that she'd given so much of herself to everyone slated for a night at the B&B.

She sat cross-legged on her bed, her white shorts doing justice to the tan she'd acquired. Even her eyes, as bright as freshly minted pennies, were accentuated by her newly bronzed skin. She patted Rosie, who settled beside her, adoration of the savior who'd come to the rescue showing in the canine's expression. Madelynn played peek-a-boo with them both. The trio of females had formed a bond that no outsider could break apart. The sight was oddly touching.

As for him, he'd fallen behind in his volunteer work, an occurrence he'd never mentioned to Emma. Not to the woman who'd altered her ambitions, even quit her job at the magazine, so she could help him realize his wish to be near his baby girl. Grant him time, that's all he asked, to watch over his daughter. Madelynn's health occupied his mind even on the best of days.

The red-ribbon cutting took place on the front porch. As the guest speaker, Bennett gave a speech that included everyone responsible for the improvements needed to make The Nightingale successful. A breeze carried the rich aromas from the sea and the herb garden as he spoke. Behind him, the inn had a sign over the door that read *The best journey takes you home*. And wondrously, a golden light shone from all the windows as if Heaven existed inside the walls.

Soon, the crowd stepped up the stone stairs past the blue-and-white porcelain pots that housed the spring flowers. Once through the doorway, the coolness enveloped Bennett like a welcoming glove, and the air smelled of fresh bread and pineapple-mango punch. People gathered about, chatting and laughing, and hours floated by, filled with Emma's sublime cookery. Even the trendy uptowners were on hand.

"Oh, look at that darling baby," a woman in periwinkle remarked with a gush.

Sucking in her cheeks and widening her already huge eyes, Madelynn made her adorable little-lamb face for her audience.

"How old is she?" asked a matronly lady with a voice like a tuba.

"She'll be a year..." Emma stopped slicing a cake and looked to Bennett for an answer.

"Tomorrow," he torpedoed back. They'd been so preoccupied they hadn't had time to catch a breath, let alone remember the date recorded on the birth certificate they'd received.

"She'll be having a birthday while we're here," a mother said, surrounded by a trio of children clapping in delight.

The newlyweds there for a surfer's convention said, "We'll have to cut our plans short. Wouldn't miss the party."

Bennett dragged Emma aside. "We better get with it." He picked up his daughter, enjoying her sweet baby smell. Not much longer, and that distinctive scent would be history, and so would her dependence on him. She might be one of those treacherous teenagers who'd rather die than be seen with their parents. He must take advantage of the time he had left.

Emma shook her head, chic in her navy dress with white polka dots. "We got lots to do."

"You're right. We have to pull this off."

"Don't look so browbeaten," she said as if reading his mind. "It's not like we've been on the beach lounging in the sun. I don't know when any of us took a day off. Oh, that's right, you, your dad, and I have been crazy busy putting together this opening-day gig. Until a few months ago, you were the man most likely slotted to leave come January for the US Capitol Building."

"When you put it that way, my prospects sound so dismal I'm glad I bailed."

"It used to be your lifelong dream. That's what your dad says about it."

"Dad! He's around here somewhere." His stomach turned over. "It's his granddaughter's birthday. He'll want to help plan it."

"And Junie Moon and the rest." She tapped a finger on her chin. "Then there are your friends…"

"They're your friends too. They like you better than me." He went into a tailspin. *How the heck are we going to pull this off?* "Do you think we can accommodate them all?"

"My family will have to get a hotel nearby. There won't be enough room otherwise."

"What will we feed them?"

"I don't know." She combed her long fingers through her new haircut. "Maybe Madelynn's favorite. She's wild about spaghetti."

He hemmed and hawed while mentally counting. "I don't think we have enough dishes."

"Haven't you heard of paper plates?"

Bennett catered to their guests, sharing Huntington's history. He added tidbits about places to go and see while silently putting together a party theme. Madelynn loved anything "princess." He ordered the decorations online for the following morning. Meanwhile, Emma did all the shopping. She was missing in action for so long that the guests started asking about her and the birthday girl. Every second he got, he invited the friends he thought would feel slighted if they were left out—which were most of them.

He met Emma in the hall right before they went their separate ways to fall into their beds around midnight. He could feel her presence more than see her in the darkness.

As always, he suffered that undisputable urge to pick her up, caveman style, and carry her to his bed.

"Do you think we can do this thing?" She sounded worried.

"We've got this," he said, but in reality, he was none too sure.

Bennett felt like he'd just fallen asleep when Emma's alarm clock blared through the wall between them. He rolled over and moaned when he saw five a.m. His body protested his lack of sleep by shooting every muscle and joint with pain. What he wouldn't give for a few more hours of shut-eye, but he couldn't let her make breakfast for the guests or a cake for Madelynn. Plus, God knew what else without his help. Determinedly, he pushed the blankets away and leaped out of bed.

When he met her in the kitchen, Emma said, "What are you doing up before the chickens?"

Did she look this way every morning? She was so easy on the eyes. Her lips were provocatively nude, the loveliest shade of natural he'd ever seen.

He yearned to run his own fingers through the hair she had whacked off herself, making disarray look like the newest fashion trend. The sun had turned her loose waves burnt sienna with lots of golden and fiery-red highlights that glistened under the kitchen's reassessed lighting.

"I have to order presents." She shoved some of her prized caramel-apple pastry into the industrial oven.

He crossed his arms in front of himself. "You need my help."

"Do I?" she quipped. "I don't remember asking for it."

"You don't think we're putting Madelynn in danger

by inviting a gang of children here to celebrate her birthday, do you?"

"What?"

"Think of the germs all those kids will bring with them."

"Bennett, she'll be fine."

"Listen, I'm here to save you and her from..." His lips brushed hers, and he fell into their sweet, buttery depths.

She closed her eyes with a soft moan, accepting his mouth over hers for the first time in months. And he wanted her so much he couldn't have stopped if it meant losing half his stocks. He'd lusted to taste more of the magic of the priceless spices that existed in her kiss.

"I think—" she started when Madelynn's wake-up call filtered downstairs and through the open doorway. Her cry hit the walls, encircled them, and broke their enchantment.

"I'll go get the birthday girl," he said, surrendering.

"You do that." Emma drew back, dreamily licking her lips as if enjoying the sensation there. "Wait." She undid her apron and tossed it on the back of a chair. "I'll go too."

Madelynn's face lit when they entered, her arms flapping at the elbows excitedly as she clutched the crib rail and stamped her feet.

"Happy birthday," he said, thinking how bad it was they'd almost forgotten. They were too busy, which was good. But he wouldn't have missed this special moment for the world.

Madelynn bounced from side to side with a smile as big as the Pacific on her sweet face.

Bennett captured her in his arms and twirled.

"Ready to party, pumpkin wonkin?"

The hours sailed by while he got the guests situated and off to their various destinations. Only a handful of problems arose. First, the kitchen drain plugged up, and Bennett had to plunge the pipes. When that didn't work, he rented a plumber's snake, which did the trick but took a good portion of time out of his morning.

Next, the dog needed to be walked, and Madelynn had to go along with her daddy to give Emma more time to prepare the food. He was lucky to get showered and shaved. Then he had to take Emma's place so she could do the same.

By three, the people arrived, filling The Nightingale with flashing smiles and laughter. Everyone had come out to party hearty. Bennett scooped up Rosie so she didn't get stepped on. Who'd have believed he'd resort to carrying around a purse dog?

Between the kids scarfing down the spaghetti and most adults preferring Chinese, the meal stretched far enough to feed the crowd, and the red and white wine flowed. The balloons swayed in the air from the open windows, and one lively kid popped a couple before his mother apprehended him. After this shindig, Bennett would have to summon one of the advertised cleaning companies for help. This bash would end up costing a mint in damages.

But when everyone assembled sang "Happy Birthday," something as hard as a rock lodged in his throat. His little angel, his Madelynn Grace, had turned a year old today. The fact that she appeared healthy warmed his heart. Emma clapped, laughing, and waved him into their close-knit circle to share in the blowing out of the twinkling candles.

Madelynn had tomato sauce from head to toe. Her crown sat askew atop her reddish-blonde curls, and one patent leather shoe was missing, but her smile, that dazzling grin, lit The Nightingale brighter than all the electric lights combined. He snapped photos with his camera. Others took pictures of her grabbing fistfuls of the sliced cake on her plate and squishing it so forcefully between her fingers that her little body shook with the effort, making everyone laugh.

"She's enthusiastic," someone commented.

Emma took a wet towel to Madelynn's hands, saying, "She's as determined as her daddy."

"Hey," he said, "I'd say she's more like her mother."

This blunder stopped some of the partygoers cold since most knew Emma wasn't the baby's birth mother.

"Her mommy," he amended, cocking his head to observe the beautiful woman holding Madelynn's sippy cup. "Our little lamb's just like her mommy."

Had he ever thought of his daughter as Rachel's child? Maybe in the beginning, when he learned of her death before he'd even set eyes on Madelynn, but that seemed long ago. He'd been another man in a different galaxy, a traveler without a home.

The rest of the night pounded on in a cloud of Audrey's uncle at the piano that only Bennett had played until now. Emma and her gang, which included Madison, Audrey, and Lucinda, sang along as Johnny Spade performed a tribute to pop songs from the last century.

Meanwhile, Bennett held Madelynn and danced. Soon, he included Emma. The trio whirled across the recently refinished floor, the hardwood cool and smooth on his bare feet. The baby nodded off, dipping her head on his shoulder. Her crown toppled to the floor with a loud ping as if to summon the end of the party.

After everyone had gone to bed or left for home, Emma's silence told him she'd heard him when he called her Madelynn's mother. He couldn't decipher her reaction, but her face looked pinched. His edginess surfaced again, his palms sweaty, stomach tensed. What did she think? Did she want to throw the rest of the birthday cake at him?

Maybe he didn't want to know. Maybe he did. Perhaps he shouldn't care so much one way or the other. That was just asking for a world of hurt, but try as he might, he couldn't get his mouth to work. Anything he said would be more important than all the hundreds of things he'd uttered in all his thirty years.

Rosie hunkered down at his feet and gazed up at him through a cloud of fur, her eyes humongous in her tiny body as she barked. With a mere twitch of her wet nose, she appeared able to tell when one of them needed a nudge. Bennett glanced at the walls, now defaced with fingerprints, glanced too at the balloons on the ceiling and at Rosie trotting away, her snout lifted as if fed up with him. He sighed, realizing he'd better speak up instead of standing there with his hands in his pockets.

"I'm sorry, Emma. I probably offended you when I called you my daughter's mother. I know how much you loved your sister, and I didn't mean any disrespect. If you want, you can go back to not speaking to me except when you have to. I wouldn't blame you if you did."

While looking everywhere but at Emma, he heard her say, "Marry me," and it was so unexpected it knocked him on his butt.

Chapter 12

Emma knelt at the high-back chair where Bennett had flopped down, staring up at her as if in shock.

"I don't think I heard you right." He cupped his hand over his ear. "For a second, I thought you said—"

"Marry me," she repeated, refusing to let her emotions show for fear he'd be able to see right through her.

"Marry *you*?"

She leaned closer to him, and his nearness made her senses spin. "We'll announce our engagement on social media." She paused, her heartbeat increasing. "Tomorrow, I think."

He blinked. "As early as that, but don't we need to discuss this first? I mean, marriage—"

"I heard some guests gossiping about me not being Madelynn's real mother, and yadda, yadda. I understand that you wanted to marry my sister and that life hasn't gone as planned, but I'm trying to make things easier."

"Wow." He rubbed his forehead. "I'm honored and blown away by your offer, but you don't have to sacrifice your happiness to stop people from talking. That's just wrong."

"Look, we're running this inn together, and we're bringing up the baby—together. Someday, you'll go back to politics. You don't want any past scandals to haunt you."

"Of course not."

"So we marry for appearance's sake." Oh, she wanted so much more than to put on a show. Had he guessed that about her? "I'm not just thinking of you but of Madelynn."

"Of course you are." He covered his mouth and shook his head as if overwhelmed. "This is so unselfish, so good of you, Emma, but…"

She leaned down and took his chin in her fingers. "What do you say?"

He shrugged with a roll of his broad shoulders. "I guess…hey, hold on. You're talking about a marriage of convenience," he said as if impressed. "How very Jane Austen of you."

Maybe so, but would he walk away after their pretense had done the trick? And how long before then—a few months, a year? Would they never see each other from that day forward, or would they run into each other on the street or at a party and reminisce about the time they played house?

Emma was breaking all her self-imposed rules to put this offer on the table. But she must rectify the problems for him that she alone had caused. If she hadn't insisted on being the nanny all those months back, if she hadn't stuck around, there'd be no need to propose. It was a bitter pill to swallow, but she only had herself to blame.

Oh, she could blame her prolonged stay on Madelynn's health. Her niece was still her number one priority, she told herself. And it was true, but Bennett was coming in at a close second. Because of this, she took the initiative by pulling him off the chair with her hands clasped around his large wrists.

"So we'll act happily married," she said—a total

oxymoron for her—this happily married theme. From her experience with her mother, she'd learned being bonded with someone in matrimony couldn't be counted on for much, and she had to keep that foremost in her mind.

That's why the next morning, when he met her in the hall with, "You still think we should tie the knot," she winced.

"You're asking me this before coffee?" What had she done? "Meet me downstairs, and we'll discuss things while you help me whip up hearty omelets to serve the guests. I'll even teach you how to make ghee that causes toast, even gluten-free, to melt in your mouth."

"Did I ever tell you I love it when you talk dirty?"

She snorted as if his remark didn't make her want to press herself against his warm body and caress the length of his lean, mean, custom-machine back. She fretted over the way her feelings betrayed her. So, blowing out a sigh, she bolted out of the hall to the safety of the downstairs kitchen and snapped on the lights.

She'd have to pull herself together, or her plans would fail before she began. "Let's set some ground rules, here and now."

"Aye, aye, Captain. What are you thinking?"

"When there are people around, we act all lovey-dovey. Behind closed doors, we'll be ourselves—friends without benefits."

His gaze connected with hers, and he breathed out a quiet, "Without benefits?" He shook his head. "Damn, and here I thought you wanted to jump my bones."

"I do…" Her blunder was out before she could snap it back. She bit her lip, took the bread dough from the fridge, and plopped it on the butcher block. The sky outside the windows had lightened to the pearl pink seen along the West Coast on many a spring morning.

"You feel the hunger too?" he whispered, making her insides quiver.

She silently cursed herself for giving him the wrong idea and turned her back on him. "We'll call our friends and family and announce the big news. Then we'll make certain we're seen together groaning and moaning."

"You make it sound like we should be headed to the doctor instead of the altar."

"Sorry," she said, inclined to add, "but if we get sick of one another, then it's over."

He snapped his fingers. "As easy as that?"

She didn't meet his stare. "Split bedsheets," she deadpanned.

Why was her belly twisting and turning like a tornado?

She punched down the bread dough for all she was worth, wanting to rid herself of her angst. As if in response, Bennett beat a dozen eggs nearly to death. They didn't speak a word to one another. When June entered, wearing a smile that quickly faded, the tension in the kitchen had gotten thick enough to hack through with a butcher knife.

June poured herself coffee. "Did you two have something go wrong this morning?"

"Bennett and I are getting married," Emma announced flatly.

June quit blowing the steam from the top of her cup. "I don't understand. I—"

"Don't worry, Auntie," Emma said. "I popped the question, and he said yes."

Bennett didn't add anything, and Emma hadn't

expected him to, but his scowl told her that something about this fake alliance didn't appeal to him.

June must have caught his brooding look too. "Is this what you want?" she asked him.

"Yeah, yeah, sure." He swung open the back door. "I need some air."

"Are you getting cold feet?" Emma called.

He turned on her. "I always thought when I married, it would be because we couldn't stand to be apart." He left, jogging down toward the shore.

Emma buried her face against June's shoulder. "He's thinking of Rachel."

"I wouldn't be too sure about that." June steered her toward the doorway. "Go after him."

She didn't need another push. She ran until she spied Bennett on the rocks worn by wind and sea. He twisted around, a cloud of wavy hair hanging seductively over his forehead.

When he saw her, his mouth dropped open. "What are you doing here? You never get this close to dangerous surf."

"I love it out here." Her attempt at courage faltered. "I just can't swim."

"And still, you ventured out where it isn't safe." He walked in her direction, and the land seemed to tip. "What's up?"

"I apologize for being so insensitive after all you've been through."

"What's that supposed to mean—*after all you've been through*?"

"You had wanted to marry Rach. You're still grieving, the same as I am—well, maybe not quite the same, but you're kind of stuck with me."

He wore that look she'd come to associate with him whenever she brought up her sister's name. He was shutting down, she thought, the way people often did while in deep mourning and unable to talk about it.

"I believe what my sister must have known before I did," she said. "The community, the state—hell, the entire nation will prosper with your leadership someday."

"Do you honestly think Rach thought like that?" Cynicism sharpened his voice.

"I know she did. She mentioned the politician she met in her voicemail to me."

His expression was...somber. All at once, he straightened. "Hey, since you like the ocean so much, how would you like to go sailing with me?"

Wishing to right a wrong had brought her to where the water roared, and the rocks were slippery. Her motivation hadn't included much forethought. He seemed to have emerged from his former funk with a gleam in his eyes, so she didn't have the heart to refuse him.

She forced a grin. "Sailing? That would be fun."

When they returned to the house, the bread was just coming out of the oven, and the lodgers, most ready to take on the theme parks, gathered around the breakfast buffet June had so skillfully put together.

Emma gave her a big hug. "You're a gem."

"I think getting away is what you both need," June said after they brought up the subject of their adult boat trip. "Where you headed?"

"Somewhere Emma will never forget," Bennett said and, a half hour later, came down the stairs dressed in a royal-blue polo shirt and a navy blazer. Sunglasses hung from a coordinating cord around his neck. White denims finished off his nautical look. He could have posed for a photoshoot for men's cologne or an ad for a cruise ship.

But nothing could be more natural than him forgetting his nice clothes and romping with his daughter around the yard. He'd set Madelynn on the top of his shoulders, and she was laughing, and so was he when Emma came out to join them. He saw her then and halted, Madelynn resting the side of her face on the top of his head.

"As far as stylish goes," he said, "Emma, you fit the bill."

"Thank you." Just a single sentence—a simple compliment—from him gave her tunnel vision. "You're quite the charmer."

She hadn't been able to resist wearing her version of bon voyage—a pair of clean white slacks, an off-the-shoulder sweater, open-toed shoes, and a straw hat. She should look like she belonged with him, she told herself—if only for appearance's sake.

All too soon, they were saying their goodbyes and slipping into the car, alone for once, and driving down the Pacific Coast Highway like two for the road.

Bennett lowered the volume on the radio. "I can't wait to introduce you to *Helen*."

Emma lifted an eyebrow for effect. "I take it *Helen's* the name of your boat?"

"*Helen of Troy*," he said like someone announcing royalty.

She had never stepped foot in a marina—why would she? But she found herself on a walkway in one sometime later. Tied to pier cleats, boats of all sizes rocked along the water's edge. Flags snapped in the wind, classic rock played from a nearby bar and grill, and engines started up with a growl that sent chills of dread up her spine.

When she heard the slap of flip-flops on the dock and the squeak of rubber soles, she realized others were in their element. She wasn't. The kelp flies buzzed near her ears, and she swatted at them as Bennett led the way, the picnic basket June had packed with goodies swinging at his side. The thought of food made Emma's stomach rebel, and she hadn't boarded yet.

He grabbed her hand. "Act like you're mad about me," he said as smooth as glass.

"Why? It's not like you're still running for office."

"I would hope people haven't forgotten me already. Besides, you were the one who insisted on being all lovey-dovey while out and about."

She could have told him nothing in her feelings for him were phony. Being this close accelerated her heartbeat and initiated thoughts she'd never had.

But that wouldn't do. "Let's take this show on the water," she said.

Dashing down the pier, hand in hand, they passed the fish, jumping through the surface and then disappearing, and everywhere she looked, bare masts stretched into the sky. Soon, he was reaching to help her onto a huge boat with tall blue sails and lots of glossy white.

Emma uttered a humble, "How do you do, *Helen*?"

She noticed that he still held her hand and could have pulled away because any future voters had gone on about their business, but her fingers were shaking, and his grip was secure. He guided her out onto his boat and got her a life jacket from the console.

"Buckle up." He helped her into the bulky vest, the likes of which she'd never worn—but then again, why would she?

In her wildest dreams, she'd never pictured herself going sailing. But the pride Bennett took in showing off the helm, the radar system, and the mic he spoke into did some funny things to her heart. He was sharing his love for this seafaring vessel with her, and she wanted him to know she appreciated it.

"Your boat's beautiful," she admitted.

"Thanks." An invisible draw seemed to pull them closer together until he stepped away. "I'll just finish our tour so we can shove off."

"Yep." She swallowed down her anxiety. "Can't wait."

"You're in for a treat, Emma." He still held her hand, pulling her down below the deck.

Seeing the cabin for the first time, she gulped. "There's a bed."

"Berth," he corrected her. "That's the term when you're on a boat."

"Ah, berth," she repeated, noticing the marine blue-and-white-striped bedspread and wooden frame with its spindle design. "People sleep in a berth."

"They do. That and other things." Bennett's voice had gotten all croaky.

"We're really alone," she said with a tight awareness of the fact in her throat.

"That's right…"

She imagined him filling that mattress, his shoulders spanning the length of a pillow, and her enjoying the feel of his body close to hers… *No, don't go there.* But his warm breath alongside her head made her hunger from the memory of his mouth on hers.

"No baby zooming around in her walker," Emma observed, "never still, not even for a moment. No hotel guests, no family, and need I mention, no clingy dog."

"Nope." He grinned wickedly. "Just you and me."

She got so rattled she didn't trust herself but slid past him and inspected the compact kitchen. She complimented him on the marble countertop and stainless-steel sink. He appeared caught up in her praise, explaining how he'd designed things. His enthusiasm excited her and intensified her feelings for him. How easy it was to get lost in the way he carried on.

Being below could prove dangerous if she didn't make a move, so she nodded toward the stairs. "I suppose we should get started."

He nodded back. Their visual interchange prompted her to reluctantly make her way up the steps into the blueness of the light above, where everything was safe.

While she watched, Bennett adjusted the sails and steered clear of the other boats with an efficiency that fascinated her. They moved swiftly, the sun sparkling on the water, the wind fingering through her hair. She could sense his desire to impress her while he steered. His allure caused her to ignore the sway of the boat beneath her feet, and that her stomach had become a little more upset.

Still, she'd never been out on the ocean. Nothing but endless blue, the beach so far off.

"Stand with me at the helm, Emma." He took her in his arms. "Here you go. You can steer the boat if you want."

Her sweaty hands clutched the magnificent wheel, and she experienced the fantasy she never knew she had until now. She was in control, which made all the difference in the hour or so that followed. Two for the road had become two for the deep blue sea, but dark clouds rolled across the sky in a matter of minutes.

"It's getting dark," he said.

Her mouth went dry at his comment, and her belly was jumpier than before. "What is it?"

"Looks like a surprise storm. We've had a few this year. This one wasn't on the radar until now."

Emma wrapped her arms around herself as if that could prevent her from shivering.

He massaged her neck with one hand. "It's fine."

She wanted to believe him.

But within a half hour, the skies were flecked with rain. A flight of pelicans flew in from the south toward a piece of land not covered yet by the rising tide. And the boat itself rocked with so much force it gave her vertigo.

"I need..." She had started to ask for a bucket, but it was too late, and she staggered as fast as she could and puked from the side of the boat. Bennett was warning her to get back when a gust of wind launched her over the rail. The water swallowed her headfirst. Her buoyant lifejacket enabled her to pop up, and she gasped. She hardly heard the boat engine cutting off in the ocean's roar.

The icy current was already dragging her off. "Bennett!" She saw him on the side of the boat.

"Emma," he shouted. "Grab hold of the life preserver!"

A floating ring attached to a cord snaked toward her. She snagged the lifeline with her frozen fingers, but in the next second, her numbed grip proved useless, and her only hope shot away from her like a slippery wonton in a bowl of soup.

"Try to get back to the boat," he yelled through cupped hands.

Terrified, she struggled to kick her legs like she'd seen swimmers do, but her limbs hadn't any memory of the motion.

A wave exploded in her face, and her lungs burned. She needed a good, strong breath but couldn't suck in any air.

Water surrounded her—not pretty and inviting like before, but shadowed and as despairingly final as a grave. Maybe she'd see Rachel if she crossed over or whatever people did after death. Vaguely, she wondered if her sister would be there to greet her—or maybe her father. He had to be dead by now. She'd never heard from him after he went to China.

"Bába." Her four-year-old self cried out the Chinese word for Daddy, wondering if it would be the last thing she said.

With renewed terror, she remembered Madelynn. Nothing could stop the surge of emotion. Their baby had celebrated her birthday—was it only last night? Balloons everywhere, all those kids, family, friends—the best moments of Emma's life.

Although only minutes had gone by since she'd been swept overboard, the seconds passed like hours. At least, Madelynn would still have her father. This fact bolstered Emma's mental state, giving her peace of mind—until she noticed Bennett, feet apart, on the pitching boat.

He'd removed his sunglasses, the maritime jacket, and beach shoes. Just then, a steel ladder rattled down the side of the vessel. "I'll save you, Emma! Stay right where you are."

Where else was she going to go?

In a flash of insight, she recalled how many would-be rescuers drowned trying to save some poor sap. She still couldn't catch her breath, let alone voice what was in her mind.

Madelynn can't lose her daddy too!

Even as she registered that, she saw Bennett swimming through the foaming peaks like one of Huntington Beach's legendary surfers. He hadn't spent his adolescence sitting on a beach towel. He took to the call of duty with all the determination of a lifeguard.

If she could have managed it, she'd have cheered.

Now she felt him behind her.

"I've got you." He wrapped his arm around her ribcage just below her breasts, her back to his front.

He kicked as if with all his strength, falling into constant movement as he struggled to keep Emma and him afloat. She rested her eyes on his brawny arm in his drenched shirt. Obviously, he was well-equipped for just such an emergency.

But she had to say through the rawness in her throat, "You shouldn't have—"

"Shut up." His sandpapery chin scratched her cheek. "Save your strength."

The sun broke through clouds and streamed down over Bennett's razor-sharp profile. The wind and water added to the illusion of a face set in stone, yet the harsh rasp of his breathing told her he was also suffering the effects of the cold water.

How much longer? She turned her head and, with a sudden lightness in her chest, saw the boat only a few yards from them. He pushed her from the mouth of the water and up the rungs of the ladder. His large hands grasped her rear and hoisted her to the top.

This was no time to mention that he shouldn't be touching her in such an inappropriate manner. Her strength had been spent so that she tumbled over the side—barefoot since the sea had robbed her of her shoes—and collapsed in a shivering heap at the bottom of the boat.

Coughing, she gave in to expelling the saltwater. Afterward, she curled into a shuddering ball, remaining as still as possible while the sailboat rocked. Her lungs smarted, and her teeth chattered. She'd never been so cold.

He dropped down beside her. He was hacking now and almost as sick as she was, his breath wheezing. She finally got enough stamina to lift her head and studied him through bleary eyes. He sat next to her, his back against some sort of storage chest.

"Get below." He urged her to her feet. "Too cold up here." He clamped her tight against his side, and his muscles flexed and tensed beneath his dripping clothes. "I've got you."

Emma was so weak she couldn't protest as he dragged her down the steps with him.

Once inside the cabin, he tore off the bedspread and grabbed the blanket. "I have to get you out of your wet things."

She frowned at him. "I can undress myself." But her knees buckled, and she collapsed on the mattress. Her shaking hand fumbled with the button on her drenched sweater.

He took over. "Friendzone—remember?"

She watched him, taken aback by the tender look in

his dark eyes. She swallowed and couldn't gaze at him anymore, suddenly fiercely aware of her nakedness and him drying her body with the towel. His hand brushed her breasts. By accident? She was afraid of seeing arousal when she looked again at his face—afraid of what that sensation might do to her.

"You better?" he murmured, wrapping her in the blanket.

She sat against the pillows and combed her fingers through her snarled hair. "Your turn."

He bunched his T-shirt up his arms and yanked it off over his head. She focused on the ceiling, telling herself she didn't need to rubberneck. Not gawking took every shred of her self-control. Well, maybe a glance, she reasoned. After all, he'd seen her. She lowered her chin.

He had stripped down to nothing. His chest was sculpted, not like he'd spent hours in a gym, but his arms and shoulders were toned. His stomach was flat, not in a six-pack sort of way—more natural than that. He had spirals of dark hair and...

"You're checking me out," he said as if pleased, though his teeth were still chattering.

Her cheeks heated with embarrassment. "Thank you for saving me."

"Are you still cold?"

"I'm freezing."

"We have to help each other warm up." He opened her blanket. "Skin to skin. It's the only way."

"I can't—"

He sat and pushed himself back up against her, and she clung to him. A welcome surge of warmth melted her humiliation. He rubbed her forearms with his palms, quieting her, and she buried her face in the back of his neck and couldn't stop it—she wept.

"I was so afraid," she admitted between sobs.

"Let you in on a little secret, so was I."

Her fears came out in a rush. "I believed I was going to die, and then when you jumped in, I thought you might not make it, and then Madelynn would have been orphaned."

"I worried about that too. Madelynn needs you... I need you."

The last part came out in a whisper that sent Emma's spirits soaring. Did she dare to hope he meant he wanted her and not just a nanny for his daughter? She was about to ask when a whirring noise sounded from above.

"It's probably the mayday I sent." He pulled a terrycloth robe from the closet and headed up the steps.

She kept the blanket around her and crept behind him. A white boat trimmed in orange was approaching.

A male voice boomed from a loudspeaker, "This is the United States Coast Guard. We got your report of a woman on your sailboat falling overboard."

Her face tingled with dread. "I'm fine," she called.

Bennett didn't pay her any heed but welcomed the medical team aboard. Two paramedics attended to her and treated Bennett while asking him questions. She allowed all the poking and probing while trying to distance herself from the scene.

Emma hadn't ever been the person who needed help. During any disaster, she had always been capable. Even as a child on the streets, she'd done everything possible to stay alive. And yet here she was a victim of circumstances because of her inadequacy.

If nothing else came out of this, she vowed to learn to swim.

Chapter 13

Bennett finished telling everyone at the dining room table about their afternoon while they all ate a feast created by June's culinary expertise. The sun had gone down, and the light from the chandelier bounced off walls as clean as they'd been before Madelynn's birthday party. The meal proved exceptional after their harrowing experience at sea. He was thankful for his recently acquired family but felt concerned about Emma.

She had listened politely as he and the others talked, saying nothing herself. She looked weary, barely able to sit up, her face snowy white against dark hair.

What could he do? She should eat something. Then he recalled the first day he'd met her, the tomato soup he'd served her.

He leaned over her chair. "Why don't we get you to bed?"

Rai signed something he couldn't make out with her hands and then voiced, "She's so tired," maybe for his benefit.

Everyone at the table agreed. Emma nodded and swayed as she got to her feet like she was still on his sailboat. He steadied her. She bent to kiss Madelynn's head, and then he and Emma ambled upstairs. June followed them to help her niece.

Much later, after the others had left for the airport and he'd tucked Madelynn into her crib, he prepared the soup. He brought it up on a tray with the rose he'd plucked from the garden.

"Emma," he softly called as he entered the room where Rosie kept watch.

Emma stirred and snapped on the lamp atop her nightstand. "What do you have there?"

"Your mother's cure-all."

"Wow…tomato soup—your specialty." Her face brightened. "And a red rose. How thoughtful of you."

"The least I can do. I should have seen you were sick to your stomach."

She sneezed. "You saved me." She sneezed again. "Life's so fragile."

Her statement was a little too real for him, so he welcomed the excuse to leave for a box of tissues from the cabinet in the hall.

"Here you go." He passed her one.

"Thanks." She began to eat the soup and gradually regained some of the color on her face. "Sit with me, will you?"

He perched on the edge of her mattress. While she ate, he remembered, too well, their last encounter on a bed, being enmeshed together in the blanket—her naked. Her body had been even nicer than he'd imagined. He'd tried not to gaze down at her perky breasts, narrow waist, and stupendous legs. Even in his weakened state, the sight had tested his willpower, then and now.

What the hell was he doing, sitting on her bed—he who claimed to be a pal? Better to get out while he still could. He bent over and scratched Rosie's tiny ears, then rushed from the room.

That night, he suffered from endless tossing and turning. The previous day's events came alive again, delivered with the same torment—the sea carrying Emma away from him, feeling himself sucked under the water, flung up again, holding her, and struggling to get back to the boat. The cold and the darkness returned relentlessly as he used every ounce of strength to save her from a watery grave.

Naturally, Madelynn started rocking her crib at 6:04 a.m. He smacked the snooze button and fell back asleep.

When the alarm went off again, drowsy and confused, he reared up on his elbows. The sounds of Emma coughing and objects hitting her floor drifted through the wall between them. He staggered into her bedroom. She tried to get into her robe but put her arm through the wrong sleeve. Failing, she collapsed on her mattress with an exhausted moan.

"Don't worry." He picked up her fallen alarm clock and tissue box. "I'll take care of the baby."

"But that's my job."

"You can't even get out of bed." He felt her forehead with the back of his hand. "We have to get you to the doctor."

"No, I'm okay," she said through a stuffy nose, and then as if on second thought, she continued, "Is your father available?"

"Dad left yesterday for Washington. He's staying with old friends. It's good for him."

"Who's going to watch the baby?"

"I just told you, that would be me." He bit his lower lip.

She hit her forehead with the heel of her hand and fell back against her pillow. "All of this is my fault."

"How do you figure?"

"If only I hadn't barfed."

He rubbed his aching forehead, a surrealness clinging to every word uttered. "We can't keep rehashing things."

She nodded in agreement. "Lucky for us there're no guests scheduled today. Not until tomorrow."

"Right. Now, you just relax. I'll take care of everything."

What he wanted more than anything was to climb in next to her soft, warm body and cuddle, soothe—and pleasure her. But that, of course, would not happen. Not in a million years.

An hour later, after feeding, bathing, and dressing Madelynn, he took a shortcut from The Nightingale into the pouring rain. He couldn't see anyone or anything in the wind that howled in from the ocean, where the horizon looked like no more than a blur. The world was drowning as he took his delicate daughter out into the storm.

He tried to lighten his mood while he maneuvered the CUV through the traffic jam caused by the accident on the highway. Emma's words earlier flooded back. "Life's so fragile…"

Besides the inconvenience, the ebb and flow of the water he saw to his left from his open car window haunted him with flashes of yesterday.

"How's Daddy's baby girl holding up?" A glance at the rearview mirror revealed Madelynn dozing. Was it his imagination, or did she look flushed?

He didn't like taking her to the supermarket with him, but what else could he do? They'd used up most of the food in the fridge. He had a gazillion B&B obligations, but if he prepared a huge meal today, he'd have enough to serve the lodgers tomorrow. To be fair, he should be warning them that he would be doing the cooking. Instead, he'd reinforced his commitment to take over for Emma. Somehow he'd get through this.

Nervously, between sips of medium roast coffee, ignoring all the missed calls and messages on his phone, he hit Liam's number on the car screen. Better to touch base now with Liam before he heard about the engagement through the grapevine.

"I've got news." Bennett smoothed his voice out to an even keel. "Emma and I are getting married to prevent any talk that could lead to trouble."

"How lovely for you both."

Liam's sarcasm made Bennett defensive. "It'll work out. It's the sensible thing to do."

"You'd better hope Emma isn't hiding any trashy little secrets like her sister did."

"It'll work out," Bennett repeated but felt like his life had turned into a three-act play. Planning a birthday party, becoming betrothed, diving from his boat to rescue his alleged fiancée. *Alleged fiancée?* Was he caught in a tragedy with no hope in sight?

Would the day dawn that Emma would admit, as her sister had, that she didn't want to marry him? He stopped himself. Comparing Emma to Rach was wrong. Terribly and completely wrong. He wouldn't go off the deep end by imagining the worst.

Emma was the polar opposite of her sister. She was a straight shooter, someone he could depend on and respect.

With Madelynn asleep against his shoulder, he entered a market where, in his agitated state, the ordinary noises were intensified. A cashier asking for a price check from an intercom sounded deranged. The usual background music, distorted by the rain on the roof, was enough to shake his psyche. He searched for a quiet corner, the wheels on his cart going *clickety-clack, clickety-clack*.

June had helped Emma prepare spaghetti so many times she would no doubt know the ingredients by heart. He didn't need to bother Emma, he decided, as he used his free hand to make the call. When June answered, he whispered what he needed and that it was kind of an emergency that he get it.

"What's wrong?" She sounded frightened. "Is Emma still sick?"

"I think she's developed a chill." He wondered how his brain had resorted to such an old-fashioned term as "a chill," yet it seemed to fit. "She's okay. She just has to rest, and Madelynn's napping while I'm holding her. I'm trying to keep her asleep for as long as I can."

"I'll text you." She paused for a few seconds. "Bennett, do you need me there?"

"I got this," he insisted, readjusting Madelynn since his arm had started tingling.

"Yes, yes. Keep me posted."

After their goodbyes, he noticed his former office assistant heading toward him from the other end of the aisle. Anne Gomes had retired about the same time his dad had. He called out her name, and she twisted around, still as dignified as ever with her salt-and-pepper hair in a bun at the nape of her neck and her tailored clothes. She looked at him like she didn't know him.

But then why would she? He hadn't had enough time this morning to shower, shave, or even comb his hair. Anne probably didn't know he'd become a father.

As he drew near her, she said tentatively, "Bennett?"

"It's me."

"I read you withdrew from the election." Her face softened. "Is this little baby why?"

He introduced Madelynn, who was emerging from sleep. He then explained all that had happened, starting with the day Emma and Madelynn had come into his life, forever altering it, adding his job at The Nightingale, and ending with yesterday's drama. Anne stretched out compassionate arms, and he handed his daughter to her.

"Let me help you." Anne once again became the best assistant ever.

She teamed with him to pick out fresh-cut flowers for vases. Next, ground Italian sausage went into the cart, and after that came all the tasty fixings mentioned in June's text. They'd just gotten up to the check stand when Madelynn started to holler.

Anne said, "She feels warm."

He laid the back of his hand along his daughter's forehead and sucked in his breath. "She's burning up. I've got to get her to her pediatrician."

Madelynn raised her hands to him, and red-faced, she wailed, "Dada!"

"I've got you." He drew her against his chest. With a quick "thank you so much for everything" to Anne, he paid for his groceries and ran.

Beyond the glass doors, the deluge awaited.

"What's wrong with you, sweet girl?" He buckled her into her car seat like the pro he'd become. "Daddy will get you all better."

He wouldn't notify Emma and alarm her. She had enough to deal with right now just caring for herself. On second thought, she might be more upset if he didn't call.

He started the phone conversation with, "First off,

Madelynn's fine."

"Are you kidding me? I hear her crying."

"She's a little warm. I'm taking her to see Dr. Nguyen."

"Did you call for an appointment?"

He hadn't had time for it. "No, but the doctor will see me."

"I hope so." She had a hysterical note in her voice. "I'll call ahead."

"No need to. I can be very convincing."

"I'll call a driver and meet you there."

"No, you're ill. Stay where you are, and I'll handle things."

He'd gotten the green light and started driving through the intersection when his CUV jerked to an immediate stop as the vehicle to his left plowed through the red light. The culprit's car swerved, skidded on the wet pavement, and ended in the lane where the oncoming traffic had already vacated. If his vehicle hadn't had the technology to brake when needed, he and Madelynn would have been T-boned.

Bennett pulled off the road, unfastened Madelynn, and hugged her while he fell apart. His daughter might have been history. All he could think about was what could have happened. He should have been more observant. He hadn't been paying attention to the road, and his ears roared as he held his sobbing daughter with one arm and wiped the sweat from his face with the other. He uttered a thankful prayer and navigated his precious, loyal vehicle down the flooded street. By the time he got his unhappy girl to the doctor, his body trembled with aftershocks.

"Do you have an appointment?" the owl-eyed

receptionist he'd never seen before asked when he ran into the office with Madelynn, the dripping diaper bag bouncing from his arm.

"She needs to see the doctor. I'll pay extra, whatever it takes."

"Calm down now, sir. Does she have a fever?"

"I'm pretty sure she does. She's hot to the touch. Would you like to see for yourself?" He held Madelynn out for careful inspection.

Ignoring his gesture, the woman squinted at her computer. "Dr. Nguyen goes to lunch in five minutes."

"Please ask her to examine my baby. Madelynn has health issues. She could be really ill. Every moment counts."

"Are you her father?"

He didn't hesitate. "I am. Name's Bennett Browning."

She turned her head toward him. "Aren't you that politician who quit the race?"

"I most certainly am, and this is my daughter Madelynn Grace."

The new receptionist, a thirtyish woman wearing a yellowish-gold nearly matching her owl-eyed stare, said, "She looks like her daddy."

"Thank you."

And when she added, "I'll see if I can catch the doctor. Be right back," he thanked her again.

If only his temples would quit their painful pounding, but what would he do if the doctor told him to come back? He'd argue, that's what. He might not be the perfect father. He was still learning, after all, but Madelynn wouldn't suffer for it. These medical professionals couldn't turn him away, could they?

His spirits skyrocketed when the nurse showed up and escorted him into a room off the hall.

"What seems to be the trouble?" she asked.

"Madelynn isn't well." His year-old daughter demonstrated this by screaming at the top of her lungs and kicking her legs.

"Was she all right when she woke up this morning?" the nurse shouted above the wailing baby.

"Not sure..." He remembered Emma was hardly able to get out of bed. "Madelynn was herself, but the nanny—my fiancée—is sick. Maybe contagious."

"When did Madelynn start acting up?"

"When I took her to the store with me."

"I see." The nurse wrinkled her brow and pressed a battery-operated thermometer against Madelynn's forehead, and the baby lunged for it but missed. "Hundred and one. That's not too high a temperature for an infant. The doctor will be with you in a moment."

Bennett sighed and sank to a stool with Madelynn. "Hear that, princess?" He laid his hand across her heart, feeling the frantic ticking. "Pretty soon, you'll be as good as new."

Oh, please make it so...

He thanked Dr. Nguyen when she walked in and assessed the situation.

"Somebody's not happy." She shook her head.

"I needed you to evaluate her because of her heart."

"Madelynn's been doing much better than we anticipated." She raised a tongue depressor and a thin flashlight. "But let's have a look."

More fits followed as if the tot admonished them, saying, "I won't put up with this at all!"

He heard the doctor's pensive "hmm" through the

commotion and angled his head to see swollen gums with tiny bits of exposed white.

"She's cutting more teeth," he said in wonder.

Dr. Nguyen filled his cupped hands with some tubes of something or other. She unscrewed a lid and applied a little, and like abracadabra, Madelynn uttered one more desolate sob and then quieted down.

"I owe you the moon," he said. "Who would have thought anything so simple could seem so harrowing?"

"Some teeth are more troublesome than others." The doctor slipped medicine from a vial into Madelynn's mouth. "If she'd been home, your nanny would have known what to do."

"Yes, but Emma's under the weather right now."

The doctor folded her arms in front of her. "What seems to be the trouble?"

"She fell off my sailboat." Heat stole into his face as an alarming thought occurred to him. "I could have lost Emma yesterday, and just before I got here, a car ran the red light, and if my car hadn't stopped automatically, I could have lost Madelynn…"

"I understand," Dr. Nguyen said, and that empathy he'd sometimes witnessed pierced through her professionalism.

"I passed a car accident on the highway this morning…" he started but didn't finish.

He couldn't bear thinking about the fickle finger of fate another second, and later, as his car migrated toward home, he did away with his could've, should've mentality. He forced his mind to go blank, but his gratefulness was still fresh in his heart when the car rounded the drive to The Nightingale.

The sun shone on the house as he got out with his

baby girl. The upper windows reflected the clouds traveling sulkily out to sea.

Up and dressed, Emma ran down the walkway. She reached Madelynn and him and threw her arms around them. "What did the doctor say?"

The salty breeze blew Emma's hair across his neck, tickling him.

And he laughed for the first time that day. "Madelynn Grace is teething."

Chapter 14

Emma thought Bennett looked like Jimmy Stewart in that Christmas movie when he discovered he's back in his own precious life. He pushed through the front entrance of The Nightingale, dropped the bag of groceries on the desk, and dipped his hand in the pocket of his damp coat. The teething ring he pulled out glistened in the soft lanterned light. Emma took Madelynn from him along with the diaper bag from his other shoulder.

She said to the baby, "You're home now, honey bunny. All is right with the world."

He retrieved the groceries. "Don't get too excited, but I'm making spaghetti for dinner. How 'bout that?"

Her instincts were to tackle him, mentioning he had zero experience with anything but toasting bread and opening a can. But he wanted to cook, and she didn't have the heart to discourage him, especially after the day she imagined he'd been through.

She sat the baby down on the carpet with a big red ball. "You don't have to bother," she told him. "I'll prepare some quinoa and poached eggs."

"How do I find a recipe?" he called from the kitchen.

Madelynn tilted her head toward his voice and cradled her hands on her cheeks as if to say, "Uh-oh."

Emma pinched the bridge of her nose and muttered, "We're in for it now." And to Bennett, she called, "Use your phone."

"Ah, of course. You know, Emma, anyone can follow a recipe. I've got it right here. I'll just whip it up since it's Madelynn's favorite. Just think. You won't have to worry about feeding the guests tomorrow night."

"Great." She rolled her eyes. "God, help us," she whispered.

While awaiting disaster, she changed the baby into her footie pajamas. "There you go." She dropped down on the floor and clapped. "C'mon, throw me the ball."

Madelynn cared more about shoving the ball in her mouth than returning it to Emma. No biggie. She had been worrying herself crazy about the baby, visualizing the worst. That her niece and her roomie were home, safe and sound, was reason to celebrate.

In an hour, Bennett appeared again, wearing oven mitts and carrying a silver chaffing dish. Rosie was scampering at his side as if for moral support.

The sight undid Emma. "Let me finish up for you, Bennett." She had a feeling this meal wouldn't go as well as he anticipated.

"Stay put," he managed to order as, next, he lugged the high chair. "Better yet, you two make yourselves comfortable in the dining room."

They did so. Soon, the Chinese table ran wild with candlelight on Ming dragon dishes. Alas, though, the aroma of garlic wafted off wimpy tomato sauce. A lifted lid and…*something squishy this way comes.*

"They're spaghetti noodles." Bennett bent over to inspect the goop. "I guess I did boil them a little too long. But they'll work. You'll see. Just douse them with sauce."

"Why did you go to all this trouble?"

"Because you deserve to be pampered."

"Me?" She stared at him, tongue-tied, her mind skewering through the strange, unpredictable thing he'd just said. "Thank you. You're the best."

"Wait until you taste it before you go praising me."

He slid onto the chair across from her, his hair a disaster, rumpled shirt spotted with tomato sauce, sleeves rolled up at uneven angles. He wasn't the well-presented senatorial candidate he used to be but more of a heartthrob—in her book anyway.

The remarkable Madelynn said, "Ba, ba, ba," then pointed across the table and clasped her hands together. "Ba, ba, ba."

Whether the baby had actually singled out the bowl of spaghetti noodles was debatable. But as if distracted, her daddy dug up a fair amount and tried to fling it onto his daughter's plate with a flick of his wrist in a flourish that couldn't be denied. A no-go. The goop stuck like glue, and he shook his head with a woe-is-me expression.

Emma used her knife to reach across the high chair and scrape the spoon clean, at which point the noodles dropped into one of the compartments of the baby dish with a loud *blop*. Consequently, Bennett's eyes filled with evident disgust. He looked so pathetic that she got up and kneaded his shoulders before retreating to her seat again.

She dipped the spoon into the sauce and poured a watery red substance over the lump on Madelynn's plate. "Here, let me mash it up."

He heaved an endless sigh and passed her the cylinder of parmesan cheese. "This might help." He gestured toward a crystal bowl. "I made Caesar salad."

Wishing to boost his waning confidence, she heaped

the romaine lettuce on her plate. How could anyone ruin salad? She soon found out when the dressing tasted so acidic that her tongue burned and her eyes watered.

"What did you use to make this?" She attempted to swallow and failed.

"The recipe called for vinegar, but when I poured it from the bottle, too much came out, as you can probably tell." His shoulders stooped.

She lowered her fork to the table, unable to take his misery a second longer. "I'll teach you to cook."

"You think there's hope for me?"

"With practice. Remember what June told you about how I tried and failed to scramble eggs correctly? And you never know—after you learn the basics, you might discover a recipe as valuable to you as scholars unearthing an ancient manuscript is to them."

"Hmm." He looked her over seductively. "Now that would be a find."

That explosive current raced through her again. "Right…did you know spaghetti supposedly originated in China?"

"No." He rubbed his unshaven face in a manner she thought thoroughly sexy.

"Could be a myth, but history buffs swear Marco Pollo discovered it. Only back then the noodles were made of rice."

"That's fascinating—not as fascinating as you, though," he murmured.

Her face burned with the X-rated images stored in her memory bank from witnessing him unclothed the day before… Time to change the subject. "Today worked out well since we didn't have people on the books. It'll take a while to build up a following. Still, it might benefit us to generate some good PR."

His eyebrow's drew together. "What about an interview in a travel magazine?"

"I don't know. When it comes down to it, we're entrepreneurs. If we use *Powell's Review*, we might get more exposure. Do you think Lucinda might be interested?"

"It wouldn't hurt to find out."

The next day, after Bennett's morning spent playing catch-up with B&B responsibilities while she attended to Madelynn, the time seemed perfect to place a call that would most likely go to voicemail. She'd put the baby down for a nap, and a good thing, since Lucinda surprised her by answering on the first ring.

"Hello?"

Emma moved with her cell phone into the privacy of the office. "Hey, Lucinda. Emma Kuan here."

"Sweetie, I heard you fell off Bennett's boat. May I suggest swim lessons?"

Emma had to laugh despite the joke being on her. "I'll let you in on a little secret I haven't told Bennett. I signed up with a good teacher in hopes of surprising him."

"You go, girl. Is there anything I can do to help promote The Nightingale? Stuff envelopes, get the word out in the neighborhoods, shout praises from the power of my pen?"

"As a matter of fact, I—we—wondered if you'd consider doing an article about the B&B and about us. I'm thinking people might want to know what happened to Bennett Browning."

"An exclusive story? I'd like that. Thanks, Emma. I could interview you in your own backyard, which would also be an excellent way to advertise the special features of The Nightingale. What do you think?"

"I like the idea."

"What say we go for chatty and relaxed, but we can discuss anything you want while prompting vacationers to book a room." Lucinda paused a beat. "But I don't want to overstep. Any taboo subjects?"

"My sister."

A sudden hush fell between them.

Then Lucinda spoke up. "The night Bennett proposed to Rachel at the teahouse, he asked me there to take pictures. Everyone had halfway raised their champagne glasses in a toast to the happy couple when she decimated him. I tried to convince him he picked the wrong woman. I just hope you're the right one."

Emma realized, then and there, that she couldn't let on about their staged marriage.

"Has it occurred to you, Em, that although I won't mention Rachel if you don't want me to, you might be able to use this interview to your advantage? There has been talk about her. You know what I mean? The main question is…why did she do what she did? And what made her disappear? And how did she die—really? It's best to stop the public from speculating now and be done with it."

"Uh…" Emma's throat closed up.

"Excuse me," Lucinda said.

Emma heard her speak into an intercom, most likely allowing Emma time to collect herself. Although Rach would have rebelled at having her name mentioned, Emma experienced an indefinable feeling it was the right thing to do. She didn't know Rach's motives for the things that had happened, and Emma couldn't ask her.

She bit her knuckle. "Okay..." It came out as uncertain.

"Listen, you've got me, Audrey, and Madison at your disposal. If you need us, we'll do what we can."

"That means a lot."

"Not so long ago, but before you, my sister and I discovered Bennett's phone had been bugged. We listened to a recording—everything he did for others daily. I told my sister I'd beg him to marry me if she didn't turn it off."

A snort escaped Emma. "He has that effect." *Oh, did he!*

"I tell you this because Bennett's a good guy, and I think you're fabulous." Lucinda cleared her throat. "I'd like to see your business venture succeed and the two of you happy."

"Thank you for that."

"And take note. Let the readers see who you both are and that you care deeply for one another. Nothing interests people more than a good love story."

And fiction is all it is, Emma thought miserably. Things had gotten wackadoodle, and she secretly dreaded—feared—it would all blow up in her face.

The Saturday before the interview, the sisterhood met at The Nightingale. They'd waited for the lodgers to leave before discussing their strategies. The living room was pulsating with lively chitchat when Lucinda grabbed Emma's hand and examined it with a critical eye.

"Browning!" Lucinda bellowed out the open door, and soon he appeared, coming from the beach with Madelynn pulling on his earlobes and Rosie barking at his heels.

"Look at your fiancée's hand," Lucinda said, "and

tell me what's missing."

He bent from the waist, the baby's head tucked under his chin. "Nail polish?"

"News flash, what will people say if they see Emma without an engagement ring?"

"Holy crap," he said. "Good thing you caught the disparity."

Balking at the notion, Emma shook her head. Bennett shouldn't spend money on her when this marriage wasn't slated to last, but Lucinda wasn't letting up anytime soon.

"Where's that rock you stuck in the cake for your big mistake?"

Ordinarily, Emma would have jumped in to protect her late sister, but she needed to hear his answer. She didn't know their history, and he'd been so evasive it had made her curious.

"It's in my bedroom," he admitted rather self-consciously.

Shock all but knocked Emma off her feet. "You still have it?"

Had he been waiting for Rachel to come back to him? She hadn't, and now she never would. Emma's chest swelled with pain for the grief she believed he'd endured.

Madison shoved her hands inside the pockets of her pleated trousers. "Talk about big bucks down the drain."

Audrey lowered her eyelids and shook her head. "Oh, Bennett."

"What's done is done," Lucinda said. "You two need to find another stone and hock Rachel's—unless, Emma, you want to claim it for your own."

"No dice," Madison said. "She can't wear glitz

intended for someone else."

Emma couldn't fathom waste—period. "I don't mind. Honestly, I don't."

"That diamond is not you, Em," Audrey said gently.

Emma wondered why. What about Emma Kuan didn't warrant her sister's ring?

Lucinda went to Bennett. "Take care of this. Today, while I have time to babysit."

"You'd do that?" he asked as his daughter batted at one of the large, hooped earrings the fashionista wore. "Careful." He lowered the baby to the floor. "Madelynn has a thing for bling."

"My kind of girl." Lucinda handed Madelynn a crayon and a coloring book. "While you two are gone, we'll make a meal for your guests' dinner tonight."

"I don't want you going to any trouble," Bennett said.

Audrey picked up Madelynn and waved goodbye to him. "No trouble. Plus, I'll get my baby fix."

Madison nodded. "Brandon requested some daddy time this morning, so I'm free to cook up a storm."

In an hour and a half timespan that included a stop to buy coffee, Emma observed the jewels through the window at Tiffany's with the eyes of a child who could never really cure that aching throb of not having enough to eat.

"I chose Rachel's ring," Bennett was saying. "Didn't give her a chance to express an opinion. That could be why she refused me the way she did."

"My sister hurt you." Emma still wondered why Rachel had walked out when she had been so taken with him. Something must have happened. But what?

"I don't want to talk about it." He turned his back on

her.

She tossed her paper cup in the trash, then encircled her arm around his. "Shall we?"

People turned to stare at them as they strolled inside, just a silver-spooned man and a woman who had come a long way, baby. Expensive wall clocks ticked, speaking for themselves, along with well-groomed sales associates and well-stocked displays.

Being recognized as the man who had been running for senate, even if briefly, had its advantages. He'd been a popular candidate—that much was clear. Within moments, a few of the customers had stepped aside. Hands raised to mouths. Murmurs followed. Emma turned to Bennett, her hair barely scraping her shoulders as she smiled up lovingly at him. She hoped the charcoal dress in place of the proverbial black had been the right choice.

Because the show must go on!

She leaned against the cold glass case while browsing. Keys jingled, and a black suit moved like a tornado to fulfill Bennett's request. Soon, the incredible smoothness of a sapphire ring slid over her finger. Every cell in her body welcomed this like an unprecedented treat.

Still, she bent over the counter and mouthed in the black suit's direction. "How much?"

The answer was discreet, and she struggled not to gasp visibly.

She raised her lips to Bennett's ear, cupping her hand. "Let's get out of here."

"Huh?" He appeared to notice her face then. "Where do you want to go?"

She raised her chin. "Meet me in your bedroom."

"Now you're talking."

"I want the diamond you bought for my sister."

He shot her a frown. "You're not going to like it."

"You're worried I'd see that solitaire as ostentatious?" She might have before today.

"You'd call it too traditional for your taste."

"You believe you know me so well." He did, to tell the truth. "Let me be the judge."

She wasn't about to allow him to squander money on their pretend matrimony. More than that, she needed to wear the symbol he had associated with eternal love— one true thing.

So they staged their great escape from Tiffany's by shamelessly flirting with each other. Soon, praise be, they were back at The Nightingale with its yummy aroma and Madelynn having the time of her life with all the grownups spoiling her. Nobody seemed to notice Bennett and Emma tiptoeing upstairs like jewel thieves.

Or if they did realize it, they didn't say.

He rolled out a drawer. Emma's cheeks fired up while spotting those good-quality briefs that stimulated the sight of him without them.

They observed each other in the mirror over the bureau, and her mortification fled.

Bennett's focus dropped to his underwear, and he removed a small black box. A knot of excitement mixed with dread grew in her belly. When he snapped it open, the exquisite gem caught the light and refracted it in rainbows.

Her breath caught when he slipped the diamond on her finger. "This has to be two carats."

His hand paused on hers, and he frowned. "Are you sure you're okay with this?"

Of course, she wasn't. "I am."

"I'm glad, Emma," he said with a total lack of emotion.

He didn't try to kiss her or even make a move, and something about his apathy struck her as him adhering to their prenuptial agreement. With that, she couldn't help being just "okay."

Any of the adoration her heart yearned for was inconsequential, which was fine by her.

It had to be.

Chapter 15

Bennett awakened that night feeling hollow inside and headed downstairs for a snack, though he didn't think food could touch what ailed him. When Emma had refused the sapphire ring, he realized she probably wanted a prop for publicity's sake. Nothing personal. As a result, she'd wear the flashy diamond, though he could tell she wouldn't have picked it for herself.

She was the type who didn't follow the crowd, and he loved that about her.

Soft lamplight came from the living room. The glitter-globe tune pierced the air with its powerful sound, drenched in images of the Orient. Memories appeared to hold Emma as incarcerated as the cherry tree inside the glass.

He cleared his throat to alert her of his presence and stepped from the shadows. He longed to know the object's grip on her and why it affected him, but he was an interloper who'd burst in on a scene he had no business witnessing.

She lifted her eyebrows. "What are you doing up?"

"I'm hungry." He couldn't stop the defiance that had moved into his voice. "Are you?"

"Nooo," she blew out through a sigh. "Ready for tomorrow's charade?"

He tensed—a knee-jerk reaction. "You bet."

At least the fog didn't hang around that morning.

The baby didn't wake up in a bad mood. The guests at the B&B chatted excitedly among themselves about the interview. After all, they might be quoted and perhaps get their picture taken.

Bennett and Emma had submitted a list of questions they wished to be asked, and they had prepared their answers, even rehearsed a little, but the most challenging part of their act would be convincing the readers that theirs was a true romance.

He wanted to appear happy and secure in their relationship but hoped to avoid looking forced. A fine line. He chose a knit shirt, a blazer, and trousers from his closet, combining professional with relaxed. He didn't want their image to fall apart because either one unknowingly said or did something wrong.

At ten sharp, Lucinda swarmed into the resort with her crew. She wore colors and an outfit that faded into the background—as much as she could fade into any location. Audrey followed along to care for Madelynn, and a makeup artist had shown up for Emma and him.

In the dining room, a man began setting up the camera equipment. Fresh fruit, herbal bread, and a generous display of garden salads lavished the table. And the smell of coffee, intense and dark, drifted in the air. Bennett's daughter exchanged worried glances with him as he entered and rolled his shoulders to loosen the muscles there.

Lucinda conversed with a cameraman, who she introduced as Jason. Bennett tagged along, appreciating the effort taken to encapsulate the elements that made The Nightingale five-star. The guestrooms shone under a subtle light, as did the grand staircase, the marble in the foyer, and the pewter in the kitchen.

Lucinda flipped on her recorder to give her introduction. "The Nightingale is a byword for elegance and Asian culture. Yet there's a low-key vibe because this is Huntington Beach. It goes without saying then, the guests are offered complimentary breakfasts, evening cocktails, and an optional dinner. All of this while Bennett Browning and his beautiful fiancée attend to the guests' every need."

Emma came into the kitchen, speaking softly to Lucinda in a language that lent itself to shared confidences, and Audrey gravitated toward Madelynn. What were they talking about? Soon, Jason snapped pictures of Emma, and Bennett drew near. Tentatively, she turned to face him.

Now his mouth fell open. "Your eyes are just...wow." He wasn't faking his adulation.

Her blush came too quickly to be anything but genuine. "Guess Lucinda's guy's a miracle worker."

"Well, considering his canvas, I'm not surprised." All the others in the room fell into scattering shadows so that Emma stood out like the main event.

Lucinda sliced her hand through the air between them. "Hey, could you tear yourselves away from each other long enough to answer a few questions?"

Bennett angled his head in Lucinda's direction but kept his gaze fixed on Emma. "Ask away," he said with the practiced ease he had displayed to all journalists—even when sweat trickled down his spine like it did now.

"Excellent. Let's start with you, Bennett. When did you realize you wanted to be a politician?"

He let his head fall back. "I can't count the times, when I was a kid, my dad and I went door-to-door. I liked hearing what people had to say, and I believed even then if someone cared and worked hard enough, they could make a difference in the lives of others."

"Do you feel pressure being Charles Browning's son?"

"A little bit. I inherited half my dad's supporters and most of his worrywarts, but I'm proud to be his son. I watched him improve our country, one conversation at a time, person by person. He had a set of unshakable principles—still does."

"How did he react when you withdrew from the race so early in the game?" Lucinda asked, as if allowing the axe to fall where it may.

"He was a little apprehensive, but when I told him why, he not only understood but wanted to join us in our pursuit to open the B&B."

Lucinda paused to jot something down. "Does he babysit?"

"Oh, yes. Dad loves to be with his granddaughter."

"And his future daughter-in-law?" Lucinda asked.

"I think this question is for you, Emma," Bennett put in, holding his breath and absently drawing close to plant a kiss on her cheek.

Her face paled, and he wondered if she feared saying anything damaging.

"Every good relationship requires sacrifice on each side. Both father and son spent long hours teaching me how to run a small business like The Nightingale. I've taught them something about Chinese food."

"I heard you're an expert cook."

"I've always had a passion for good cuisine. That helps."

Lucinda waved for Jason to move closer for a shot of the guests still lingering on the premises. "What do you all think?"

They gave the thumbs-up, adding a great deal of compliments. Lucinda asked Audrey to watch over Madelynn while she and Jason followed Emma and Bennett walking hand in hand to the beach. The extravagantly blue skies glowed with sunshine, and the sea racing in hit the rocks and fanned out with a rainbowed spray.

Lucinda motioned the camera closer as Bennett pressed a small pink shell against Emma's ear, striking an intimate pose among all the sunbathers and scampering children. She listened as acutely as she had earlier to the musical globe. Then, like an actual newly-in-love couple, they settled together, side by side, for a stroll down the coastline toward where the beach was vacant. There, the water glistened in sapphires, darkening along the cliffs to charcoal.

She pointed a finger. "Look at the way that tide pool sparkles."

Click went the camera, catching the look he'd seen on her face outside of Tiffany's. A longing, he'd have to call it. He wished to know what was happening inside her head, but this wasn't the time to bring it up.

"Tell us more about yourself, Emma," Lucinda said. "You worked for a feminist magazine in San Francisco. How has that experience prepared you for your new role?"

"It enabled me to write about issues that plague women today."

And Bennett said, "Emma's still writing articles—still working to create equality for all."

Lucinda glanced up from her tape recorder. "Do you think that sums it up, Emma?"

"I do. Let me add that women want the ability to make their own decisions in the same way men have for so many years."

"Nicely put," Lucinda said. "Bennett, how are you different here in Huntington Beach than you were on the campaign trail?"

"Can't you tell? I'm more relaxed." He ran his hands through his hair. "I'll probably go back to politics in the future, but right now I enjoy running The Nightingale."

They were alone with only the warbling birds whose wings flapped against the wind, and the waves pounding the shore. With an awakened sense of wonder, he forgot about all else. He basked in the evident awareness of Emma and himself.

Only the two of them…

Click…

Was that the camera?

He added, "I love being seaside…with my sweetheart."

"People are saying you two came here to hide out," Lucinda said. "Any truth to that statement?"

"Huntington is a great place to escape. The seashore goes on forever, and you can kick back and beach it up for all you're worth, but the truth is we came here for my daughter. You see, Madelynn started life with a defective heart. Living oceanside is the best thing for her."

"Her illness must have been tough for you and Emma since she is the baby's aunt."

The conversation had just strayed into unsafe terrain, and he felt unstrung and off his game. He gripped Emma's hand as she turned her head toward Lucinda.

"I chose to leave my job at the magazine to become the nanny," she said. "I wanted to be part of my niece's life. I'm not sorry I did it."

Lucinda squinted as if deep in thought. "Your late sister, Madelynn's mother, is rumored to have committed suicide. Do you believe that's true?"

The beach muted as if even nature strained to hear, and Emma's back stiffened against him. He longed to answer the unrehearsed question for her, but he had no retort. He couldn't see her face but imagined her confusion. It made him want to postpone the interview. He started to say as much, but she prevented him with a gentle tug of his arm.

"I don't know," Emma said, "but Rachel suffered from depression. She was diagnosed as bipolar when she was quite young."

Her announcement seemed to materialize from the ether. Nobody had told him about her illness. Rachel herself had never breathed a word. In all their practice runs for this interview, Rach's state of mind hadn't come up, but when he thought it through, bipolar made perfect sense, especially when he considered her highs and lows. Plus... "If you read Emma's magazine pieces," he said, connecting the dots, "you'll see how serious she is about mental illness and its effects on families and society as a whole."

Lucinda said, "It's a subject worth pursuing, don't you agree, Bennett?"

Emma twisted around to look at him, and he nodded but was surprised that he hadn't put two and two together before.

"So, Emma, you have an opportunity to contribute to the better good, as well as contributing to your life together." Lucinda didn't wait for a reply but seemed ready to lighten the subject. "Can you tell me what

Bennett said when he proposed?"

Jason drew even nearer, adjusting the camera lens. Was he getting a shot of the diamond? Good thing Bennett had given Emma the ring. This subject had the power to lighten the dark road the interview had taken.

"He said…" Emma smiled as if recalling the scene that had never happened. " 'You're my best friend, and if you'll let me, I want to be your husband.' "

Lucinda clapped him on the back. "Nicely done, Bennett. When is the big day?"

He nearly fell into the ocean, but Emma piped up as if on cue. "May 3rd."

That's only two months away. Usually, a wedding took a year in the making. There's a reception hall to book, the caterer to secure, and the wedding cake to order.

Click…

He hoped his shock wouldn't show in the photo—such a short time until he slid a wedding ring on Emma's finger. He cradled her face in his hands and ran his mouth over hers. She deepened the kiss, and for now it felt as natural as breathing.

****

Emma was flabbergasted when the story took off. Podcasters came out of the woodwork, along with media influencers. The popularity of The Nightingale tripled. Still, no news was good news since a tabloid mentioned Rachel Bellamy with speculation about her having all that money and how it hadn't made her happy. That caused Emma to rant and rave. But then again, she'd always reacted badly when anyone criticized her sister.

The weeks before the wedding were far from calm. Emma's nerves rolled and leaped.

She had committed herself to promoting the lodge. Lucinda had gone above and beyond, printing photos that drove people to book a stay at the B&B weeks in advance. Emma left a week open after the wedding to include a honeymoon on Catalina Island, but that was about it as far as her plans went. When their clientele disappeared into their rooms each night, she began to list what needed to be done for the wedding but fell asleep every time.

Meanwhile, her vow to teach Bennett how to cook turned out more difficult than she'd predicted. Because of the demands he put on himself, he expected to fix a sublime meal in a matter of days. He snuck into the kitchen when she wasn't looking, intending to prepare some julienned carrots and onions for a garnish. It couldn't have been simpler, but when he fried them up, somehow Madelynn diverted him. While he attended to her, the veggies burned. The stench drifted out just as a handful of guests were checking in.

"What stinks?" asked a man in a haughty voice.

Bennett sped out of the kitchen with his daughter clinging to his neck and her face pressed against his chest. "My mistake," he called.

To smooth his ruffled ego, Emma included him while she made supper. He followed her, keeping a safe distance, his hands clasped behind his back. Madelynn watched them from the corner of her eye as she pounded pie dough on the tray of her high chair. And Rosie sat politely, or slyly, off to the side, awaiting any accidental food spillage.

Emma heated the wok. "Interesting fact." She incorporated her instructor's voice. "It's a Chinese belief that shrimp is an aphrodisiac."

Bennett angled his head. "Really," he drawled, eyelids lowered to half-mast.

"Shrimp helps circulate the blood, bringing heat and energy throughout the body." At the moment, she didn't need any shellfish to get her hot.

He leaned forward and curved his arms around her waist. "Just keep talking," he murmured, making her skin tingle.

But before she could respond with something to cool her jets, one of the guests, a big-haired woman, poked her head inside the kitchen.

"The toilet in our room is overflowing," she cried.

"Ah," Bennett said the slightest bit begrudgingly. "That's where I come in."

****

With no warning, the sisterhood kidnapped Emma from The Nightingale when she least expected it. She caught their destination in whispers. The plotters planned to make a "bride" out of her. Just as well. If left to her own devices, she would have chosen an outfit from her closet and called it good. Now she had bridesmaids to help her.

The hijacking left her no time to change out of her black jeans and a T-shirt with the slogan *Sorry If My Feminism Ruins Your Sexist Jokes*. So when her three conspirators deposited her in a bridal shop called *Enchanté*, she felt herself spiraling into self-doubt.

Matters didn't improve when a consultant slid behind the admissions desk and sized Emma up with a frown. Before she could speak, a lady with an upsweep of white hair, kind eyes, soft wrinkles, and a lovely French accent introduced herself as Estelle, the proprietor of *Enchanté*.

"You are Emma Kuan, yes?" she asked, and Emma felt she should curtsey.

Madison took charge. "That's right. She's the bride I made the appointment for."

Her friends whisked Emma to a circular sofa where she sat as if on display, awkwardly for her, while Estelle, while listening to the trio, crossed the room like a beautiful white cloud.

"Perhaps a gown that brings to mind Hepburn in the film *Funny Face*," Madison said.

Audrey rested her hands on her very pregnant belly. "We hoped you, Estelle, could help Emma create her own look."

And Lucinda added, "This is her red-carpet moment, after all."

Estelle tilted her head and called across the shop. "Ah, Emma! What is your preference?"

Emma sweltered under the scrutiny. "I don't know exactly."

When it came down to it, she'd never pictured herself walking down the aisle, let alone getting married. She still didn't.

Estelle drew closer. "Let's get inventive, shall we? How do you describe yourself?"

I'm the snot-nosed kid who worked the streets in the hood, now the grown-up who'd just as soon not tap into my already dwindling bank account.

"Do you have a bargain rack?" Emma choked out.

Estelle squinted at Emma as if trying to read her. "I may have something just for you. We order a few exports in Paris from a designer who shakes the customary wedding codes to bring 'attitude' into our industry. These creators take a stand not to use any animal skin—

no feathers, leather, wool, or silk."

"I admire that," Emma said, and the others nodded.

Estelle guided Emma inside a dressing room where original pieces hung at her fingertips.

Emma blew through each unique creation until she found the one that she'd rob her bank account to own. A soft gasp escaped her. "There…" She pointed to a jumpsuit.

"*C'est très magnifique!*" Estelle helped Emma into the outfit with its strapless calypso style that hugged her waist and enhanced her bust. In addition, it had removable, blousy sleeves positioned just above the elbows. Then, as if saving the best for last, Estelle attached a long train that saluted tradition.

Emma self-consciously stepped out from behind the drape to the eruption of applause.

Madison pushed away from the pillar she'd been leaning against. "This is wild and yet sets a new standard for sophistication."

Audrey teetered to her feet from the loveseat. "It represents a partnership."

Lucinda said, "And it makes a statement both defiant and sensual."

Emma's heart pitter-patted with pleasure, but then she realized the sad truth. "I don't have any idea where to hold the ceremony."

Madison poured glasses of champagne. "It's best if it's somewhere you adore. I tied the knot on the beach where I live, and Audrey exchanged vows in the British woodlands."

Emma hadn't had time to think about it. "At this stage, it's too late to rent a hall. I suppose we could have the wedding at The Nightingale."

Madison took a generous swig of bubbly from a crystal flute. "That's your happy place."

"The Nightingale would be fantastic," Lucinda said, then added to Estelle, "Shouldn't we be dressed in a way to complement the bride?"

They put their heads together in that pursuit while romantic instrumentals floated in the background and champagne flowed behind the closed doors. The women chose aqua gowns with straight lines and very little detail. Estelle made adjustments she said would require more than one fitting, especially for Audrey.

Everyone got into the act as they tried on shoes, headpieces, sashes, and jewelry. It would be a day Emma would always recall with joy—this being with friends and kicking up her heels like she never had before.

"I know it's a break in tradition," Emma said, overtaken with emotion, "but I want all of you to be my maids of honor."

"What a novel idea," Audrey said. "We'll be goddesses. Mere mortals will bow."

Later, when they were outside the boutique, Madison asked, "Have you thought about what kind of cake you want?"

"Cake tasting is something she should do with Bennett," Audrey said.

Emma didn't want to put him through all that fuss. "I don't think so. He's too busy."

Lucinda looked at Emma directly. "You love him?"
Love him?

How could she? Her conception of herself with him didn't include something as slippery as love. After all, months ago, she hadn't wanted any man. After her sister's death, Bennett and she had come together as two people who had loved Rachel. They needed the comfort of finding each other. Images of all their times together flickered through her mind. Had love entered through some hidden door in Emma's heart?

The ladies were watching her with less than glee in their faces.

She couldn't lie to them.

"I don't know if I have it in me," she felt obligated to admit. "But after people started gossiping about the two of us, I wanted to nip it in the bud."

"So that's it," Audrey said, her voice thick with disappointment.

Lucinda frowned. "You and I already talked about the earth-shattering effect your sister had on him."

"It took him more than a year to recover," Audrey put in, moving carefully to a sitting position in the front seat of Lucinda's sports car.

Bennett still hadn't gotten over Rachel. Emma didn't admit this because it made the wedding an even bigger farce.

Madison sat in the seat next to her and patted the back of her hand. "What they're trying to say is, none of us wants to see him hurt."

Emma had to make them understand. "Please, there's no reason for your concern. I'd do anything to keep the sky from falling on him again."

"Just so we're clear," Lucinda said. "Now gather up that man of yours and go eat cake."

Chapter 16

Monday morning, just shy of Bennett leaving to stock up on groceries, he heard the entrance door open and turned to look.

Alexis Nathan's high-top sneakers squeaked as he entered and set a battered suitcase down in the foyer. "I am here to fulfill my promise to you and Emma."

Bennett thought back to all the poet had said to him. "Your promise?"

Alexis Nathan removed his shabby raincoat and folded it over his arm, exposing jeans faded to mere threads and a tattered gray sweater. This incongruity wasn't the typical attire for Huntington Beach, but somehow statement-worthy just the same. "I am here to assist you and the future Mrs. Browning so that you have more time to prepare for your wedding ceremony— starting now if you would like."

"That's cool, buddy. There's so much left to do, and we don't know where to start." He waved Alexis Nathan into the interior of the quiet house. "Emma, look who's here!"

After welcoming the poet wholeheartedly, the couple left and spent the next hour sorting through wedding rings at Tiffany's. Emma suggested a more modest jewelry store. They patronized a little shop on the Sunset Strip where they bought matching eternity bands studded with small glittering emeralds. Neither he nor

Emma mentioned that this purchase would have to be returned when their bogus union ended. The impermanence of their actions had to be foremost in her mind too, since she insisted on paying for hers.

Once inside the car, he locked the rings in the glove compartment. "They'll be safe there, don't you think?"

"I would hope so. We don't want to accrue another bill."

She sounded worried, and the thought occurred to him, not for the first time, that she was reluctant when it came to spending money. That was why he paid for things whenever she let him. Considering that, he had come up with an idea to save them a bundle.

"You realize the living room at The Nightingale is too small to hold all the people we've invited." When she nodded, he continued, "I want to build a gazebo on the west side of the property where the ocean views are amazing."

"There you go again. Talk about a small fortune." She strapped on her seat belt. "Why don't we get married by the justice of the peace?"

It wasn't an option—not in his book, anyway. "We've got to think about Madelynn. Besides, we can't take all our friends and family to some drafty courthouse."

"Why not?"

"It's not right."

"What do you mean?"

"I want my daughter to see our wedding photos." His insides twisted, and he would have liked to erase the pain. "My mom and dad were in love, and it shows in each and every picture."

"Okay, Bennett, I get it. But you said it yourself—

they were in love. You and me—I don't know what we are."

"Oh, yeah, the friend thing." He fell into a funk.

"Well, we're a little more than friends by now." Her teeth were buried in the plumpness of her bottom lip. "Build your gazebo. I'm in. I'm all for it."

"I built houses in China."

"I read you did—back when you were in the Peace Corps. Are you planning on getting one of those ready-to-assemble kits?"

"Nah." He recalled his failed cooking attempts and wanted to impress her. "I'll construct my own. It will be a beauty. Wait and see."

"Great." Frustration sharpened her tone.

He decided to feign a thrill for helping her pick out a bouquet. "You want to take care of the flowers right now?"

She brightened. "Sure."

When they entered a florist shop, the bell above jangled discordantly, and the mélange of blooms threatened to take him down. He'd forgotten the burning sensation he'd always had in his nostrils whenever he came into contact with too much flora.

A woman with a round face, spiked yellow hair, and a reed-thin body popped up from a row of daffodils. "Hello," she sang out amicably. "What can I do for you?"

Emma merged into the jungle, a step at a time as if testing the ground for stability. "We'd like to place an order for our wedding," she said cheerily.

The florist tugged a pen from the top of her ear. "When's the big day?" She opened a calendar surrounded by orchids atop a counter.

"Uh, a month and a half from now?"

The florist drew in a sharp breath, her tongue between her teeth. "We need a nine-month advance, at least. Sorry…"

By this point, all the flowers squeezed into such a tiny space made Bennett sneeze repeatedly, and both women blessed him each time.

Emma handed him a tissue while addressing the florist. "Do you know if there are any other shops that can work with us at this late date?"

"I doubt it." The florist slumped her shoulders as if genuinely sorry. "Maybe you two can make your own arrangements and bouquets with store-bought flowers."

Just put me out of my misery. The colors and shapes in the shop ran together. "I have to get out of here," he said with watery eyes.

Emma snatched his keys. "I'll drive."

The wind had picked up outside, and the skies darkened. When they got home, a thundercloud opened and flooded them as they exited the car. The couple shared an umbrella and raced inside. They greeted the feisty Madelynn and their guests with revived spirits.

Alexis Nathan announced he'd cooked an Indian dish called murgh makhani and carried it into the dining room. "Please be seated," he said to the new arrivals.

One of them, a businesswoman from Chicago, staying just one night, turned off her phone and sniffed the air. "Ah, it smells wonderful."

Alexis Nathan bowed. "I hope you will like my humble attempt to please you."

One of the things Bennett loved about The Nightingale, which made him glad they'd opened it up to visitors, was the community atmosphere. As he sipped his port from a ruby-red wineglass of Oriental design, he spoke to these new visitors on his turf. He talked about the dog park and mentioned the Huntington Beach pier, how it was one of the longest on the West Coast, and how their town had the coolest surf shops around. And upon request, halfway through their spicy chicken, Alexis Nathan recited a poem that lent keen insight into human nature.

When the meal was nearly over, Emma laid down her fork. "Bennett, would you like to go with me to sample wedding cake tomorrow?"

"Wedding cake?" Was she just being nice, or did she really want him to go? "Didn't Lucinda set you up with that appointment? Maybe you should be asking her. After all, she and the rest of your peeps got a kick out of whisking you off to the bridal shop."

"A bride doesn't let her groom see her gown before the wedding."

He laughed and sat back. "I never thought of you as being superstitious, Em."

"If you don't want to go…"

To tell the truth, he liked the romantic idea of feeding her cake but didn't want her to feel obligated to include him whenever she did something for their wedding. He'd proceed with caution, discover on his own what was what. "Wouldn't you feel more comfortable getting the female take?"

"I think that question is discriminative."

Bennett took a bite of his lemon custard, trying to decide if the nasal quality he thought he detected in her reply was criticism. "Em, if you'd rather go with Alexis Nathan, you won't offend me." He was giving her another out in case she wanted one.

But her chin trembled, and he wondered if he'd

unintentionally hurt her feelings.

The businesswoman glared at him as she lowered her spoon into her coffee and stirred with a loud clanging noise that seemed to shatter her former pleasantries. His daughter threw her dinner roll at him, smacking him in the chest.

In the uncomfortable silence that followed, Alexis Nathan lowered his eyes. "Accompanying you would be my pleasure, Emma."

Her glance fell to her lap. "No big deal."

"I beg to differ," the woman fired off with fed-up looks at Bennett that seemed to inaudibly trill. "I wouldn't marry you if you were the last man on earth."

Maybe if he were more obliging, he decided. "Pick whatever—chocolate, vanilla. Doesn't matter. Get a receipt, and I'll pay the bill."

"It does matter," Alexis Nathan said in a sharp tone Bennett had never heard him use.

Later, though, when the two men were alone and Emma had gone upstairs to get Madelynn ready for bed, the poet waved a hand toward the bar.

"Would you care for a drink?" Alexis Nathan gestured toward the wonderfully comfortable sofa as if he owned the place. "I think we should talk man to man."

Something in the level of disapproval in his dark eyes caused Bennett to squirm and think up an excuse. "I should work on plans for the gazebo."

"I do not say this lightly, but with much deliberation." Alexis Nathan poured them scotch and handed one to Bennett. "To me, kind sir, in lieu of Emma's request to go eat cake, you've been acting like…how do you say it?"

"Wish I knew…please, give me a hint."

Alexis Nathan scrunched up his forehead deep in thought. "A jackass," he said as if it had just come to him, raising his glass to emphasize the point. "I believe that's what you are."

What? Bennett cleared his throat. "Is something lost in translation? Calling me a jackass? Do you even know what that is?"

"A fool—jackass," Alexis Nathan stated. "No offense, but I believe the term fits you very, very well."

Bennett drained his drink, feeling the burn. "You say this because?"

"Because you are like a man with smoke in his eyes. You do not see the obvious, the—how do you say it?—the writing on the wall."

"What exactly are you referring to?"

"Emma Kuan is the woman of whom I preface. She is the subject of most of my poetry."

The shock of this had Bennett sitting on his hands so that he couldn't act on his impulse to punch the daylights out of his favorite poet. "You're saying you're in love with my fiancée?"

"I am—regretfully, as she does not feel as I do." Alexis Nathan's face had clouded. "You are a lucky man, fortunate beyond measure, yet you act like a—"

"I don't deserve your digs. What did I ever do to you besides suggest you take my place tomorrow?"

"And therein lies the problem."

"What do you mean?"

"You have been offered a banquet with a beautiful and compassionate woman, and what do you do? You give it away like it is rubbish."

"But I don't think Emma wants any part in all these rituals. She'd rather we had our ceremony at the courthouse. The only reason she's agreed to this cake tasting is—"

"For you, you misguided ignoramus. Emma does it all for you. Have you not stopped to figure that out?"

"What are you trying to say?"

Alexis Nathan set both his hands flat on the table. "If you hurt her by not loving her, good sir, you will have to answer to me."

"Hey, pal, you've got it all wrong. Emma's only going through with this charade to keep me from being the brunt of rumors."

"And why has she volunteered to do such a thing?"

"Because she somehow feels responsible for all the talk. She's not, of course. Not at all. I'm indebted to her. She's first-rate."

"If you do not love her with all your heart, then do not go through with this wedding. Marriage is a sacred act not to be entered lightly."

"She's only doing it for show."

"Have you seen the way she looks at you?"

Stumped, Bennett rubbed his temples. "You honestly think she cares?"

"I believe you are a fortunate man," he repeated. "Emma made a good life for herself, a life full of reward in mind and spirit. She gave it up for you and your precious baby."

"I never really thought—"

"Again, therein lies the problem. An unthinking man is a…"

"You've got me pegged." Why hadn't he ever stopped to figure it out? But could it be true that Emma had genuine feelings for him?

When he first met her, he'd thought he saw a spark

168

of attraction in her eyes, but then she demanded nothing but a business relationship. There had been times in the past months when they had almost connected, but something always happened to make him believe he'd gotten the wrong idea. Her proposal of the marriage scheme had seemed proof enough of her indifference toward him, but if Alexis Nathan was correct, then Bennett had been a fool—a jackass.

No wonder women didn't stick around when they were with him. And how could he have gone to Harvard and be such a goober?

"Tell you what. I'll accompany the delightful Ms. Kuan to the baker's and any other place her heart desires."

****

Emma found Bennett waiting for her at the bottom of the stairs. She became very aware of his male body and found herself adrift in his warm brown eyes. So much awareness in those eyes, in that face, an absolute contradiction from the insensitivity he'd shown at dinner.

"Emma, I was a total jerk earlier. I shouldn't have tried to pass my responsibility off to someone else."

She shook her head in defiance. "Your only responsibility is running The Nightingale and putting up your gazebo. You didn't do anything wrong."

"I didn't see what was right in front of me. When I think I almost missed sharing something so special with you..." His voice was clipped and troubled. "I got the impression you might be tired of always being around me. I didn't want you to feel trapped."

"That's crazy." Her stomach clenched. "Here, I thought you were passing the buck because you were tired of our pretending to be engaged."

He rubbed his forehead and sighed. "I am tired—of pretending, I mean."

She glanced away, feeling that familiar ache, that almost panicky helplessness. "I know, you said so before. If you still had Rachel, everything would be perfect."

"Don't, Emma," he growled. "Don't talk about her. Please."

She gently stroked his strong jawline with her fingertips. "Okay, I understand. It hurts you to think about her. You're still mourning your loss. But I'm glad you decided to go along."

He lifted her hand to his mouth and kissed it. "I'm glad you included me." Then he winked at her. "Who knows? You might need my expertise."

She arched an amused brow. "Oh, you've been cake sampling before?"

"No, but I know what I like." He hugged her. "What I really like is you."

"I see." Although she couldn't fathom why he changed his mind, pleasure bubbled inside her. She'd rather eat cake with him than anyone else, had all along.

The next day, the skies brightened, and the landscape outside the window looked washed clean. Emma giddily reached for a fun outfit—sunglasses, dark and oversized, a wide-brimmed straw hat, a quarter-sleeved blouse, and a skirt that floated above her ballerina flats.

Bennett's dark eyes brightened, and he grinned. "Looks like you're ready for another one of our adventurous quests."

His words whisked her back to their days of

discovering places to see and things to do in Huntington. Their many outings had begun after a period of inactivity and disagreement. They seemed to have come a long way since then. They'd gotten a dog, opened The Nightingale for business, and worked together on the same goals. To others, they must seem caught in a whirlwind romance, but in truth, they'd advanced in drawing closer to one another only to slip back again and again.

"You look fantastic," Bennett was saying. "Love this new you, Em."

Em? She loved it when he called her that. The nickname sounded like an endearment, but no one else was around—no reason to put on an act. He accompanied her to the car like someone on an actual date.

They got out under a sparkling sun at a cake shop in Malibu. Because Lucinda knew the proprietor, Emma had secured an appointment without the usual six-month wait. *Imagine owning such a prize*, she thought as they entered the tall Victorian with its back to the sea.

Inside, along marble counters, wedding cakes towered in spools of ivory, pure white, gold, and even black. These were distinctive creations that set to mind the whimsical and the daring, but they weren't real, of course. How could they be? Just a large display composed of cardboard, but Emma fell back to a time when pastry, seen through a bakery window on Market Street, had the power to make her weep.

They were seated beneath framed pictures of the multitude of couples who'd sat at this very same table. Happy people. Expectant. Waiting to pick out that crown jewel that would set their wedding apart.

The lean, red-headed advisor, who had introduced himself as Stuart, settled down with them and glanced at his notepad. He asked a few questions, and after getting answers that seemed to satisfy him, he knitted his brow as if ready to dig deeper. "So how do you want your wedding cake to look?" When they shrugged, he handed them a photo album, adding, "Do you prefer fondant over buttercream? Fresh or sugar flowers? Simple or ornate designs?"

Emma hadn't had time to consider any of this beforehand. "Sorry, but I'm not sure. What do you think, Bennett?"

"To be honest, I haven't a clue."

This wasn't how she'd dreamed their afternoon would go. The pair nervously adjusted and readjusted themselves in their chairs. That she hadn't taken notes before the appointment went against her nature, no check-off list. In her defense, she'd been so busy running the B&B with Bennett and caring for Madelynn that she had no time to consider cake flavors.

Stuart grimaced. "What's the theme of your wedding?"

"We don't have any yet," she said.

"Who's the planner?"

"There isn't any." Her heart sank a little. "I guess it's just us."

"The florist?"

"We can't find one."

"Isn't your date a month from now?"

Bennett said, "We seem to be failing the test. Are we a lost cause?"

"Let's try a different approach," Stuart said with a never-say-die straightening of his thin shoulders. "Where will your wedding reception be held?"

"That's easy." Bennett's eyes dazzled from beneath

his thick lashes. "At our home in The Nightingale where our love story began."

"Aha!" Stuart whooped. "The Nightingale with its lovely Asian décor. Hmm, I think I have the perfect option for you."

He opened the album to a snapshot of a cake with four tiers in an ombré design. The bottom structure was a bold jade color that gradually faded with every inch, leaving the small top layer a mint green. A sprig of pink cherry blossoms was the only decoration, and the branch wove up the entire side of the three levels like an embrace.

"Esthetically stunning." Her throat was tight. Something about the cake, the color, and the flower branch brought her music globe to mind.

"I think we found ourselves a cake," Bennett said.

Stuart was rubbing his hands together in evident delight. "Now for the main event." He leaned forward and eyed them. "Are you ready?"

"We're both foodies at heart," Bennett admitted.

"Food excites us," she added.

Bennett whispered, "You excite me, lady."

And all her senses heightened. "We're ready."

Soon, the champagne arrived like an opening curtain. "Rhapsody on a Theme from Paganini" courted them from hidden speakers as the master chef greeted them with an assortment of samples.

The twosome participated in the traditional arm-entwined manner of feeding each other—not for show on her part but because the smells and the tastes aroused her.

Being with Bennett was like being with no other man. The current was so great she knew the memory of it would fix itself in her mind evermore. The day, the time. Just a single, hot moment when they discovered their unique connection by way of cake.

She slipped off her shoes and played footsie with him under the table. The murmurs of "oh, yum, so good. I love it" came after each bite as her passion multiplied and engulfed her. He licked her fingers of the chocolate, and her lust almost devoured her. He appeared enmeshed with her conception of feeding the empty places inside her with the magical confections. The rest of the world faded away, leaving only the two in sweet rapture and pure enchantment.

Stuart said, "Why have one cake flavor when you can have two or more?"

Bennett nodded at a cake sample. "I thought I tasted a hint of cheese in this."

Emma pointed her fork. "And is that wasabi in the buttercream?"

"Nudging people out of their comfort zones is our specialty," Stuart said proudly, lifting his pointed chin. "Any taste that holds a special meaning to you as a couple?"

She didn't need any time at all to think. "Tomato soup."

"Right," Bennett agreed.

"Well, you're in luck. Tomato soup cake is one of our specialties."

Thus, they settled on separate tiers of their favorite flavors—peanut butter cup, key lime, and tomato soup. When they left, Emma had slipped into a food coma. She relished the ocean breeze on her face as they strolled to the car.

"Do you mind if I drive?" she asked giddily.

"Not at all. Where to?"

"I'd like to order some traditional baked goods for my family to enjoy at the wedding."

"Great idea."

She drove them to a bakery on the streets of Chinatown in Los Angeles. The yeasty aroma of freshly baked longevity buns, usually purchased for birthdays, wafted in the air. A few customers and the proprietor appeared impressed when Bennett spoke in their native tongue. With her family in mind, Emma preordered the wedding pastries that came in all shapes and bore Chinese motifs—symbols for double happiness, luck, and prosperity.

When she took out her wallet, Bennett stopped her. "If I'm not mistaken, it's the groom and his family that pays for the wedding—in China, that is."

"But we're not in China."

"I insist."

Money in the bank meant everything to her, even though hers had shrunk since she'd proposed. The absence of a nest egg gave her a hollow feeling in her stomach. Still, she had to live with herself. "Okay, but I mean to pick up the bill for the flowers we order."

He steered her over to a quiet corner. "Not on your life. I told you I was paying for the wedding. That includes the flowers. Cake. Organist. Food. The honeymoon. The whole shebang, even the gazebo—definitely the gazebo."

She stuck her hands on her hips. "I can't let you do that."

"You have no choice."

"Oh, yeah? Just try and stop me."

"If you recall, I am your employer. You're my employee."

"So you're playing the boss card." She glared at him, furious with herself for being relieved he aimed to pick up the tab.

"That's right, I'm the boss," he reiterated.

"Aren't you afraid of me walking out if I don't get my way?"

He squinted and groaned. Had she unwittingly struck a nerve? Had his abandonment issues flared up yet again? The two of them were not without hang-ups.

Feeling guilty, she lifted her hands to his arms and massaged his elbows. "Well, you can't lose me that easily," she amended, her throat squeezing with emotion.

All at once, he dropped to one knee. "Marry me."

She tried to lift him to his feet without success. "Okay, you can get up now. We've already been there, done that."

Refusing to budge, he remained in a kneeling position. "Marry me tomorrow."

"Wait, what?" She wilted a little. "The justice of the peace?"

"Screw the courthouse. I'm talking Vegas, baby."

But she was shaking her head. "You want to elope?"

"There's no time like the present. We forget all this stress, and neither of us has to spend another dime."

"But you wanted a big wedding, Bennett."

"I know, I know. But ours is a marriage of convenience, right? So why are we killing ourselves to put on a performance?"

Did he actually believe this? Or had she pushed him into a corner—literally?

"What about the cake we just ordered?" She cracked her knuckles—an old habit she'd thought she'd broken years ago.

He shrugged. "It's early enough to cancel it."

"But my wedding gown isn't altered yet, and my bridesmaid's, what about them?"

"I'll pay for everything, no big deal." He tapped his chin. "Don't you have anything else you could wear tomorrow?"

She paused to think it over. "I have a dress I wore to receive a writing award last year."

"Well, there you go. And I just happen to own a tux. We're good. We even have our wedding bands."

"Right." She should be jumping for joy. This was what she'd wanted, this no-fuss union. A paint by numbers couldn't be more straightforward. Yet she felt very close to shedding disappointed tears. Why did getting married have to be so fricking complicated?

Chapter 17

Bennett couldn't tie his damned tie. His hands were not cooperating as he contemplated the next few hours. Today had the power to change his future for good or bad. He struggled again with his tie, but the knot turned out too big and lopsided. They were due soon to show up at the airport, but the egg he'd eaten for breakfast threatened to come back up.

"There you are," Emma called from the doorway. She held Madelynn's hands and guided her tiny footsteps into his bedroom. "Your daddy looks like he could use some help."

He dropped his arms to his sides. "I'm all thumbs this morning."

"I think I can remedy that."

His daughter smiled at him, warming his heart with the banner across her T-shirt that read *I love my daddy.*

Forgetting his troubles, he bent down and hugged her. "Such a big girl. You'll be walking on your own soon. Then we're in for it."

He thought about what a precious gift she'd been to him and how much she'd gone through in her young life. If this realization made him soft soapy, he could only speculate what it did to Emma.

Carefully, he stood and thrust his chest toward Emma, remaining as still as possible while she tied a perfect Windsor knot, and his daughter lifted her sweet face, observing the giants hovering above her. How incredibly lucky he was to have been entrusted with Madelynn Grace. This realization calmed his nerves and steadied his pulse.

"Good job." He gave Emma a grateful smile before he moved in and brushed his lips against her petal-soft cheek. She was nearer to him than they'd been in quite a while—if he didn't count the foot-spooning while sampling cake yesterday.

She sent him a flirtatious wink that looked a little too showy. "Why don't we just stay in today?"

He gave it right back. "Don't tempt me, babe, or I just might take you up on it."

Her eyes widened. "What did you say? I dare you to call me that again, dude."

He guessed she was trying to make them forget their anxiety, playing like he was a surfer dude, and she was his babe instead of a couple headed to Vegas for a quickie wedding. They planned to go straight to the Clark County Bureau, no tiptoeing through the tulips for them. It would be wham, bam, and slap them with a marriage certificate. Then find a chapel, and they'd be home before Madelynn finished napping.

"Guess we'd better get a move on." He nudged Emma's arm with his own and gathered up his daughter. "See you downstairs."

Alexis Nathan greeted Bennett with a wrinkled brow. "If it's the money," he said, taking the baby, "I have too much of it. I give—"

"No!" Bennett cut him off, horrified but touched by his kindness. "Thank you for your offer, but the cash isn't a problem. It's just that the stress of our wedding is putting too much emotional strain on Emma."

"So you are running off to the Marriage Capital of the World because you believe this is what she wants?"

"I need to make things easier for her."

"I see." Alexis Nathan sat Madelynn in her high chair. "Sometimes easier is not the best."

Bennett had just started to respond when Emma entered in a teal gown that did incredible things to her skin and body, and he wolf-whistled. "You better not let Madison see you dressed like that. She'll have you auditioning for some blockbuster."

"I'd have to tell her no—too busy." She winked at him. "But not after today."

She slipped on a fancy wrap, and together with Bennett, they kissed the baby goodbye, patted the dog's shaggy head, and strode out, arm in arm, with the best intentions. By rights, they should have booked a room for after the service. He couldn't think of anything that would brighten his day more. The thoughts of them being alone in a hotel suite brought back memories of seeing her naked and his unsatisfied desire. To think he might get lucky with her—finally—might be too good to be true. Or maybe not.

As the narrow-body airliner lifted from the runway, he remembered the last time he'd flown with Emma. He'd forgotten her fear of flying. He covered her hand with his own as turbulence rocked the plane and the jets roared.

"We'll be there before you can blink." He'd go for casual conversation. "You said you won an award for your writing?"

"It wasn't the Pulitzer or anything that prestigious, but it was an honor to be recognized just the same."

He had to ask, "Do you miss your job, Em?"

"I do," she said in a low tone. "Writing's addictive for me, especially when the subject matter is something I care about."

And there it was. Bennett was a selfish SOB, keeping her from the work she loved. Maybe they should call the whole thing off, but the original matrimony idea was hers.

A couple of hours later, they had their marriage license in hand. Their driver dropped them off on the Las Vegas Strip. Huntington might be known for its stretch of silvery beaches, but here, resort hotels and casinos spread as far as the eye could see. A garish, strikingly vibrant fantasy lured poor suckers in and sometimes never let them go. Bennett swore he wouldn't fall into the temptation of winning jackpots and keno tickets. Not him. His allegiance was to do one thing only—an in-and-out wedding ceremony.

His stomach reacted to the savory food smells wafting from an open doorway, reminding him he hadn't touched a bite since four a.m. Neither had Emma.

"Do you want to get a sandwich or something?" he asked.

She froze, her eyes searing into his, her chest rising and falling like it was a life-or-death question. "Yes," she finally allotted to his suggestion of altering their single-minded itinerary. "I could eat."

"Let's find a restaurant inside one of the casinos. Maybe we could relax a little and take advantage of being in Vegas."

"Excuse me?"

"You know, the slot machines."

"I'm *not* a gambler."

"We'll have to fix that," he teased, but she didn't

laugh, so he added in all earnestness, "You are, too, a gambler. You gambled when you opened The Nightingale for business."

She gave him the thumbs-up. "You're absolutely right. Let's go."

He led her across a marble entrance, and the glass doors yawned open. At once, dinging bells pierced his ears. A guy, no older than twenty-one, was jumping up and down, laughing, as coins spilled into the slot machine tray.

Bennett urged Emma past the dealer calling out bids to a roulette table where the wheel *click-click-clicked*. And they both got their chips. She nervously swiped hers along the green felt before placing it on the number five. He went for two.

The clicking circle fired up, multiplying many times, dizzying him, before it stopped on five. She went wild, and so did he. To celebrate, he ordered champagne. Soon, they hugged each other after every roll of the dice and kissed like lovers. Her voice was alarmingly high, as if she'd lost control. This might not be a good sign. And when they began to lose more than they won, he had to end things.

"Let's get lunch," he suggested.

"But I have to win back my money," she insisted with glazed eyes.

"Emma, it's just a little lost income."

"Maybe for you…but not for me… I… You have no idea what it's like…" She was fuming in a way she never had before.

"Emma?" Should he be concerned?

Her magnificent eyes had darkened like midnight. "I don't want to wind up broke…" Her cheeks flushed.

"Sorry, guess I'm being kind of unreasonable."

She took his arm and, with her usual grace, turned away from the table.

The roller coaster they'd been riding since the first moment they'd rolled the dice stopped. Emma wouldn't have to worry her pretty head about a cash flow after today. Why would she be so weirded out about spending money when she'd grown up with June? After all, her aunt hadn't had to beg, borrow, or steal to make ends meet.

"You just need some food in your belly," he explained, for his own sake as much as hers.

Bennett wasted no time locating a buffet. Emma loaded her plate with mac and cheese, the lights returning to her eyes as she ate. He scarfed down a burger, pocketed some mints, and fetched his untouched water bottle.

"Are we better?" He rose to his feet.

Nodding, she gulped the rest of her coffee.

"So are you ready for our... Ready for our really big..." Unable to find a suitable finish, he left his sentence dangling.

She bent to slip the strap of her sexy sandal up her heel and stood elegantly next to him.

Before long, they'd gone outdoors. The noonday sun reflected off all the chrome and glass, making his eyeballs ache. The rising heat penetrated his monkey suit, causing him to sweat like the devil. They should have stuck to their guns and went straight to the altar, but—oh, that's right—he'd gotten the brilliant idea to introduce Emma to Sin City.

He must have needed to postpone the inevitable. He didn't know all there was to know about her. Yet here they were, going to the chapel, and they were going to get m-a-r-r-i-e-d.

"Do you have the rings?" He wished she'd forgotten them.

"They're tucked inside their box in the zippered compartment of my purse."

"Well done."

"There's the chapel," she burst out suddenly. "What do you think?"

What did he think? He longed to retreat to The Nightingale, something raw and elemental tightening in his chest. The Nightingale, he loved the thought of it, the sound of it—home and everything good in the world. Ah, just to savor the meaning of it for a while, but out of necessity, he turned his throbbing head toward Emma's pointed finger.

A mini Victorian with loads of gingerbread trim on the gables, eaves, and windows looked as out of place in this plethora as the Eiffel Tower, the Canals of Venice, and the Statue of Liberty. He was pledging his life to Emma in a fabricated world—but theirs were fabricated promises, weren't they?

"Isn't it something?" She attached herself to his arm.

Perspiration damped his already wet tux. "It's something all right."

"And guess what?" she sang off-key. "My bouquet will be made out of silk, not even real. So you won't sneeze. I thought of everything. Isn't that terrific?"

"Terrific," he repeated, his scalp as tight as a latex swim cap. He gazed at the chapel in horror. "Don't make a move," he was tempted beyond reason to warn, but she did, and strangely, her eyes filled with tears.

She clutched the doorknob and immediately

released it like it had burned her.

"What's wrong?" He believed she was about to say she didn't want to marry him, and that was somehow worse than venturing inside.

"I can't do this."

"Why?" He hoped he hadn't come off as desperate.

"I want Madelynn and our family and friends to be at our wedding. Eloping without them just feels wrong."

He felt the corners of his mouth lifting. "I want the same thing."

"But you proposed to me, so I thought you were tired of all the hassle."

"Not at all. I only wanted to free you from the stress of organizing a wedding in such a short time."

"Oh, Bennett…" Her hand traced the skin along his jaw. "You're such a nice person."

"Thank you." A thought dawned on him then. "We don't have to go to the market to find the flowers. There's no need to visit a nursery or fly to Ecuador. Not when we've got all we need in our own backyard."

"Fantastic idea." She raised a triumphant fist.

After their misunderstanding, he resisted the urge to mention how much he admired her for admitting her error in judgment. She had character. So what if she was a little neurotic when it came to money? That could turn out to be an attribute, couldn't it? Besides, no one could ask for a better partner, mate—woman. He couldn't see himself ever going solo again. "There's something else that needs to be at The Nightingale."

"What's that?"

His chest lurched with the thrill of it all. "Our wedding gazebo."

Chapter 18

Emma came downstairs to the smell of coffee. Ah, the euphoria of anticipation. Nothing could please her more, but who was up at five a.m. besides her?

She should have known it was Bennett. She'd spied her betrothed burning the midnight oil in his office. He had been drafting a blueprint of "The Gazebo." Rather than converse about his pet project, she'd slipped back into bed. Her enthusiasm was hard to muster when the lumber alone would cost him plenty. And for what? The living room would have sufficed. It would have been somewhat cramped, but they could have made it work.

He set a cup before her at the table. "Coffee for the chief cook and bottle washer?"

Too weary to say or do anything else, she nodded.

If anything, he looked more rugged than she'd ever seen him, even if gaunt. A bit tired, probably, but his big dark eyes appeared stoked as they met hers. Should she mention their wedding was in two weeks? Emma would have liked to have him helping her with what really counted. She hadn't even picked a flower girl or a ring bearer. She didn't know any kids, but maybe he did. Somebody had to play the piano since Bennett couldn't, and what songs did they both agree on?

A hundred details needed attention, but she wouldn't say so—she who only yesterday called off their chapel service. Instead, she rested an elbow on the table and twisted a strand of her hair around her finger.

"Sooo," she began languidly. "What are your plans?" As if she hadn't figured it out.

Victoriously, he drum-rolled the table with his index fingers. "We break ground today."

"That's productive." No, it wasn't.

"I have just one request to make of you, Em."

She folded her arms on the table and leaned forward. "Yes?"

"If you have to go out, I want you to be blindfolded, and don't peek out the windows on the west side of the house."

Was he kidding her? "Why?"

"I want the finished product to be a surprise."

She sucked in her bottom lip. "Got it."

As soon as he left her alone, Emma soldiered on. With baking powder flying, she stirred the ingredients for sweet potato muffins, spooned them into paper liners, and tossed the tin in the oven. Her waffle attempt failed when she threw too much liquid into the batter. She broke a few eggs and dropped them into a pan to sizzle. Some of the yokes ran wild.

While she cussed under her breath, Alexis Nathan entered, saying, "Good morning."

Fortunately, she didn't have to return the greeting because through the open window came the hissing of truck brakes and the sharp thuds of wood being unloaded on cement.

"It's here." He sounded as awestruck as a kid when the circus came to town. He opened the door and looked at the spectacle. "Isn't it exciting?"

She didn't turn around. "I wouldn't know since Bennett wants to keep it secret from me."

"Ahh, says the woman who herself has many, many secrets."

"That's not fair." The stove timer beeped, and the muffin tin shrieked across the wire rack as she yanked it from the oven.

He deposited the mini-packaged cereals in a basket. "Have you told Bennett about your and Rachel's life before you came to live with Madam?"

"I haven't, and I probably won't." She gathered the earthenware she needed. "He wouldn't understand, not ever having to want for a thing."

Blocking her path, Alexis Nathan tilted his chin and frowned at her. "I believe you underestimate your beloved."

His comment took the fight out of Emma. Was he right? Had she misjudged her husband-to-be? Ruminating over this, she took the plates, utensils, and laundered napkins into the sunny dining room. She shut the blinds without peering out the window. Besides, all was quiet on the western front. Bennett must be leveling the ground. She summoned up all her willpower not to find out.

People moseyed down for breakfast while Emma attended to Madelynn and Rosie supervised. Emma managed to direct the vacationers to their destinations, even suggesting a write-home-worthy detour she had gleaned on blogs written by Huntington's own.

By ten o'clock, Alexis Nathan had cleaned the top and bottom story. He was sticking his head out the back door when Emma caught him.

"Why don't you just go out there?" she said. "I know you're dying to."

He straightened. "You have to work on the

wedding."

"I can do it all." She waved him out. "Now shoo, fly."

But the sad truth was she didn't get time to do much more than care for the baby and the guests who, as if instructed, didn't breathe a word to her about the goings-on in the side yard. The hammering and sawing made her want to shout, "Stop it!" The noise went on for not just one day but two and then three. She saw little of her fiancé, but his praises were sung by one and all. As for Emma, the gazebo had become a damned nuisance. She'd gotten used to working with Bennett at her side, but since he'd started his "project," he was almost always out of sight but not out of mind. How could he be with all the commotion?

At last, on the afternoon of day number four, Bennett found her in the kitchen and started to say something but then appeared to spot Madelynn rushing around in her walker. He let out a yelp. "How did I not notice her new tooth? Nobody should be this kind of busy."

He jimmied Madelynn out and lifted her into the air as if to better examine her while she giggled. Emma's heart squeezed as she watched their interaction.

After sitting Madelynn in her high chair and bestowing her with a pretzel to gnaw, he wrapped an arm around Emma's shoulders. "I couldn't have built the gazebo without you, Em."

She looked down at the floor and said nothing.

"I want you to take a refreshing shower and change into that knockout of a dress you wore in Vegas. I'll meet you back here. Alexis Nathan has volunteered to take over for us. The night is ours."

She nodded, her tummy full of butterflies.

An hour later, he enveloped her hand in his warm grip. They walked outside, he in step with her, matching her stride for stride. Although he was fleet-footed by nature, he never plunged ahead without her. To her way of thinking, his consideration of her made him sexy— without a doubt, the sexiest man she'd ever known.

The ocean air refreshed her as they strolled into the warm evening. She spotted a soft glow from the side of the house. "What's that?"

"Don't know." He rested his hand on her lower back. "Maybe Martians have landed."

A playfulness hung in his voice. He escorted Emma to where twinkle lights lit the orange trees and the dwarfed palms. Rhythm and blues rumbled softly from speakers, and she instinctively moved her body, losing herself to the beat.

The gazebo was a white octagon with lots of latticework and a cupola-style roof composed of natural wood. The design projected beauty cohesively integrated into the surrounding plants and flowers. Red rose petals had been scattered down the path that led to the structure. A table set for two awaited them.

Bereft of words, she glanced around. Bennett had put everything together with such attention to detail, from the many tealights burning everywhere to the bottle of zinfandel chilling in the silver bucket.

"You're amazing, Bennett…you know that?"

"I wanted to celebrate you, for all that you do."

He had done this for her. No man had ever given her such an unexpected surprise, and it wasn't the first time he'd been good to her, nor would it be the last. Doing things for others was who he was. This interlude had come when she needed it the most, and that made her eyes sting. She had to get ahold of herself.

Drinking the wine calmed her. Eating tri-tips and veggies steamed to perfection took her mind off everything but the man sitting across from her. Moonlight flooded the evening sky with brilliance, making her heart break for all she couldn't say.

He took her hand. "I'm so glad we didn't elope."

Her stomach contracted. "We almost made a big mistake, and while we're on that subject, I just want to tell you how sorry I am that I thought you were wasting time and money by building this work of art."

"It's not the first time you've freaked out about money. I wish I knew the reason so I could understand." He adjusted the collar of his shirt. "I didn't mean to pry."

She forced a laugh. "It's totally fine. I go bonkers when it comes to losing a cent. I think it warrants a question." Emma swallowed hard, her stomach turning over before she admitted, "My sister and I lived on the streets when we were little."

"Oh?"

"Yeah. We had a cardboard box in an alley in the Tenderloin."

He squeezed the hand he still held and looked her square in the eye. "I'm sorry."

"You want to ask how we ended up there?" she asked with contrived nonchalance.

His handsome face reddened. "Yeah, I do. I can't picture you and Rach like that. Now that you told me, I want to know more about it. If you don't want to talk, just say so. It's not anyone's business but yours. I've overstepped, and I—"

"No, you didn't do anything wrong." She sank

against the back of her chair. "My mother was addicted to opioids. She started with Fentanyl, a doctor's prescription, and it got out of hand. So much so she forgot about anything else."

"That must have been hell." Bennett's expressive eyes were full of empathy.

"Yeah. Rachel and I were stuck. Mom wasn't around much, you know? Junkies don't think about anything but their next fix. She was rushed to the hospital after some bad shit. I guess the doctors did everything, but there's some stuff you can't come back from. We waited for her to return to the alley, but she never did."

"Wow." His eyes were glassy. "I'm so sorry you and Rach had to go through that. I can't imagine what that must feel like."

"We were almost always hungry."

His hand on hers was strong, firm, and protective. "Thank you for telling me."

The black sea danced, silver-tipped waves rolling back and forth over the sand, and the calm allowed Emma to reflect on her prospective husband.

Before Bennett came into her life, she'd believed she'd never give herself to a man. Her conviction was the result of her mother's many affairs and breakups. The perverts Emma had known when they were homeless only added to her conjecture. The fact that her father had left when she was very young had intensified matters. No wonder self-preservation had given her the restraint to turn down any opportunities for a sexual experience.

But even on the first day she'd met Bennett, whenever they were together, heat had risen in waves along her skin and penetrated deep inside. The ice around her heart had melted, and she had found comfort in his solicitude, making him even more desirable. But with her past, could she learn to care about him so much she could honestly call it love? She didn't know.

Chapter 19

Bennett had set Sunday morning aside from his hectic schedule to watch Madelynn. The lodgers had checked out, and no more had been scheduled until after the honeymoon. Alexis Nathan had to give a poetry reading at a bookshop in Venice Beach. Emma holed up in the office with only the dog for company. The seating chart for the reception needed wrapping up along with the menu choices. Bennett volunteered to help her, but she turned him down flat.

"The best thing you can do is to take care of the baby," she'd said.

"You're assigning me the easy part."

He gave Madelynn the run of the downstairs. Touching objects, putting stuff in her mouth, and getting into things was her job. His job was keeping her quiet so Emma could concentrate—a cinch. Or so he'd believed, fool that he was.

He sat with her on the piano bench, and her tiny fingers found the keys and struck them with a single blow. *Boom!* Her giggles rippled throughout the house.

He moved her to the floor and slammed a shushing finger to his lips. "We have to be quiet so Mommy can work."

Crawling away, then walking with the aid of furniture, and—

Clang went the bell on top of the front desk. *Clang,*

clang, clang!

His hand cupped over her busy fingers. "No, no. Mommy's trying to think."

Thwack went one of the books she threw on the floor. *Thwack* went another. *Thwack!*

"Madelynn Grace!"

A toy locomotive left her grip with a *tooooot!*

Then she was off again. "Wait for me," Bennett called, chasing behind.

Before he could catch up with her, all at once, she took a tumble. And oh, how she wailed at the top of her lungs. *Waaah! Wah! Wah!*

He snapped her up into his arms, determined to quiet her as quickly as possible. "There, there, sugar pie." He dried her wet cheeks with a tissue.

He sank to his easy chair with her on his lap. She rested her head against his chest, and they rocked. With her thumb in her mouth, she conked out cold. They both napped. After about an hour, he awoke to find her looking up at him. Her little fists scoured the sleep from her eyes, and she grinned up at him adoringly.

He gave her a big hug. "Daddy loves you."

She was already down and about to scoot away when he picked her up and hauled her into the kitchen. He considered asking Emma for advice on what to serve for lunch. But she'd waited till he finished the gazebo to take care of the last-minute wedding details. He wanted to give her as much space as she needed. Still, he should at least tell her he planned to take Madelynn outside in case she came down and found them gone.

Just as he was about to text her, his phone rang. "Hello?"

"Bennett?"

"Yes, Em. How's it going? You good?"

"Yeah, I'm good." A hesitation. "What about Madelynn?"

She always worried about the baby, and so did he. Although Madelynn appeared super healthy—that quintessential energizer bunny—the threat of the hole in her heart never ceased to invade their thoughts. Would it mend on its own as the doctors had hoped?

"I'm getting her veggies from the fridge as we speak," he said to ease Emma's mind. "Thought I'd take her to the beach."

"That's nice. Madelynn loves hanging out with her daddy."

He could hear the tremor in her voice, and it tempted him to ask about the father she never mentioned. But she'd already confessed enough bad stuff to him. He'd take away every tragic thing that had ever happened to her if he could.

"Well, see you," she said with the vagueness of the isolated.

"Oh, uh, of course." He paused. "Do you need anything? A fresh pencil, a phone charger, some lunch?"

"I'm fine."

"Okay then, bye." He felt useless. She had sounded out of sorts. But if he bonded with her over these final arrangements, his interference might hinder her from getting her dream wedding—if she'd fathomed such a thing. He hadn't asked her if their marriage was still a show. He didn't want to put her on the spot, or maybe he didn't want to know the answer. Even after Vegas, he might exist in the friendzone, never to get any higher in her estimation.

Worrying about where he stood had become

habitual. They needed to have a serious talk, but the moment never seemed right. His overthinking wasn't doing him any good.

And so he said to his daughter, "Let's get out of here."

Madelynn clapped her hands and rocked from side to side in her high chair, clearly understanding his words. Fair to admit, she was by far the sharpest baby on the planet.

As for him, he prided himself on knowing how to get his daughter ready for an outing. Be it holiday or weekend, her swimming gear was the same. He made sure she wore loads of sunscreen, a swimsuit, a sunhat, and her florescent-pink water wings. He packed a duffle bag with more quality nourishment than she could ever need.

Then off they went into that briny sea air, the umbrella stroller zipping over the terrain. They passed the low stone wall where fragrant yellow jasmine was anchored against the wind. Emma loved those flowers. He turned and caught a glimpse of her in the upstairs window.

She waved, and he longed to beckon her to join them with the vacationers taking advantage of the clear blue of sea and sky. He cupped his hands to his mouth to call out, but she'd already disappeared. Just as well.

He lifted his daughter from the stroller and positioned her where the water lapped at her beach shoes, amazed at how hard she clung to his index fingers. Then she let go of him and balanced herself on the wet sand.

"Look at you!" he said in amazement.

Her feet were so dinky in proportion to her body that he wondered how standing on her own was even possible. He wondered, too, if Madelynn had forgotten all about her birth mother. Rachel—this was the first time he'd thought of her in a long while. In his mind's eye, he saw her as if he were looking down from the ceiling of the teahouse.

He'd had such high hopes back in those days. In honor of Valentine's Day, white tablecloths, red candles, and homemade cards spruced up the tables. While eating a delicious dinner, he and Rachel had talked.

Well, to be honest, he talked—and talked. He told her how he planned to stamp out poverty in the US as if he could even make a dent. Her eyes, big and dark, glanced away as if bored with him. He should have taken it as a sign.

As soon as Audrey had served the chocolate cake with its diamond ring atop, he'd gotten down on one knee. People stopped eating to stare at them with curiosity. He'd written and memorized his proposal but, in the heat of the moment, forgot it. It was unusual for the speech giver, but sad to say, he should have noted the many bad omens before popping the question.

When he had, Rachel had uttered the unexpected but deplorable, "I'd rather be shot in the head than marry you."

Now here he was with his daughter, on the verge of taking her first step and reliving all the pain and disgrace he'd experienced. "Rachel could be brutal."

Madelynn angled her head as if she understood. "Dada."

From behind him, he heard Emma say, "I'm sorry she hurt you."

He startled. Despite the storm in his chest, he inhaled the calming scent of her perfume. Once again, she'd misunderstood and thought he'd been mooning over Rachel. How could he admit that those long-ago feelings had been a case of puppy love? The truth was, Rach and his differences would have been impossible to live with.

Madelynn was swaying on those little feet. "Momma," she said with a happy grin.

Emma's eyes widened. "Did you hear her? She called me Momma. I swear she did. Can you believe it?"

Before he could respond, Emma reached for Madelynn's hand, and all danced in place—the woman, the man, and the baby that had brought them together.

Maybe Emma would grow to love him. She'd gotten over their initial terms of strictly business, of that he felt sure. More than all their stolen kisses was the fact she'd confided her secrets. Plus, Alexis Nathan had insisted she cared for him.

Had their make-believe engagement turned real when he wasn't looking? Bennett wanted their marriage to succeed. Oh, he didn't care about being a big cheese at his wedding. He just wanted to be an effectual groom for her.

Was that too much to ask?

He booked an appointment on Tuesday for a tuxedo fitting with his tailor for himself and his groomsmen. The shop was tucked into the second floor of a townhouse in North Hollywood and supported checkerboard floors, spare wooden shelving, and a retro diner-drip coffee machine.

His father's tailor had a distinguished silvery hairline and a low, throaty voice. He talked politics while snipping and taking out the stitches in the sleeves of the tux he'd turned inside out, then pinning so that Bennett stood with his arms straight up in the air. That's when Liam entered for his fitting, as did Brandon and Alexis Nathan.

The groomsmen were staring at him quizzically.

"What are you doing there, mate?" Liam asked with a grin. "Stopping traffic?"

The tailor had put pins under both arms, rendering it impossible for Bennett to move, let alone get a word in of explanation.

His predicament appeared to drive Liam to barge ahead. "Can you fancy getting married in the courthouse? That way, the ceremony would be done and over with in no time."

"Of course, Liam would opt for a quick marriage," Brandon said to Alexis Nathan. "This is the man who organized a wedding in four days."

"Actually, I think it turned out quite well." Liam shook a finger at the group. "It's a good thing Bennett's not getting hitched in his church. That way, if he finds out he's made a mistake, he can bail without any consequences."

His groomsmen were talking about him as if he weren't there. He couldn't get a word in.

With bushy eyebrows lowered, Alexis Nathan was glaring at Liam. "What is wrong with you? Someone does not go into this blissful sacrament with such a bad attitude."

"He does if his prospective bride's sister was Rachel Bellamy," Liam said. "Her rich father employed staff members to kill any negative stories about his daughter. If I hadn't spent a decade as a spy, I would have come away empty-handed."

"You didn't know her," Alexis Nathan said. "And

you certainly don't know Emma."

Bennett managed to clear his throat and gesture toward his immobile arms with his chin.

The tailor glanced up from the pants he'd been hemming and nodded. "Pardon me, sir." He hurried to accommodate him.

Bennett was uncomfortable about speaking ill of the dead. "Both Emma and I want the wedding to take place at The Nightingale."

On the level, he didn't know if Emma would stick to her original plan and file for divorce if things didn't work out. If that happened, he would be glad they hadn't married in the church since the marriage wouldn't be recognized and quickly annulled. As much as it killed him to consider her leaving him, he had to be realistic.

"I believe we should change this controversial subject," Alexis Nathan said. "Bennett looks upset, and who can blame him?"

"I'm all right," Bennett said. "I've got a lot on my mind. Um, anything we should go over while we're all together?"

"What about the bachelor party?" Liam asked. "What are your thoughts?"

Alexis Nathan sat on the edge of a chair. "In India, we take a party bus, go for dinner at the groom's favorite restaurant, and have a room reserved at a resort on the night before the wedding. We enjoy good drinks and soulful talks and take pleasure in each other's company."

"I don't think the alcohol's such a good idea, especially if the party is the night before," Brandon put in. "Bennett, isn't it better to be at your best on your wedding day?"

"Agreed. My luck, I'd manage to get myself

arrested." The prospect of that made his throat clench.

"What if we have the bachelor party at the teahouse," Liam said, "so that the drinks are tea? Then there would be no worries, eh?"

Bennett remembered when a veteran had suffered an attack of PTSD and all the customers had fled the teahouse in a mad dash. Not to mention, the Tea and Poetry had been where Rachel dumped him. But all in all, it was a wiser location for the get-together—if there had to be one. He supposed adhering to tradition was all part of the marriage bargain, though he didn't care for the bad vibes he'd gotten from their discussion.

Liam gestured a hand as if the teahouse existed next door and not in Venice Beach. "We can have it on a Sunday when we're closed. Bennett, list the blokes you'd like me to include. I'll send out the invites and do the cooking myself."

"Good. Then it's all set."

But Bennett had a sick feeling in his gut the bachelor party wouldn't go well.

Chapter 20

These days, Charles Browning had earned Emma's respect. He had proved a great asset by helping Bennett and her run the B&B. Still, she could tell by the rigidity of his normally limber frame that something bothered him this morning.

He got himself a coffee and took a seat at the kitchen table. "I need to talk to you," he said to her with solemnity.

With dread, she sat like a student summoned to the principal's office. He probably wanted to ask her why she hadn't finished the last-minute wedding details. Did she dare tell him she couldn't see spending a fortune on the live band Bennett wanted when a DJ would be adequate? Also, why hire multiple photographers when one would do? And why get some big-name caterer when she and June could whip up a feast themselves at no cost?

"I come from a long line of politicians," Charles said unexpectedly. "We lived by a motto passed down to us. Simply put, it's 'no bad press.' So when I first heard about you and Madelynn, I reacted the same as all the Brownings who came before me. Determined to stop bad press at any cost. But then I met my granddaughter and worked with you."

"I appreciate you taking the time to get to know us," Emma said, meaning it. "I don't know what I would have done without you."

"It's kind of you to say so."

"It's the truth." Even if Bennett was still in love with her sister.

"Rachel could be brutal," he'd said, and, well, of course, he felt that way. The universe had taken her from him, and he would never get over it. What else could Emma expect?

The bottom line was that he had loved her sister with all his heart. Emma was only a stand-in, a substitute for the real thing. How could she complain when the idea of a "wedding of convenience" had been hers? And hers alone. It had made perfect sense at the time.

And now? She wasn't sure about anything any longer.

"I have something to ask you." Charles whisked her back to the present. "Please just hear me out. Your father is out of the picture. I don't know why, and you don't have to tell me. But somebody's got to walk you down the aisle. Now, you might favor Alexis Nathan since he's like a brother to you, or even Eddie Wong, who has always been there when you needed him. You may wish to ask your aunt, even though she's a woman. But if you're on the fence, I hope you'll consider me a worthy candidate."

She didn't know what to say, though her heart ached for the father who had disappeared so many years ago. Who'd accompany her down the aisle to her groom? She couldn't imagine picking any of them but didn't want to hurt Charles. After all, she'd come to care about him. He was family. Yet she didn't want to offend her other loved ones.

Besides, if she could have her heart's desire, her

father would magically appear for her on the day she was to marry, but that would be a fairy-tale wedding. Hers was not.

"Don't give me an answer now," Charles was saying. "Just think about it and know I'm here for you. I would be delighted if you chose me."

"That means a lot, and I will consider it." She cleared her throat. "Bennett's having a bachelor party, and I'd like to host a bridesmaid's luncheon."

"I see." He leaned forward and tagged her with his keen blue-eyed stare. "A bridesmaid's luncheon?"

"It's where I honor all the women I care about."

"You would have invited my late wife. I wish you could have known Maura. Bennett is so much like her…" He broke off and smiled sadly, then conspiratorially. "You could have the luncheon outdoors in the gazebo."

"Maybe right before Bennett's bachelor party." Mentioning the pavilion reminded her of the trials and tribulations before Bennett had surprised her with dinner and how elegant the atmosphere had been. "You're right. The gazebo is the ideal place to have it."

And so Emma threw herself into organizing the event, inviting the aunties and her three besties. With recipes from a pile of wrinkled and stained pages, she devised a menu she imagined, in short, a triumph. The dishes were garnered from June's notebooks and Emma's experiments. As a result, she felt confident the luncheon would be a hit.

How could anything go wrong?

For starters, a rare, unpredicted atmospheric river fueled a storm along the coast. The garden party decorations had to be rushed inside at the last minute. Brandon had planned a playdate for his son and

Madelynn. Bennett whistled as he and his daughter left the B&B like it was another sunny Sunday in paradise.

Rosie had no more sprung after them when Emma caught her and raced back for cover from the downpour.

"Great day for ducks," Madison said, sliding by Emma, towel-drying the dog in the foyer.

"I'll say." Lucinda's voice rang out, hair and attire in the chaos only the former cover girl could exude with panache. "Build us an ark, and we'll party on."

Audrey waddled into the house, holding a hand on her lower back. "You might want to kick me out of your wedding," she said woefully. "I look like a rotisserie chicken."

"You'll always be beautiful no matter what shape you're in." Emma steered her to the comfiest chair in the living room.

Lucinda rubbed her twin sister's very pregnant belly. "I think they miscalculated her due date."

Madison chimed in, "Dear Lord, let's hope not."

June and Rai came from the kitchen, and the group chatted about everything from pregnancies to the flooding and mudslides California had endured this year.

Soon, though, they were in the dining room. The tone was light, though the day outside the window appeared almost as dark as night. As they ate, they discussed movies, news, and fashion. Mostly, though, they talked about the wedding while Emma inwardly cringed.

A thunderbolt caused Rosie to scamper up her legs and onto her lap.

"Audrey, are you all ready for the baby?" Emma asked, trying to comfort the dog cowering beneath the tablecloth while drawing the conversation away from herself.

"Jack," Lucinda said discreetly behind a raised hand. "The baby's name is Jack."

"Oh, right." She should have remembered that detail. What kind of friend was she?

Starry-eyed, Audrey answered Emma. "Liam painted dancing bears on one of the walls in the nursery and children's verses on the other, and now he's decorating the teahouse for the bachelor party tonight."

Blah, blah, blah was all Emma registered because the topic pertained to her nemesis. No matter how much Bennett tried, Liam and her mending their differences was a lost cause.

"Everything is beyond delish," Madison said with a swoop of her fork. "Hats off to Emma for putting this affair together." She turned to Rai. "Now that you'll be here for the week, would you allow me to arrange a screen test?"

Rai sat up as tall as her four foot ten inches would allow. "I want to work. For you. Do not know if I am classy enough for TV."

"Rai," Madison signed with her expressive hands, "in that dress, with your new hairdo, no one else is as classy as you."

Emma valued Madison's friendship the same as she did the rest of the women. She'd bought satin, monogrammed robes, but it didn't seem enough, though the group appeared delighted when they opened their presents. Even the candles she'd crafted and placed in colored glass holders as party favors couldn't—well, couldn't hold a candle to what the women deserved.

"I lost my sister," Emma said. "My life has changed, and there is another, or to be accurate, others. I have all of you. You're different and yet so important to me. There's also June—my rock. She took Rachel and me in when we were at our lowest."

Her bridesmaids were listening with sympathy.

"I've never had the strength to go through Rachel's things." Emma had to think of something or totally lose it. "Would everyone care for dessert?"

Audrey rose to stand, not spryly when her back was clearly bothering her. "I'll help."

"We've got this. You stay put." Emma lowered Rosie to the floor and went into the kitchen with Rai and June. The women cleaned up the kitchen, talking about how, despite the weather and the abrupt change of plans, all seemed to have gone well.

Emma disagreed, though she kept this to herself. She had wanted to applaud her tribe. But nothing had been celebratory. Not her mood as black as the clouds in the sky—not her speech that had poured out from some bottled-up place inside her. Considering it all, she had to suck up the fact she hadn't been a good hostess.

June had no more sliced the lemon cake when a frightened Lucinda entered.

"My sister's water broke!" she cried. "Do any of you know what to do next?"

June dropped the tray on the counter. "My niece does. Emma?"

"I do, but did you call 911?"

"Yes. There's been an accident, a pile-up on the Pacific Coast Highway. Nobody can get through." Lucinda wrung her hands. "Please…help."

Emma recalled the babies she'd brought into the world to calm herself and hesitated a few seconds before saying, "Of course."

In the living room, she discovered a frantic Audrey.

"I can't get Liam." Audrey's mouth opened, closed, then opened again. "He probably put his phone down on the other side of the teahouse. He does that. Gets preoccupied when he's working on a project."

Madison lowered her wristwatch. "Her contractions are five minutes apart."

"Everything will be fine," Emma said and, when a bolt of lightning lit the room, added, "June, there's a bathroom to the left of my bedroom. Rip down the plastic shower curtain and cover my bed with it. Madison and Lucinda, help Audrey up the stairs. Rai, put all the candles I gave out on the tray and bring them up, along with a lighter from the kitchen."

Emma unlocked the front door so the EMTs could enter. She retrieved sheets, towels, and the box full of instruments she'd packed and stored in the linen closet.

Just, please, let there be no complications.

As Emma got to the second story, she heard Audrey asking for Liam again and her twin telling her to breathe.

Audrey's hair had become damp as time passed, and her face contorted with pain during every contraction. When the next came even more intensely, she cried, "It hurts!"

Lucinda extended her arm. "Hold on to me."

Audrey clung to her sister. "Don't let go."

"I won't." Lucinda's gaze got hold of Emma's and beseeched her.

Panting, Audrey lay in a nest of blankets, her back propped up with pillows. The women kept giving encouragement, and not that much later, Audrey uttered an anguished cry and then another. She thrashed her head against the pillow, and with a washcloth, Rai dabbed cold water on her forehead and temples, and Audrey stilled with a moan. Then she gave one more loud bellow, and the baby's head started to crown.

Emma sanitized her hands again and inserted clean towels beneath Audrey's hips. "All right. Time to push."

Lucinda bent over her sister. "Come on, Jack!"

Madison followed suit. "This is your show, Jackie boy."

Jack's head emerged, which Emma gently cradled in her hands. Then a shoulder slipped out of the womb with the next contraction.

"Way to go," Emma said. "Keep it up, Audrey. You're almost there."

June said, "Not much longer."

After another contraction, the other shoulder slid out, and the rest of the body quickly followed. Emma stroked downward on the tiny nose and cleared the air passages.

Everyone waited for that strong, healthy cry.

Come on, Jack, breathe!

But he didn't obey, and Audrey looked up in utter terror. Emma knew only a short window existed in which to save the baby. The tension in the room increased, the women watching with terrified eyes.

The electricity blinked intermittently and went out, leaving them in an artificial night.

Lucinda drifted to the window, a solitary figure in the darkness, her head lifted to the sky.

"Pass out the lit candles," Emma said, and Rai didn't hesitate.

The women skirted around the bed, united by the flickering flames. Emma massaged Jack's body, trying to stimulate him. In a few seconds, he suddenly gasped and wailed loudly enough to scare off any angel of death. Sighs of relief filled the air, followed by cheers.

Lucinda held her nephew's tiny foot while he kicked like mad. "Looks like we've got a star running back on our hands."

"He's a keeper all right," Madison said.

Emma bathed the now whimpering Jack. She wrapped him in the receiving blanket she'd reverently kept. The one Madelynn had been swaddled in when the social worker dropped her off on that pivotal first day.

Sobbing, Audrey stretched her arms toward Emma. "Let me see him."

Emma placed him on Audrey's breast. "Here's your mother, Jack," she managed to say with a throat so tight her words were gravelly, and the baby began to suckle.

The blaring approach of the ambulance caused everyone to clap. Within minutes, the electricity returned, and paramedics attended to the mother and son. The fastener tearing loose after they took Audrey's blood pressure seemed loud beyond belief. The comforting voice of the robust man in charge reassured Emma. The stretcher they used to transport Audrey and Jack creaked as the crew passed by Emma, cold metal rails brushing against her, and she flinched.

They filed out and down the steps into the drizzle, and she stood by as they lifted the cot into the idling ambulance. The overhead lighting inside appeared unusually bright against the darkness. Lucinda had just started climbing aboard when a vehicle suddenly stopped, and a frantic Liam raced toward them.

"Well, it's about time you showed up," teased Lucinda, stepping aside.

When Liam saw his wife and son, his shoulders

shook as he wept. Audrey said something to him. He twisted around and saluted Emma, all previous animosity forgotten. She gave him a nod, and something in the transparency of his emotions touched her. Then the doors slammed shut, and the ambulance headed down the highway.

Madison said, "Looks like you could use another mimosa."

"Hell with mimosas." Lucinda rolled her eyes. "What she needs is a pint of whiskey. It's what we all need."

Madison embraced Emma. "You did good, sweetie."

"Yeah," Lucinda said. "You're my new hero."

Her friends left, and shivering, Emma started through the rain back to The Nightingale. The coastline rumbled with wind and waves—a sight akin to the uncommon weather this year. No one could predict the storms or their outcome, but this afternoon, they hadn't mattered, and she would be ever grateful for that.

June was waiting for her at the door and ushered her inside. Emma took two steps into the entry and hesitated. June tucked a lock of her niece's hair behind her ear. The gesture melted something inside Emma. She was nine again and had just found out her mother had died, and she wanted her father, needed him to come back— wanted it more than anything.

Chapter 21

By the time Bennett returned to The Nightingale with a sleeping Madelynn in his arms, June and Rai had left to catch their flight back to the city. He found Emma sitting in the dark.

"Hey, you," he said gently.

"Hey, yourself." Her voice was thick and unsteady. Had she been crying?

"Guess all those survival skills of yours paid off."

"It could have easily gone the other way."

"Could have…" He laid Madelynn on the couch, plumped some pillows around her, and turned, wanting to comfort Emma. "But it didn't."

"Hey…don't you have a bachelor party with your name on it?"

"I don't know. It just might be called off." He allowed a grin. "You know the host's wife just gave birth to a baby boy."

"Jack," she supplied. "The baby's name is Jack."

He felt proud of her. "And you should know, right?"

His phone rang, and he nodded at her. "It's Liam," he announced and tapped the speaker icon. "I guess I should say congratulations."

"Thanks, mate, but I didn't do anything. Your fiancée did it all, thank God." Liam cleared his throat. "Hey, I'm still at the hospital. Johnny Spade said he'd take over for me, but I guess we should cancel it."

Emma was shaking her head. "No. I had my party. It's only fair you have yours too."

"I invited your mates from your school days," Liam said. "Some of them came a long way. Maybe you could take them, I don't know—bowling."

"Bowling?" Bennett met Emma's eyes and shrugged. "What the hell, Liam?"

"I'd flip the bill," Liam said anxiously.

"No one needs to spend any more money," Emma said. "Liam, Audrey told us you've been decorating and cooking all day. Your hard work shouldn't go to waste."

Bennett patted the back of her hand. "Em, I'd rather stay home and take care of you."

"You go. I'm fine."

"Liam, they're bringing Jack in for feeding," Bennett heard Audrey saying. "You'll get to hold him."

"That's my cue," Liam said. "You do what you want." He sounded resigned, giving Bennett cause to wonder why.

But an hour later, the driver had swung down Abbot Kinney Boulevard and parked in front of the teahouse. Bennett slashed through the rain to the entrance door and into the warmth and noise. The aroma of Liam's finger-licking chicken wings, spring rolls, and cheesy quesadillas lured him toward the table.

He'd only gotten halfway there when his frat brothers from college bear-hugged him. Some were already hurling darts on a circular board illustrated with a tattooed, bikini-clad sex goddess.

Ralph, Bennett's best buddy going back to elementary school and wearing white skinny jeans that matched his shock of bleached hair, slapped Bennett's shoulder.

A clown he recognized from the boardwalk stuck a party pin on him that read *The Groom*—as if he needed a reminder of who he was in the herd.

A few close political connections shook his hand, congratulating him, while neon signs told him how and what he was supposed to feel.

Tying the knot...showed a man hanging from the gallows.

Under new management...displayed a man on his knees before his bride.

The same vagina forever...needed no description.

This depravity would have been history if Liam had returned here instead of accompanying his wife and baby to the hospital. Like a dagger to the gut, Bennett noted that everywhere he looked, the decorations reflected his last hurrah. So this was why Liam tried to call off the party—this disrespectful slur on Emma. He hadn't wanted Bennett to marry her. And now Liam had changed his tune. A little too late.

As Bennett drifted to the tea bar, he spotted specialty teas listed on a blackboard—a fair share spiked with alcohol. The inconsistency set his teeth on edge. He found Johnny Spade bartending and went to him to state his concerns.

Spade brightened when he saw Bennett. "Ah, the man of the hour."

"I thought we'd decided on no booze."

"It was Liam's idea." Of course, it was.

"I didn't want—"

"These medicinal teas are for buffering the temperatures outside. You wouldn't want to send your bros into the cold without a little nip, would you?"

"But we—"

"Be right back."

"Spade, we've got to take down that blackboard."

But he was gone. This setup was a shitstorm waiting to happen.

Alerted, Bennett was more determined not to drink too much. He joined the dart tournament and the laughter and carousing, but he felt outside his own party and looking in.

It was his bash, on second thought, and he was, at heart, a SoCal dude. And these were the guys from his alma mater. He ordered a white rum daiquiri a la Hemingway to prove he could be a good sport. Just one doctored tea, what harm could it do?

By the time he'd polished off his—um...*tea*, Audrey's uncle had traveled down the long mahogany bar and back, refreshing drinks and providing new orders. Just as he'd filled another empty glass, Spade's long-lost parrot flew through the open window and landed on his shoulder. Bennett nearly fell off his stool. No one had seen the bird since he disappeared when Liam and Audrey married over a year ago.

With bright-green feathers ruffling, Kubla warbled, "Bottoms up."

Unable to believe his eyes, Bennett guzzled another daiquiri. "Bottoms up!"

Spade had cocked his head and was gazing open-mouthed at his former sidekick. "You've returned to me, you goldarn parrot. Returned from that dome in the air, those caves of ice. A marvel, I do declare." Raising his glass and taking a jaunty, theatrical stance, he added, "To Kubla Khan!"

Cups were lifted from one side of the teahouse to the other. "To Kubla!"

"Back from where the sacred river ran," said the poet Alexis Nathan.

"Through caverns measureless to man," said the fitness guru and philosopher Brandon.

"Down to the sunless sea," Bennett finished, dazed. "Beware!"

"Before I forget," Spade said, "I wish to toast Emma. Thanks to her, my great-nephew made his much-anticipated debut this afternoon." He turned to Bennett. "To your bride."

And Kubla rasped, "To your bride."

Bennett nodded and drank up. He couldn't wait to get back to her.

But as the night wore on in the teahouse, the frat boys reverted to their younger selves. When they weren't bragging about the crazy antics that had bonded them, they were roasting Bennett, poking fun at him for giving up his freedom. They arm-wrestled and placed bets and pushed at each other. Fights flamed up for no apparent reason. By the time someone let in the scantily dressed females, his former classmates had gotten wild and raunchy.

"Benny, my man." One bro slapped Bennett on the back. "How 'bout one more fling before you're saddled with the old ball and chain?"

"One last night of good lovin' before the fall," said another.

A few guys were already trying to woo women like they were twenty, not thirty.

From outside the open window, Ralph hollered, "I dare you to jump…"

The challenge set off alarm bells in Bennett's head. "Uh-oh."

The crowd rolled into the Oriental garden in the back and looked up through the rain at the shit-faced man on the balcony between the first and second story. Ralph's hair hung in dripping shards over his wet, slack face, and his lanky body fluttered on the wooden rail.

He steadied himself for one regal moment. "Remember when we flew like eagles?"

"We were twelve when we jumped off the school roof," Bennett shouted through cupped hands, his temples thudding. "And we landed in the sand. There's just grass down here—lots of slippery grass. Come down. It's dangerous."

From a distance, the parrot echoed, "Dangerous."

"Double dare you," Ralph yelled, rocking back and forth just before falling to the ground with a *splash*. His scream of pain sliced the air as he lay, his leg at a weird angle.

A shrieking ambulance stole him away. The partygoers fell silent and long-faced as they sauntered off, most shocked sober, including Bennett. His groomsmen remained on the scene to help Spade clean up. Meanwhile, Bennett got a ride to the hospital to be with Ralph.

In his drunken state, Ralph had lucked out with a mere bruised rib and a broken leg. Nothing, though, could hide his scarlet cheeks when he saw Bennett.

"Sorry, man," Ralph muttered. "Don't know what got into me."

Bennett's fears about his bachelor party had come to pass, but he didn't say anything for the first few seconds. Ralph's face appeared less splotchy, the redness gone, but he slouched and bowed his head.

"A bunch of screwups, all of us." Bennett wanted to

let him off the hook.

"Good thing you're not still running for office."

"Right." Hopefully, if and when he signed on for another election, he wouldn't be getting married, praise be. Vegas was looking better after tonight.

He was counting the minutes until he arrived back home. When he finally got inside and out of the rain, that enigmatic song from Emma's glitter globe greeted him. He was grateful for the tune's hypnotic spell and drew nearer, taking comfort in emptying his weary mind. The tinkling slowed and stopped, glitter encircling the glass sphere.

Emma glanced up at him. "I thought I heard you. Did you have fun?"

He didn't answer, couldn't. How dark her eyes were, bronzed in the lantern light, and how tangled her hair, with the wick's flame brightening its natural blaze.

He hung up his wet coat and plunked onto the high-back wooden chair across from her. "I didn't mean to disturb you. The day we moved in here, you said you'd tell me the story behind the musical globe. Would you now?"

Pinching her beautiful lips together, she nodded. "You must have noticed I pick it up whenever I'm feeling sad."

"Yes, the tune seems to soothe you somehow."

"The day my father left, he sat me down." She gulped hard. "He said he was going away and gave me this gift. He told me he'd return soon but to listen to it when I felt low. I didn't know why he hadn't come back home until I heard my mother talking to a neighbor. He'd been summoned to China by his brother to fight in a revolt. My father was shot and captured by the communist regime and held as a political prisoner. I never saw him again."

She got up and started past Bennett, but he rose, catching her with his hand and pulling her close. She rested in his arms, pressing her face against his chest, her breath warm and smelling faintly of wintergreen.

A sob sounded in her throat. "I don't know why I'm crying. I've been such a mess. There's no reason. It's not like I lost my dad yesterday. It happened years ago."

He tried to dry her tears with his fingers. "I shouldn't have asked you about it. You're not a crier, but you're getting married and want your father."

She seemed to allow herself to drown in his arms. She was letting him comfort her as she did him. Both of them had suffered their share of misfortune, she a lot more than he had. Then they kissed, and he got lost in the moment.

Until Emma said, "You loved my sister so much and still do."

Was it a question?

He longed to announce *no, that's not true*. But he'd have to tell her why he didn't give a damn about Rachel, who he believed, by her negligence, had caused Madelynn's health problems. If he started in, he couldn't stop from letting Emma know of all his pent-up grievances. She didn't need him blowing off steam, not now of all times.

Still, his silence denied nothing.

Consequently, she ran from him as if she believed the worst. She headed up the stairs, with him lagging behind. Her bedroom door slammed shut, and by the time he caught up with her, he had no choice but to cross the hall—a bridge that left him alone in the dark and so far away from her.

At the wedding rehearsal six days later, Bennett went through the motions. He should have taken something for the burning pain in his chest. People moved around the garden and gazebo, shadows he couldn't see clearly except for Emma.

She was the source of all his discontent.

Leave it to him. He'd injured the woman he was about to marry by not speaking up. Since then, he'd been committed to rectifying his mistake. But sadly, she was no longer on the same wavelength as him, and since people were around them all the time, he couldn't begin to tell her the truth. He felt at a frustrating loss. Her smile was stiff, her face expressionless, her eyes unwilling to meet his. Her behavior had driven him up the wall. Didn't help that they were making things legal tomorrow, the marriage nothing but a farce.

The entire wedding party was patting him on the back. At the rehearsal dinner, they would utter speeches about how well the couple fit together. Pitiful, just pitiful.

Maybe they could work things out after they were married. Right. And perhaps it would never rain again in California. The state had experienced an unprecedented wet year. Climate change? Atmospheric rivers? El Niño? Whatever the crap it was, it appeared to epitomize the chaotic time he was having, running a bed-and-breakfast while trying to win over Emma.

All his life, he'd wanted to be loved by a woman— lusted over. But he was destined to remain single, even in marriage. If only Emma had reassured him that she cared, but she hadn't given him that, and why the hell would she?

No one knew of his problems, as Madison, usually behind the scenes, had stepped in to direct the practice run for tomorrow's grand production. She'd given instructions for the past half hour, standing back to watch them played out, then adding her input. When she asked who planned to walk Emma down the aisle, three men had approached her—Eddie Wong, Alexis Nathan, and Bennett's father.

"Dad..." he started to say in amazement but stopped.

His father and Emma had grown close, so his volunteering made sense. Externally, Bennett kept his cool. Internally, he was moved by his father's gesture.

She seemed to consider each member of the trio for the important role—and a role was all it was when it came down to it.

She finally shrugged. "No one's going to walk me anywhere. I'm breaking tradition and will await my groom at the altar. The groomsmen can walk down the aisle. Maybe, Charles, you can accompany your son instead of me."

Bennett wouldn't have understood her strange request if she hadn't told him about her father going to China, never to return. But she had, and he wanted to help her.

Without hesitation, he said, "How gender-neutral of you, Em. I love it!"

She snickered, and her eyes lit with warmth before the spark went out of them and the chill came back. With a stab in his chest, he realized she had responded to him before remembering the lie he'd unintentionally made her believe. He didn't still love her sister. Quite the opposite. But if he were to tell her and explain all the all the reasons why, it would hurt her deeply.

By ten o'clock the next day, decked out in his tuxedo, he stood before his bedroom mirror. "I can't go through with this," he said to the teensy beast at his feet.

Rosie glowered at him through her fuzzy mop of dog hair.

"Don't look at me like that. I'm not the bad guy here." When the little fur ball continued to give him the stink eye, he said, "I know I inadvertently injured your mom, and now I don't know what to do."

She yawned as if trying to speak, her pint-sized body tensed and her expression one of fierce intent. "Gaw," the dog got out after much exertion.

"If I didn't know better, I'd think you were trying to speak, telling me to go."

"Gaw," the stubborn little cuss repeated.

"Go? Go where? To hell? But wait. Go to my wedding? Of course, that's it." He crouched to scratch her chest and rub behind her ears, his insides a little shaken when he realized he owned a talking dog. "You made your point."

When he stood, she tugged on his pant leg. He didn't have to be told again.

A half hour later, the song "In My Life" played softly. The groomsmen started down the path as the bridesmaids entered from the side of the yard in a stream of flowing aquamarine.

From behind Bennett, he heard, "Dada," and turned to find his daughter, her hands reaching out to him like tiny starfish as Madison's sister struggled to hold her.

"Sorry," Harper said. "I'm in charge of Madelynn, but she's a daddy's girl. I shouldn't have brought her back here. She just couldn't sit still—poor thing."

He absently took his daughter from Harper and held her. Madelynn immediately reverted to her stretching act, signaling she wanted to be set free. He gave in, and she positioned herself before her father and bounced at the knees as he held her hands.

"Daddy had better get a move on, or he's going to be late," he said as the traditional wedding march burst forth with all its fervor.

Madelynn lifted her head full of copper spirals, and her gaze centered on Emma standing before the gazebo. Overwhelmed, Bennett stilled, taking in the sight of his bride.

"Emma..." he murmured through the lump in his throat.

Her bridal outfit had transformed her into a goddess...the way her hair had been swept up and twisted into soft swirls beneath the veil...the way her magnificent face was all but hidden. Helen of Troy, the mythological woman, had nothing over her. Emma's look was esthetically perfect, openly rebellious, and so prone to make him lose his sense of everything happening around him. He had to get to her side before it was too late and he ruined everything.

He noticed Madelynn toddling woodenly on one foot, then the other. She took to the pathway like a miniature flower girl without her flowers.

"Madelynn!" Emma cried. "You're walking!" She whooped and pointed her bouquet of blue dahlias at the miracle before them. "Bennett, look at our baby!"

"Her first steps!" He wildly chased after his toddler.

The couple met at the entrance, dropped to their knees, and embraced their wayward lamb and each other. And he was back on track. Any concerns he had beforehand dissolved in the elation his daughter had left in her wake.

Nothing else meant as much to him. Seeing the moisture in Emma's eyes, he knew she was just as affected as he was over the miracle.

No matter what happened from now on, no matter how much rain fell or trouble knocked at their door, the image of this moment would be forever seared in his brain. He would keep it at the forefront, come what may.

Chapter 22

Emma rested her head against Bennett's shoulder as the ferry headed toward Hamilton Cove on Catalina Island, the memory of their wedding lingering in her mind.

When Madelynn had stolen the show, Emma had lowered her lashes to hide the happy tears that formed regardless of all her doubts.

June took the baby, and on their knees, Bennett bent and pressed a kiss on the top of Emma's veiled head before grabbing her arm and urging her to her feet.

They stood at the altar surrounded by friends and loved ones, her eyes drinking in his lean body immaculately dressed in his tuxedo, his bowtie adorably crooked at his throat. She straightened it and tilted her head back to look into his face.

He lifted her veil, and his lips met hers in a long, tender kiss. She was trembling when he stopped and pushed her away from him, his strong hands clasping her upper arms.

"Ben—" she began, but he cut her off.

"The past is over and done with, Emma. More than anything, I want you to be my wife, and I plan to spend the rest of my life with you. I have to know that you feel the same way about me." His dark eyes bored into hers as if daring her to deny it.

"Yes," she'd confessed with a glorious smile,

realizing he wasn't marrying her in name only and for a short duration. He was in it for the long haul.

When they arrived at the hillside community in the late afternoon, she was glad she'd decided to skip the cramped and "rustic" boutique hotels. Instead, she had insisted and splurged more of her savings on a small villa.

The cab driver dropped them off on the driveway.

Bennett opened the garage door. "Look. This unit comes with a golf cart—as if we're going to be playing golf."

She took note of his implication that they wouldn't be leaving the bedroom. She turned quickly away from him, pretending to be consumed with the views.

Not that Emma would have changed anything about their wedding, but she had barely enough time to throw her bouquet. At least she'd gotten to exchange her bridal gown for the floaty cream-colored dress the sisterhood had chosen for her "going away" outfit.

"Stupendous," Bennett had announced when he saw her.

The sultry look he'd given her throughout the reception and trip to the island weakened her knees and caused her to question herself at length.

In short, she was kind of old to lose her virginity, but that hadn't mattered to her until she felt sure she was giving herself to the right man in the right place at the right time. To her, their marriage ceremony had traversed into the realm of sacred, from the fine-plaited platinum wedding band he'd slid onto her finger to his kiss that sealed the deal. She hoped Bennett would feel the same as she about sex and not be slighted because of her inexperience.

"Are you ready for some action, you action figure, you?"

"I'm not a superhero." Far from it.

"You are to me."

Yes, well, what if she didn't satisfy him in bed?

"I didn't eat at the reception," she said in an attempt to postpone the inevitable.

"Why does that not surprise me?" His voice had an edge. "You want to get dinner?" A stiffness existed in his tone.

"Please."

He didn't quite frown, but he didn't look happy either. Was he peeved with her for not jumping into the sack with him right away? They were newlyweds, after all—newlyweds who'd never had sex, newlyweds who, presumedly, shouldn't be able to keep their hands off each other. Yet, although her hunger knew no limits, she felt cautious.

"I know of a place not far from here," he said. "That is if what you really want to do is eat—is it?"

What kind of question was that? Another innuendo, to be sure. Frankly, she'd been yearning to be with him but had developed stage fright. If she entered the seaside villa now, they'd end up together. Would that result in her failure to go through with being with him when that was all she could think about? What if early childhood memories rose to destroy her passion, making her frigid? Even more intolerable…what if she disappointed him?

Here she was on her honeymoon, feeling indecisive. Rachel would know what to do. She'd always had a way with men—unlike Emma.

She struggled to prevent her painful hiccup of a sigh. She'd missed her sister so much today. Would the pain of losing her ever stop? But then no one had the answer regarding how long grief lasted. "Everyone is different," the experts claimed.

Unable to deal with her emotions another second, she pushed all thought away and traveled with Bennett in the golf cart through the quaint streets. *Keep the topic safely on the sights.* They were just tourists, along with day-trippers and other getaway vacationers spending a few days on the island and seeking out delicious cuisine.

The restaurant was upscale, with wicker furniture and a laid-back yet refined ambiance. Pearly beige walls and bleached wooden floors. Everything high-end. People turned and looked at her husband with, if not sudden recognition, a lingering glance. Men, she noted self-consciously, girl-watched her as she crossed the room.

Bennett took her hand in his. "Other men are admiring what's mine—or am I allowed to say that? I suppose I've gone all macho on you."

"It wouldn't be the first time." She found it hard to conceal the pleasure that flooded through her despite her attempts to downplay his comment.

The waiter, a stout man of Latin descent, spoke with a romantic accent, maybe Portuguese or Italian. "What you have-ah to drink?" He laid a towel over his arm. "Some wine?"

"Wine would be perfect." Bennett canted his head at an angle, the recessed lighting touching his hair and producing shiny copper highlights. "Do you mind if I choose?"

"Please do."

"We'll have…" He pointed to the list as if his choice was meant to be a surprise. "This one."

"Dis is good, sir." The waiter bowed. "Will dat be all?"

"Yes, thank you. We'll look at the menu now."

Bennett was taking the lead, something Emma could have done herself. But in this case, she welcomed his assertiveness. If anything, he'd taught her that she didn't always need to insist on complete equality. Instead, she could bask in his expertise on subjects like wine, sit back, and take advantage of his ability to let her rest. And she needed to decompress after the tension leading up to their wedding.

"What do you feel like eating?" she asked languidly.

And he gave her a devilish grin. Now, what had he been about to utter? And why did his near obsession with sex make her damp in her panties? She was testing unfamiliar ground and enjoying it in a way she'd never thought possible, but what would come of it?

She pointed to an entree on the menu. "I'll order some of these sea scallops."

"And I'll go for the T-bone. I haven't had steak in decades."

"That's because I don't prepare beef. Well, hardly ever."

"You don't see me complaining."

A quiet pause crept in as she sipped the wine that tasted rich and spicey on the palate. They were running out of things to talk about. It offered the perfect time to speak up about her lack of sexual prowess, but with people close by, it didn't seem appropriate dinner conversation.

"Is there something wrong?" he asked. "You've hardly said a word."

"No." She shook her head. "I need to eat, that's all."

As if the waiter had heard her, he appeared to take their orders. "I will bring your salad," he added like he thought she might pass out if not nourished. Pronto.

The food was above and beyond her expectations. Looking around at the other diners, she felt glad she hadn't settled for a more casual look. The clothes she'd packed—the fluid outfits in cotton, voile, poplin, linen—weren't what she'd wear to navigate drugstore diaper aisles in Huntington, yet ideal for this locale.

After dinner, Bennett said, "Would you like to move to the patio? I hear the sunset there is beyond compare."

"Wouldn't want to miss a Catalina sunset."

Was he stalling too? Putting off the unavoidable question—would they sleep together?

The orange sky burst forth with streaks of dark purple and hints of the night to come as the fireball sank below the horizon. The picture-perfect prelude to an evening full of…what? While he sat looking at her as if totally into her, she felt his need for her seeping from his pores. Or was this just wishful thinking?

A single test question. "Should I sleep on the sofa?"

Bennett blinked like she'd asked him if she should jump into a volcano. "I'd rather you didn't." He downed his scotch in a single gulp. "But if you feel you have to…"

They were getting nowhere. "I guess what will be will be."

She knew so much about him, yet so little. If asked about his political goals, she'd spout, "To effect change, to inspire, to make a difference." But inquiring about his private affairs, such as asking why he had been so troubled after his bachelor party, made her uneasy.

He gave her an odd look as if he suspected

something. "Ready to leave?"

A line of sweat had settled between her brows. "Okay."

She insisted on getting behind the wheel and took to the twisty roads in the golf cart. Wind fingered through her hair in an evening so alive with tension it snapped and crackled. Lights from windows in the terraced hillsides dazzled against the darkness like fireflies.

The sight of the ocean, ebony in the moonlight, struck her with a grand idea. Breathing sharp air deeply into her lungs, she braked to a stop. The coast. Her. Alone. With Bennett. This island and him. Beside her, his very presence got her blood pumping. With this inspiration, she slipped off her silver sandals, and swallowing down any fear, she ran toward the waves, sand flying from her bare feet.

"What are you doing?" he called after her.

She'd never mentioned her swim lessons since she'd wanted to take him by surprise. The water in this part of Catalina was warm this time of year. She couldn't wait to show him her newly acquired skill, so she shoved into the agitating surf like she was in a triathlon.

He shouted, "Stop, I get it. You'd rather kill yourself than sleep with me!"

She twisted around in utter shock. "You've got it all wrong."

He'd done away with his Italian loafers, chucked his jacket and his pants, and was leaping through the current. "You don't have to do this, Emma."

In a mere second, she realized he planned to rescue her—again. What could she do? Words wouldn't be quick enough, so she flipped over on her stomach and swam away from him, hearing her teacher's "you've got this" in her head.

"You're swimming!" he cried, coming up behind her. "How could that be?"

She turned and trod the water like she'd learned. "I know how to swim."

He was laughing. "I've never... I thought you...were intending to drown yourself."

"Aww." She nodded as his misunderstanding dawned on her. "You figured I'd pulled a Rachel." She strung her hands around his neck. "Not a chance, buddy."

The sky above seemed to open for them alone, exposing a night spread with stars, the scene full of a million little things that Emma knew she wouldn't ever forget. The tickle of Bennett's hair against the side of her neck, the fresh, lemony scent of his aftershave, the headlights of the golf cart casting a glow across black water.

He snagged her hands, and they glided into the shadows where they were hidden from view. There, in their own private world, he kissed her. His mouth held a hint of scotch and the frenzy of abstinence. Her body throbbed with heat even in the cool ocean. She felt the hardness of his arousal against her, and some of the worry about not knowing how to please him diminished in its power over her.

He murmured in her ear, "Are you game?"

"No." She surprised herself with her comeback, not meaning to be so abrupt, but to have sex with him, she had to be in control. "Not here. I want to see what I've been missing."

His breath blew out in huffs. "You mean that?"

With an easy freestyle stroke, she headed back to shore to show the seriousness of her intent. He kept in sync with her. As they rose out of the water, drenched and dripping, his face was glossy with wetness in the beam from the headlights. His shirt stuck to his chest and arms, transparent against his bronze skin, and his eyes were dilated under damp lashes as he turned toward her. She shivered with cold in the evening breeze. Clinging to one another like wartime lovers, they staggered to the golf cart, and she managed to drive the short distance to their private villa.

He dimmed the lights inside, and she recalled when he'd taken off her clothes below the deck of his boat. Their frantic need for each other had been interrupted. Tonight would be different. Nothing could stop them from connecting, not if she kept hold of the reins. When she was a child and some street degenerate tried to grope her, she had fought back. Things were not as they had been but as she'd always wanted.

She unbuckled his belt and snapped it before dropping it. She lifted a shoulder in his direction, inviting him to slip the dress from her body, and it fell in a soaked heap on the floor. As she yanked down the zipper in his slacks, the harsh scrape of it echoed in the quiet, and she unfastened the waistband and reached to the placket of his oxford shirt. Her fingers smarted as she struggled with the wet cotton to release the buttons from their tight hold. Finally, yes, *finally*, she had stripped him, and he did the same to her.

"You're more beautiful than I ever imagined," he said.

Her arms hung at her sides. For once, she had the freedom to observe Bennett in the nude. He was a rainfall in the desert that had been her life until now. Her hands moved along his sternum where the silky hair curled around her fingers. She hadn't touched his chest before, not in this intimate way, though she had been tempted beyond reason—driven out of her head when she saw him after his everyday swim, passing her in the hall half-naked. On the stairs or heading to the shower, his body toned and shining with suntan oil, leaving behind the scent of coconut.

"Do you like what you see?" he asked.

"I do."

"I love the sound of that, 'I do.' "

"You really like it?"

"You bet, Mrs. Browning."

"I love the sound of that, 'Mrs. Browning.' "

For some reason, perhaps the reminder of their sacred vows, she dropped her gaze and trailed her fingertips down the soft line of hair to his rock-hard erection. Her touching this was at first timid, as if afraid of breaking a priceless gift, but she eventually molded her hand around the length of his shaft. When she heard his sharp intake of breath, she hesitated.

"To cherish?" She raised her eyes to look at him.

"God, yes, till death do us part...and beyond if I have anything to do with it."

His eyes shone as he observed her with such total absorption she decided then not to mention this was her first time. If she did, he'd become afraid of hurting her, and she longed to feel all of what she'd been dreaming about since day one.

His mouth found the pulse in her neck. She let out a soft cry, releasing pent-up emotion as she threw back her head, and the floor shook beneath her feet. Feeling as if she might fall to the Earth's center, she caught his shoulders and braced herself as he kissed her throat, jaw, and cheek, and she burrowed her fingers in his damp hair.

He paused to ask, "Want me to stop?"

"I'd rather you didn't."

"Okay, then. Let the seduction begin."

That word "seduction" stirred images of the night Bennett's father had told him to dump her, the sexual urges she'd felt when Bennett had possessively held her. Of the time she'd been stranded in that forsaken ghetto, and he had come for her like a knight on a white steed. Of the night after she'd delivered Audrey's baby—how badly she'd needed him to hold her. But not as much as she did now. As she came to terms with her desire, the restraint she'd practiced for all these months died away, and she surrendered to what had been forbidden.

She pulled him down and nibbled on his lip, trapping it between her teeth, and her act was unexpected even to herself. He groaned, his eyes glazing over. His breath increased, jagged and raw. Although she didn't actually know what she was doing, she'd read articles and watched movies. Feeling more confident, she pressed her breasts against his chest and gyrated her hips like she had seen women do on the dance floor.

"You've got to slow down, Emma."

"Do I?"

"Yeah…" His voice was low and savage.

She had the feeling she'd nearly pushed him over some sort of brink. "Did I do the wrong thing?"

"No, you're perfect." He bent over and kissed her nose. "But I don't want to lose it too early and ruin everything. I need a breather." He looked around and paused as if spotting a welcomed distraction. "Remember the fun we had cake-tasting?"

She'd never been as turned on as that afternoon. "How could I forget?"

"I know. A shame we didn't get a slice at our reception."

"We ran out of time."

"That we did." He crossed the room, and she watched him. He was magnificently endowed. He paused at a table that she hadn't noticed set now with flutes and champagne. He picked up a cardboard box and presented it to her like it held a king's ransom.

"What's this?" She didn't need his answer to realize what she'd find. Before she could respond, he fed her a bite-sized spice cake. In turn, she smashed a sliver of key-lime cake against his mouth, crumbs falling, both laughing like—*shock*, like newlyweds. She tore off another sample, and he licked his lips, then her fingers, and the feel and sight of that was so hot she did the same, savoring the flavor of caramel and the salt from the sea still on his skin.

"Sweet and salty." She dabbed a napkin on his lips and allowed him to reciprocate.

The ocean sounds came through the open window, and the memory of their swim still lingered. The heat of his flesh and her own warmed their bodies. She ran her tongue along his jaw, amazed at her need to devour the taste of him, the cake remembered, her past with him seasoned with countless temptations.

He moaned and hugged her tighter, and that hunger grew inside her. A yearning so deep that the more she sampled of him, the more she wanted, and he seemed to go half mad as he drove his palms down over her buttocks, squeezing softly and then harder. Her tormenting need meshed with his, and their breaths came as they had when they'd reeled from the sea, weak-kneed and gasping for air.

"I'm ready for bed," she whispered in his ear.

He bent and scooped her into his arms and carried her. He glanced at the fruitwood tables flanking a Renaissance-style bed with a gold-curtained crown. "Such an elegant villa, Em. You'll have to choose every place we go from now on."

She poked a finger on his chest. "I choose you."

"Darling," he said with such tenderness it brought tears to her eyes, and his lips brushed hers one more time before he hurled back the bedspread and lowered her onto sheets so soft and smooth she felt she'd come to rest on gossamer.

Their breaths increased as they fell into a freewheeling exploration of each other's highly sensitive spots—the shell of her ear, the hollow in her throat, his glutes, and the incredible span of his shoulders. She couldn't say for sure when his finger had slipped between her legs and inside her, but her muscles instinctively tightened, and she moaned. A pleasurable, almost unbearable, ticking pulse rose and increased until she couldn't stand it any longer.

"I need to be inside you." He groaned against her ear.

The tables had turned, and she was no longer the seducer. How could she be when she didn't know quite what came next?

"Spread your legs for me, my love."

She obeyed, noticing that the muscles in her calves had tightened in readiness, but as he gripped her hips and tipped her back gently, he looked puzzled. Most likely aware of the inadequacy she'd fought so hard to hide.

She felt seconds of panic. She should stop this mistake before it began, walk out, and never see him again, and what? Stay safe inside her chrysalis—never break out and fly?

He rubbed the tip of his shaft, hard, smooth, and wet, against her entrance. This act lessened her concern, and stripped of her inhibitions, she relaxed. Bit by bit, he plunged deeper until, all at once, a stinging sensation shot through her lower body. Her cry betrayed her, and his eyes welded to hers. Then he lifted his hips and froze in evident surprise and disbelief.

"I'm sorry," she whimpered. "I'm so sorry."

"Sorry for what? For giving me the honor of being your first?"

"I don't want you to think I'm made of glass. I'm not."

"No, you are not. You're more precious than anything created by human hands."

He adjusted her limbs and appeared to contort himself to fit inside her narrow passage. With the momentum of his thrusts, at first gentle, then harder, she felt spurred to new heights by pleasure. She instinctively pulled him closer and arched her hips, calling out his name and becoming lost in sensations. Her passion built and begged for release. When the quake hit, she held on to him with all her might as they peaked together, and he planted soft kisses on her face while murmuring endearments, and her body responded in glorious tremors.

"That was…" Panting, she lay spent in his arms.

"The best sex of all time," he finished for her.

And she laughed. "I couldn't have said it better."

He helped her to her feet. "Let's get you cleaned

up."

A half hour later, after changing the sheets and taking a warm shower, they were tucked back into bed. Bennett rolled on his side, wrapping a leg around her and holding her pressed up against him. She had given him not only her body but her belief in him, and he hadn't failed her.

Yet.

Chapter 23

Unable to sleep, Bennett rose before sunrise. Emma's sensual, slow-moving grace centered in his consciousness—Emma as they'd made the bed last night after replacing the sheets, her fabulous legs appearing as weak as a newborn colt's. Hard to believe no man had had her before him. Her virginity would have baffled him if she hadn't revealed her past.

She'd put all her faith in him. He wanted to be the perfect husband, whatever that entailed. So that she never became bored or tired of him. In addition, she deserved everything he could give her. He jumped out of bed, dressed, and bicycled to the coast, the sea hidden under a white mist.

He surprised Emma with a breakfast of strawberries he picked out himself from a boy selling them on a street corner in the dawn's light. He purchased some healthy-looking bread and the organic butter she preferred. He entered their room with the bed tray he'd discovered in one of the kitchen cabinets.

She sat up with a lazy smile and spread her fingers through her hair. "Ah." She luxuriously stretched her arms above her head. "What have you got there?"

He parked the tray across her lap. "Breakfast for my lady."

"You conjured up a meal?" She shook her head in mock disbelief. "I'm impressed."

In the next week, wanting to please Emma, he chose the activities from the brochure. Nothing proved too challenging for the couple most likely to make the society pages. People watched the lovebirds, some romantics getting photos and videos of them hiking and taking advantage of the fantastic ecosystem of natural wonders. The newlyweds attempted standup paddling, fell off into the water, laughed, and got up again to zip-line through canyons all glittery through the rays of the sun, which led to the relaxing spa trip she'd arranged. Next, he wooed her on a glass-bottom boat tour, rented a pickup, explored the off-the-beaten-path places, and experienced another head rush in an escape room.

They graciously spoke to other vacationers, endorsing The Nightingale whenever they could. Their one-on-one advertising paid off. Who didn't love lovers? Especially when they were the most into-each-other couple on Earth.

The people they met readily made plans for a trip to Huntington where the swells, up to six feet and more, were perfect for surfing, prompting them to say, "Surf City, here we come!"

Yet here he was, having the best time of his life on that silver-sequined island a mere thirty miles away from home. If their days were chock-full of adventure, their nights were packed with exploration. Behind closed doors, Bennett quickly learned what pleased Emma, what aroused and satisfied her. One small space behind her ear drove her wild when he touched his mouth to the skin there, teasing her toward ecstasy.

She turned out to be ticklish and giggled when he accidentally touched her tummy. That caused an explosion of roughhousing, with them rolling across the bed and chasing each other around the villa. The couple called their home away from home their sugar shack. Never in his life had he had as much fun with a lover. In her sexy trousseau, with her spunk and sexual appetite, she exceeded all his dreams and expectations.

Since they'd said their vows, he'd begun to see himself growing old with her. Thinking like this was new for him. Maybe he was pushing through his former phobias to a reinvented Bennett Browning, a man who didn't believe every woman he cared for would leave him.

The following morning, he ate chicken and waffles while sitting across from his wife. The sunlight through the café window displayed her supreme bone structure. Her stylish shirt bared her kiss-me shoulder. The mind-blowing sex they'd had the night before and again this morning had to be the reason for her rosy glow.

He watched her and spoke to her, but his mind reeled back to the feel of her firm, silky body as they'd made love. All his fantasies of her before their marriage fell short. She denoted the worldly, lovely, and oh, so worth the wait.

He stirred cream into his coffee. "The wedding's behind us, and tomorrow we're returning to our real life of waiting for guests to arrive, waiting for them to leave, and then cleaning up all their crap."

"Need I remind you we don't have to worry about childcare for our daughter. We get to spend all day with our dog. Our commute is a minute's walk downstairs to the kitchen, and we get to enjoy the sea. Get to live in a beautiful home. To top it off, we get to do all this together."

"You have no idea how much you turn me on."

She laughed, clearly enjoying herself. "You know, not until I had a lot—*a lot*—of sex, thank you very much, did I realize equal didn't mean the same thing to me anymore."

"Really?" He lifted his chin, meeting her sultry gaze. "What does equal mean to you now, may I ask?"

She boldly met his eyes. "Equal means we have different roles to play to complement each other at work, at home—and in bed."

In awe of her, he typed her reply into his phone notes. "Can I quote you someday in a speech?"

"Yeah, but leave out the 'a lot, a lot of sex' and the part about bed."

His turn to laugh. "Hmm, if only the walls in the villa could talk."

"It's the perfect hideaway." She linked her fingers with his in the middle of the table. "I'm going to miss our sugar shack. I've never been as happy."

"Me either." He kissed her palm. "Maybe we should check in for a year."

"It still wouldn't be enough time. Although I can't wait to see Madelynn."

"Me too." He paid their bill, and they walked hand in hand through the sparkling spring in Avalon. "What do you want to do on our last day here?"

"We need to buy souvenirs for our family."

"Of course we do." His lips brushed her knuckles. "I couldn't exist without you."

And that seemingly harmless remark had him floundering. The thought of life without her or his daughter turned his gut inside out.

Emma must have noticed his discomfort because she pivoted around to face him. "No one is dropping dead anytime soon. Not on my watch."

"You're right as rain." He zipped his lip as they patronized a book shop, a craft fair, and an old-fashioned candy shop where the sweets came in glass jars.

Emma talked to the locals, the tourists, and the staff. She shared his interest in the citizens and their stories. One man mentioned the water shortage and how it affected the people on the island. A lady worried about the constant flow of newcomers and how it caused food shortages. Young people waved protest signs opposing the needless deer slaughter.

"You can't live on our planet and be blind to the needs of others," Bennett said later.

She nodded. "Everyone has to do their part."

Day was almost done. It was time to head back to the villa for the last night of their honeymoon. He wanted to top his gazebo unveiling—make a splash for her bigger and better than anything that had come before. She didn't like him spending money carelessly. It had made him thriftier and more creative if he did say so himself. Whenever she'd turned her back on him today, he'd woven his plans like the maestro of a husband he'd begun to consider himself.

Her cooking lessons had paid off with dividends. He could prepare a supper for his lovely wife, but he was ready for a new undertaking. Secretly, he'd worked out a deal with a beach-club restaurant near the water.

So after slipping into the villa and engaging in a lover's romp in the shower, they dressed to the nines. The golf cart's wheels snicked over pebbles as he drove down the slope and crossed a paved strip of waterfront highway to where the surf rippled and creamed. Candlelight marked the spot on the wet sand where a table and two chairs beckoned them.

Tonight, the world was theirs.

He switched off the headlights and moved to the middle of the seat. "Well?"

"What have you done?" Emma closed the gap, sinking into his arms.

"I'm bringing the ocean to you, the moon and stars."

She closed her eyes and kissed him long and slow. "Thank you," she said, her minty breath going into his mouth.

He tightened his grip on her, and she opened eyes that flashed in the darkness like blinking stars. He got out of the cart and ushered her to the table where they drank chilled wine and ate French cuisine to their hearts' content. Not that far off, pier lights glittered in a haze over a hub of activity, people living the life while the newlyweds, as he loved to think of them, huddled together in bliss.

"I've got something for you." Heat rose to his face.

"You've outdone yourself yet again."

"Not a big deal." He readjusted his weight on the chair. "It's something I dashed off while you were sleeping."

She angled her head. "What is it?"

"Let me warn you, Alexis Nathan I am not." He shrugged. "But I wrote you a poem."

"You told me you used to compose poetry for readings at the teahouse."

"I did." He slid a paper from his pocket and unfolded it, his hands suddenly sweaty. "Not for a long time, though. It's just a little jingle."

"Don't just sit there," she clamored.

Standing, he recited.

"Upside down in a field of clouds and a daisy sky
Your face appears and
Spring goes by.
Alone with you in a sailboat on a stormy sea
You smile and
The sun comes out for you and me."

She leaped to her feet and kissed his cheek. "I love it! You're a poet, Bennett."

"Well, I don't know about that," he said sheepishly.

"That's the best gift I've ever gotten." A tear made its way down her cheek. "I only wish I had something for you."

"You've already given me the best thing I could have ever received."

"What's that?"

"Your trust."

Chapter 24

By late afternoon, loaded down with luggage and gifts, the newlyweds were making their way down the path toward The Nightingale.

Emma couldn't stand it a second longer and shrieked, "We're home!"

Almost on demand, an ecstatic Rosie sprang out the door and encircled them. The dog joyfully exercised her tiny lungs loudly enough for the whole seaside to hear, and Emma's heart pumped with love for her little fluffball.

Madelynn toddled out to meet and greet. Pink-rimmed, cat-eyed sunglasses partially covered her face as gingery ringlets bounced around her head.

Both parents dropped their suitcases, and Bennett lifted his daughter up, saying, "There's our little princess."

And princess she was with her entourage of family following and making over the honeymooners like they'd gone off to war. Hugs, kisses, and everyone talking all at once.

Inside the house, after presenting the souvenirs and all the pageantry that went with that, Bennett drew Emma close. "I've got to get to that meeting I told you about."

"Are you really ready to sell your business?"

"I haven't been involved in it in eons. It's time to

move on."

"I guess so."

"Walk with me to the car? It will be a while. Wait for me in our bed?"

"Okay." She posed with a flirtatious tilt of her head. "Your room or mine?"

His eyes gleamed with pricks of gold. "You pick."

She winked. "I'll surprise you."

He nodded and dipped his hand into his pocket for his car keys. "See you, my love."

Honestly, he was so irresistible she had to tear her gaze off him. Finally, she returned to The Nightingale, taking refuge—the door closed on the outside world, her memories of her past week suspended as she studied the scene. Madelynn had been well cared for.

Rai's handcrafted puppets lingered in a small theater. June's contribution of children's books, written in both Chinese and English, were scattered on a table. Charles, Eddie, and Alexis Nathan had constructed and painted wooden blocks stacked in towers across the hardwood.

What Emma witnessed in all this was a family affair. It warmed her spirits and made all else small and irrelevant in comparison. With a spoon in Madelynn's hand and a bowl in the other, she fed her doll pretend food, which seemed perfectly natural. But Emma kept watching her instead of attentively listening to the others talk about their week. Madelynn had always been small for her age, but her cerise shirt looked somehow bigger and baggier on her than it had before.

Shouldn't the opposite be true?

Emma approached June in the kitchen. "Did Madelynn eat well while we were gone?"

What looked like hoisin sauce spotted her auntie's apron, the splatter unusual for the tidy June. "You know how she is…she procrastinates about everything lately. Puts off taking a nap or going down at night."

"But she's never been a picky eater. How did she sleep?"

June frowned. "She slept more, but she plays so hard…"

"And then tires out?" When June gave a slight shake of the head, Emma concluded, "Just to be safe, I'll make an appointment with her doctor."

"Good idea."

Emma wanted Bennett to come home. She had to tell him that Madelynn might be ill. She suddenly felt like a neglectful parent for leaving a sick child to run off on a honeymoon. She should have known somehow. But then another nearly hidden but revealing part of her longed to say, *Come home, Bennett, and hold me. I'm scared.*

After everyone but Alexis Nathan had left and Madelynn had gone down for the night, Emma settled in Bennett's room. He was still gone. She tried to get some sleep. Unable to shut off her brain, she tossed, turned, and stared at the ceiling. Sometime later, he eased onto the mattress as if not wanting to disturb her.

With the moonlight streaming through the window, she noted he hadn't pulled up the covers and was completely naked except for a pair of boxers endearingly covered with sailboats.

She remembered how badly she'd wanted him to make love to her when they were on his boat. They hadn't gotten together sexually until Catalina, and now they were home with a potential problem brewing, but it didn't mean she didn't still want him. She needed the intimacy they shared on their honeymoon while the world had stepped aside.

Later, she felt his eyes on her before she turned her head. He was looking at her with such entreaty it made her swallow down the lump in her throat. Then and there, she decided not to tell him about Madelynn until tomorrow. Why should he lose sleep along with her?

"Hold me, will you?" she said.

"Don't mind if I do." His tender smile comforted her.

She slipped her arms around his neck, and in turn, he clutched her waist and pulled her to him. He smelled of sex and that unidentifiably splendid scent that was unique to him. After a long, staggering breath, she closed her eyes. With his gentleness, their cuddling turned into more. She was still shuddering when she fell into a restless sleep.

****

Bennett packed his lunch bag. Last-minute details in his business transactions needed his attention this morning. He had agreed to meet again with the qualified man who'd purchased the firm Bennett had established before Emma and Madelynn had happened on the scene and altered the rest of his life.

Watching his wife scurry around the kitchen and his daughter testing her newfound ability to walk on tippy-toes, he wouldn't have it any other way. He'd change his life again and again if it would keep them both safe and happy.

"Thank you for being you." He kissed Emma's neck, feeling the thrill of sexual excitement in his every cell. "I'll probably be gone most of the day."

A disconcerting quiet followed his statement as she lifted Madelynn and deposited her in the high chair. She avoided looking at him, and her hands trembled.

"Emma, sweetheart, what is it?"

She cleared her throat. "I made an appointment for Madelynn to see Dr. Nguyen."

"Is something wrong?" He twisted around to his daughter, who looked up at him from her breakfast, banged her back against her high chair, and reached her hands toward him.

"Probably not," Emma said as if measuring her words. "She's lost a little weight, that's all. She's more active since she started walking."

"What time?" He raised his daughter into his arms. "I'll adjust my schedule."

"No, you have your work cut out for you today. You don't have to go. I can handle a simple office visit, and by tomorrow, or maybe even today, we'll find out she's fine."

He knew his wife so well by now. She was trying to come off like she wasn't concerned, but he noticed the slight tremor of her God's-gift-to-lips.

"The time?" he repeated.

"This afternoon. One o'clock."

"I'll be there."

"Okay," she said, no change in inflection, but her slumping posture spoke of her relief.

The morning passed with him struggling to keep his mind on the life-altering move he'd made to let go of his former career, but his thoughts strayed to his daughter. Maybe all babies lost weight when they started walking. Bennett could only hope and pray this was the case.

Precisely at one, he met Emma in the doctor's office

they'd come to know so well. He read to Madelynn just as he had at every visit. Only now, having had many appointments, she no longer screamed at the top of her lungs at the sight of Dr. Nguyen.

Emma chewed a cuticle, a habit she indulged in whenever she was anxious. God willing, they'd leave the office after hearing good news.

A knock on the door, and Dr. Nguyen stepped inside the room. "Sorry, I'm running late."

"That's all right," Bennett said. "We already owe you more than we could ever repay for always agreeing to see Madelynn on such short notice."

"For sure," Emma seconded.

"Congratulations on your recent marriage," the doctor said, and after they thanked her, she took a seat. "You wanted to talk to me?"

Emma relayed the exchange she'd had with her aunt, and Bennett longed to lean over and throw his arms around his brave bride, but this wasn't the time or place.

"Let's take a look," the doctor said.

He sat his daughter down on the exam table. The perceptive Dr. Nguyen spoke softly, engaging Madelynn in a series of age-appropriate toys as she conducted her examination.

"Good job, Madelynn," she said when finished. "She has some warning signs we need to check out. I'll order X-rays and lab work to find out more, and we'll go from there."

"I take it her condition isn't going to improve with a few vials of a numbing agent." He recalled when the feared prognosis had turned out to be a case of teething.

"Let's wait and see," Dr. Nguyen urged in a calm tone. "I'll have the results of the tests for you by tonight."

The hours dragged on like a week.

He ate dinner with his family at five. Afterward, Emma got Madelynn into the bathtub while he did the dishes. Next, they played with Madelynn while glancing at their cell phones. Bennett rocked his daughter until she fell asleep, then Emma and he put her to bed. He left the nightlight glowing while Emma recovered the monitor receiver, and they tiptoed back downstairs.

He had just sat down in his easy chair when his phone rang, and he put it on speaker mode. "Hello—Dr. Nguyen?"

"Yes, I have the results for you."

He typed the medical terms the doctor gave him into his phone. He'd have to look them up later. One thing came out disturbingly clear.

"Madelynn needs reparative surgery."

His mouth had gone dry. "This operation…is it…serious?"

"The procedure is minimally invasive. Madelynn will need to start taking prescribed medications to treat some of her symptoms and to build up her immune system. They'll be ready for pickup in the hospital pharmacy."

Emma asked, "When will she have her surgery?"

"Preferably, the middle of next month."

"In June." Emma's voice sounded strained.

"I hope that's convenient," the doctor said.

Bennett slapped his knees. "Of course it is. Nothing's more important than getting Madelynn well."

Emma closed her eyes, her hands clenched as if to keep them from visibly shaking.

"And she will…get well…won't she?" he asked.

"She should," Dr. Nguyen said, offering

encouragement in a conversation laden with uncertainties.

After they got off the phone, he rose to comfort Emma, who looked like she needed his embrace, but he halted. The distance to where she stood had become a road too wide to cross.

Her gaze drifted to his left hand. "Would you look at that," she said sadly.

He noticed then. He still held the teddy bear he'd bought after discovering the baby he had fathered, the infant who'd won his heart at first glance. He breathed in and out, striving to keep some control and find a place inside himself where he could retreat.

She threw her arms around him. Numbly, he stared over her head at a shadow on the wall shaped like some giant gorilla who ate kids like his for breakfast.

Tenderly, she took the well-loved toy from him. "If Madelynn wakes up and can't find Mr. Bear, she'll be upset."

Minutes later, they hovered over the crib. Emma tucked the stuffed animal within cuddling reach. "You don't think she'll…uh…"

Die? Bennett had been about to blurt but shut his mouth just in time. She always thought the worst, most likely because of her traumatic beginnings. He wanted to give her a happy ending. And, okay, maybe ten-foot gorillas who ate kids didn't exist, but he was frightened too, shaking in his boots, as they said.

Before he knew what was happening, the dog had positioned herself crib-side and looked up with liquid eyes full of knowing. He trusted Rosie enough these days to let her do her job.

The least he could manage was to pick up

Madelynn's prescriptions. He drove automatically while the town spun by without him. Didn't matter what the rest of humanity had in store when his daughter's health was at stake.

Back home, he allowed Emma to steer him to the room they now shared. Once there, she helped him undress and climb into bed. He lay still, not daring to move. But he became aware of her thrashing against the mattress during the night as if searching for a spot comfortable enough to enable sleep. He longed to take her in his arms and provide reassurance, give her guarantees. Be the husband she needed, but he couldn't muster it.

Chapter 25

Just after sunrise, Emma ambled into the kitchen. She dropped a coffee pod in the pot, let Rosie out, filled the dog bowl with kibble, and switched on the TV for background noise.

Bennett didn't come bopping down the stairs, singing show tunes like he usually did on any given morning. He had shut himself off from her and everything around him. He'd always coped like this when he couldn't handle his feelings, so she brought him a cup of coffee and mixed up some waffles she hoped he'd eat, but odds were he wouldn't.

She kissed his cheek after he collapsed in a chair. "Good morning," she said, her forced behavior like a throwback from the women of the 1950s, but she didn't care. Anything to spur him back to action and make him alive again in his own skin.

In reality, there seemed nothing good about the morning. Even the refrigerator begged to differ with a groan when Emma opened it. And that's when she discovered all the food for tomorrow's guests was gone. "I've got to get groceries. Want to come? Bring Madelynn?"

"She can't go out." Bennett looked at her like the sky had fallen. "The germs on a shopping cart are enough to disable the top team in the NFL."

"Exaggerate much?"

"I'm just saying…" He rubbed the scruff of his neck. "We need to make sure Madelynn wears a mask whenever she leaves the house or comes in contact with strangers."

Alexis Nathan strolled into the kitchen. He carted a yawning Madelynn in his arms. "Look who I encountered on this beautiful morning." He stopped smiling as he surveyed their faces and slid Madelynn into her high chair. "What's happened?"

Bennett rose, shoving his hands in the back pockets of his jeans. He opened his mouth, but when nothing came out, he started gathering the breakfast dishes. "You tell him, Em."

"Madelynn needs surgery."

"Eeek," Alexis Nathan uttered as if she'd just let all the air out of him. He bent over and held on to the kitchen chair as she gave him the details. When she finished, he slowly stood up straight and rattled off, "I'll cancel my flight back to India. If you'd be so kind as to make a list, I shall conduct the shopping." He paused to study them both. "Better yet, you two go. That way, you can talk things out…"

"Sounds like a plan," she said.

A plan that would take some time to execute. Bennett was going through the motions a person made to get out the door, but it proved slow going. Emma kept stopping midstream to obsess over the baby they all adored. Was Madelynn eating enough food? Should they keep her in a bubble—maybe in her room, allowing no one else to enter?

While she awaited her husband, her doubts consumed her. What if something happened and they couldn't get Madelynn to the hospital? After all, a few weeks ago, an accident had prevented Audrey from getting help when she gave birth to Jack. Things were known to go south.

"Don't you think you should call Madam?" Alexis Nathan asked, probably trying to break Emma out of her destructive thoughts.

"I already did."

She'd phoned her auntie last night after Bennett had gone to the pharmacy. June had asked if Emma wanted her to take a leave of absence to come help out, but she had declined the offer. Emma considered herself someone who could handle setbacks. She was coping with her sister's death, wasn't she?

Yeah, right.

To any casual observer, she was failing miserably at putting her sister's demise in the past. And now, worrying about Madelynn—it was all too much.

Bennett appeared in her line of vision—a sloppy and rather absent-minded version of himself that she'd never seen before.

"You're wearing a white sock and a navy blue," she commented.

"Who cares?" He strode toward the door. "Ready?"

But she had trouble getting into the car and worse difficulty getting out, as if she'd become a centenarian overnight. Inside the market, the produce, usually so bright and colorful, had gone dull. Her mind refused to grasp the simple list she'd scribbled before they left home.

Bennett, too, looked trapped in a fog. He picked up items, read their ingredients, and repositioned each back on the shelf as if it had the potential to blow sky-high. He bent over the seat in the shopping cart like he couldn't hold himself up without support. She'd never seen him trip over his own two feet—an action so foreign to his nature she'd have let out a gasp if she'd been herself.

At dinner that night, Alexis Nathan eyed them with disdain and put down his fork. His black eyes stared at them across the table like he could see through to their deepest fears. "Where are those honeymooners who burst through the door a couple days back—so in love, so resplendently happy?"

"We're upset." Why shouldn't it be crystal clear? And why didn't he understand? She shouldn't have to explain.

But Alexis Nathan propped his elbow on the table and waved a finger. "Do you think, for one moment, any of your fretting will help your precious baby?"

Madelynn banged her fist against the tray of her high chair. "Gooshah, ya, to," she reacted as if to say, "Get it together, you two."

Rosie shook her head, giving them the raspberries.

And Emma shriveled a little. "We need to break out of our funk."

"We do," Bennett admitted.

Alexis Nathan squinted as if deep in thought. "May I suggest you two go out for a drink?"

"To a bar?" they fired off at the same time.

The poet nodded. "You—what is the American expression?" He tapped his chin. "Ah, yes. You *let down your hair* in order to express yourselves. Used wisely and with discretion, a shot of whiskey is very effective at loosening the tongue."

"I guess…" Bennett started and halted. "There's a club in Brentwood I used to go to with Rachel that has good vibes."

Emma nodded, surprised he'd brought up her sister's name without her mentioning it first, and within the following hour or so, they were seated at a table in an atmosphere of quiet luxury. A waiter, no doubt used to hundred-dollar tips, bowed and returned with a Jack and ginger for her and an old-fashioned for him. Bennett didn't comment on the prices of hors d'oeuvres when ordering them, but then he was used to spending big bucks—not so for Emma.

Her gaze fell into the gold sparkle of her swirling drink and got trapped there as she struggled to tell him how scared she felt.

"I don't know how to handle what's happening to Madelynn," he jumped right in.

She chewed on the slivers of ice, wishing for something brilliant to say. "I guess we just go through it… What else can we do?"

"It doesn't seem fair. Madelynn doesn't deserve this."

"No babies deserve to be sick." How weak her observation sounded.

He downed his drink and ordered another. "How are we going to get through this?"

She didn't have the answer. "I guess a step at a time."

"We need a blueprint, a way to cope." He suddenly banged his fist on the table, shaking their drinks, obviously feeling more than a buzz. "You know what burns me?"

She swallowed, dreading his answer. "No."

He gulped his third old-fashioned like it was water. "I'm so angry I can't stand it."

"That won't—"

She'd been about to add "help" when someone bumped into their table, startling her.

A man loomed over them. He wore a black tie, but his shirt was untucked and wrinkled. He had to be forty, not a day younger. Sad blue irises swam in reddened whites, attesting to the probability of his having slammed down too much booze. He mopped the sweat from his face with a cocktail napkin—dabbing, too, at his balding head. "Aren't you that guy who used to go with Rachel Bellamy?"

"Yeah," Bennett said. "What of it?"

"Name's Paul Harvey. Sound familiar?"

"No," Bennett answered in a warning voice. "Paul, I think you need some fresh air." He got to his feet and swayed a little. "Maybe I do too."

Paul wasn't having it, shoving Bennett off. "Yeah, you're that political baboon. Heard you married her sister." He angled his head at Emma. "That must be you."

"That's right." Her hands tightened.

"Well, sis, I fell for Rachel's lies. I lost my wife, lost my kids. The bitch got bored with me. Said she needed something new. Said she'd lost her desire for married men. That's when she found your man here. Wouldn't surprise me if one of her former tomcats did her in."

"Shut the hell up!" Bennett shouted so loudly that half the clientele twisted around and gawked, some scrambling off like he'd cocked a six-shooter.

Emma's stomach fell as the gravity hit her. "What's he talking about?"

Paul got in her face, the stench of cigarettes and alcohol gagging her. "Don't play dumb," he said. "Not when you're most likely nothing but a whoring gold digger, same as she was."

Before Emma could retaliate, Bennett had slung back a fist and threw a right hook at Paul. With it came the sound of bones crunching. Blood spurted from his nose as he wilted to the floor. From there, he shrieked and cursed. Moving in fast, she assessed his injury. She dipped a napkin into a water glass and knelt to attend to him. She asked the busboy for a clean towel and made an ice pack to prevent the swelling from getting worse.

Within minutes, Bennett had called for a ride and navigated Paul out of the club while the looky-loos stood around, pointing fingers and mumbling.

"Good thing you're not still running for office," Emma said.

Bennett flushed. "It's not the first time someone's told me that." He gave the driver a fistful of bills to cover Paul's trip to the ER.

They soon headed down the road in the CUV, Emma at the wheel. "I might have gone after Paul," she said, "but I wouldn't have rearranged his face."

"I lost control." He was shaking his hand, and the light flashing through the dark revealed his black-and-blue knuckles. "He was disrespecting you, Em."

"At least you broke out of the paralysis you've been in since last night." At the stop sign, she tapped the steering wheel with her fingertips. "Any truth to the things he said?"

He opened the window and leaned out. He could be trying to sober himself up, but she figured he was stalling, which added to her angst.

They'd gotten halfway down the next block when she demanded, "Tell me."

He fell back inside. "Nothing to tell."

Silence filled the car. A fill so thick Emma felt stuck in it.

That night, she slept. Well, honestly, she stewed. And when her eyes opened the next day, she was angrier than ever, convinced Bennett had been keeping things from her. No matter how ugly and disturbing, she had to find out if any of what Paul said was true.

So she decided to hunt for proof in the only place she could think of. "I'm going to visit Rach's storage unit this morning."

Bennett quit stirring his coffee. "Okay," he said, drawing out the word.

"I need to do this."

"Okay," he repeated, his tone one of resignation.

She was dressed and raring to get started, so forty minutes after she'd announced her intentions, she drove into Evening Breeze Storage—a facility that wasn't what its name suggested. No moonlight and roses here. Just miles of steel roll-up doors. Most hid the gluttony in people's lives. *Wasteful.* Once, all her possessions had fit into a grocery cart. She recalled her dependence on the moving company she'd hired, thinking she would deal with this stuff when she was stronger. Well, Emma wasn't as much stronger now as livid.

A padlock was the only thing dividing her from what felt like a violation of her sister's privacy. She had a moment to consider getting back into the car, leaving well enough alone. But if she did, the answers would continue to elude her. She had to see if anything inside the unit would clear her sister. Or incriminate her, for that matter.

Resolved, she turned the key in the cylinder lock, and the door clattered open.

Emma used a boxcutter and rummaged through the fallout from Rachel's stint in the Big Apple for confirmation that Paul, a jilted lover, was delusional. She'd adjusted to Rach's death, or so she'd told herself. But now the air pulsed with jasmine and gardenia—an achingly familiar scent. And Rachel's essence filtered back like a phantom.

Still, Emma couldn't help removing the clothes, shaking them out, and refolding them. It was what she did, what she'd always done, this rearranging things to make her sister's life easier. Some habits were impossible to break. She paused, though, on one of Rach's favorite articles of clothing. A shawl now faded and worn. June had given it to her. The back of Emma's eyes burned as she traced her hand over the satiny material, recalling the little girl.

With her emotions all but doing her in, she reached into another box and found a leatherbound photo album she had never seen.

Inside were pictures of Rachel with her father. Rach playing soccer, her father in the distance. Both of them walking together barefoot in the sand. Father and daughter on the dance floor. At an outdoor café. Riding horses on the beach.

This album projected a devoted father to anyone else. But Emma knew better. These empty images aided her sister's fantasy of what she wanted in a father who was, in reality, unavailable. These same pictures plastered all over social media were an illusion, an attempt by Rach to believe her father loved her.

Unable to continue, Emma opted for a break. Taking deep breaths, she phoned Bennett. Her first instinct was to admit she shouldn't have come here, but she didn't act on it. "How's the baby?"

"Fine…we have the house to ourselves. We've been playing with the puppets, drawing pictures, and baking a cake."

Emma heard Madelynn babbling in the background and smiled.

"What about you, Em…you find anything, uh, uh…" He sounded breathless.

"I'm almost done here. I'll be home soon."

"Good…but take your time. We really are fine. If you need to talk, call me back."

"Works for me." She cringed as she ended the call. The truth was nothing worked for her. Coming here had been a mistake. Paul, Liam, and even the sisterhood had been slamming her sister for no good reason.

With that, she turned to exit the tomb-like space but noticed a box she'd opened but hadn't explored. The contents inside looked like somebody had emptied a desk. Pencils, pens, notebooks, and unlabeled files that weren't alphabetized or put in any order.

On further examination, she came across Rachel's graduate certificate from UC Santa Barbara. Student loans her father paid off. The title to the car she'd died in.

Shivering, Emma dropped the file and went on to seize another that held a phony driver's license and social security card. Her sister planned to hide her identity. But why? Emma had just started to ask herself more questions when her pulse quickened. An envelope stuck out from the side of the folder. She recognized her own name and the Chinatown address.

Chapter 26

Dearest Emma,

I can't count how often I picked up my phone to call you. We used to talk every day. You've always been bigger than life in my eyes. When we were homeless, you were my mother, my father, my everything. I was—what? Five? But my nerves would jump all over the place whenever you left me to find food. I wanted to cry but couldn't. I didn't want some sicko to hear. Even after the cops rescued us, I never overcame my fear.

I thought things would improve when I learned I had a father. Too bad he didn't know how to handle me. He tried, buying me everything under the sun. Junie Moon was different. When I got cranky, she knew just what to say. I don't know how I would have gotten through elementary school if it hadn't been for Rai and Eddie. And the poet, with all his fancy talk, had the patience of Job with me. But I could be laughing and having a great time with them, yet I'd want to curl up in the fetal position and cry. There wasn't anything to be sad about, but my brain told me that I was a loser, that no one in the house wanted me around. And the worst thing...that no one got me.

Do you remember when I leveled with you about my bad thoughts? You told Junie Moon, and she took me to the psychiatrist, who started me on what he called a cocktail. My sadness decreased for the first time. Fifth and sixth grade was a breeze. When I graduated with honors, my dad insisted I move in with him to attend high school and college.

You and I got together whenever we could. We used to stay up all night talking. I never told you or anyone else that my meds kept me at an even keel, which bored me silly. That's why I rode the highest and scariest rides in all the amusement parks. Skydiving helped, and so did racing cars. Eventually, I craved a different kind of excitement—that of not getting caught. I couldn't admit to you I dated married men. Looking back, I think I only wanted to get Daddy's attention. I got it all right. He spent a fortune trying to avoid a scandal.

I met Bennett Browning at a pep rally. He was way older, twenty-eight, and talking about running for the senate when he turned thirty. I hung on to his every word. We started falling for one another, so I cut back on my meds. I wanted to experience the full measure of a normal relationship. But I realized something when he spoke that night in the teahouse about everything he planned to do when he won the election. This man would see his hopes and dreams dashed because of me. I was bad news. So when he proposed, I shouted things that were stupid and untrue. It caused a scene. And I ran.

I hid in New York. Weeks later, though, I found out I was pregnant. Going off my meds had left me confused, and I'd forgotten to take my birth control pills. That all-encompassing anxiety took hold. I'd gone through my late father's money, so a lot of the time, I went hungry. I wanted you to deliver my baby, but I couldn't call and take the chance of anyone finding out.

By the time of Madelynn's birth, I had resorted to cutting myself to feel something—anything. I kept my habit confined to places on my body that no one could see. But now that I'm back in my dingy apartment, I'm failing. Changing the baby's diaper, not to mention her clothes, is an impossibility.

But, oh, my God, your niece is beautiful. She deserves a mother who can care for her. She looks at me sometimes with her telltale eyes as if she's aware of my inadequacy. Afterward, she sobs like she doesn't like me. I don't blame her. I don't like me either.

I've been cutting myself deeper than usual. Pretty soon, I'll work up the nerve to slice an artery and end my pathetic life. It's the best possible thing I can do for my daughter.

Love always and forever, no matter what,
Rachel

Emma felt her heart breaking but read the letter over and over. On some level, she thought if she took each sentence by itself, she could delay finishing, and doing so gave her seconds to believe Rachel was still alive. Emma willed herself to find answers as if her solutions could turn back time. But the last paragraph continued to interfere with her magical thinking. So eventually, she stopped her search, folded the letter, and saved it in her pocket.

Emma never spoke about the car accident—that's what the police called it. But no skid marks had existed on the street, nothing to prove she'd tried to stop or swerve. She hadn't been wearing a seat belt when she drove straight into a concrete wall at full speed.

Emma pressed a hand to her chest, the pain growing till it was hard to catch her breath. As the car wheels rounded the lot and headed away from Evening Breeze Storage, her temples beat faster and harder. She longed to calm down, but everyone had known about Rachel's indiscretions, yet no one had filled her in, not even Bennett.

Back home, she slammed through the doorway and avoided his waiting embrace.

"Madelynn just went down for a nap," he said. "She had a good morning."

"You knew all along, didn't you?" She paused, collecting herself against her fury. "Everything that bastard said last night was true."

"Sweetheart…" His reply came out in a tender whisper.

"You should have told me what you knew about my sister at her funeral. Better yet, you could have contacted me after Rach dropped out of sight. We might have been able to do something then. Rachel was out of her head, but I—I could have helped her."

"Don't," he said miserably. "Don't go all should've, could've. It's a road to nowhere. And I'm so sorry. I just…I didn't want to hurt you."

Emma was all too aware of him moving toward her. She pressed the letter into his hands. "Read this. Maybe then you'll get why I'm so upset."

"You're trembling." His dark eyes probed hers for explanations.

She had a lot more to say to him. But of all the rotten timing, the front door opened, and a young couple walked in. The pair were loaded down with suitcases, swim bags, and books.

"We're early by several hours," said the man with earnest eyes and a kind smile. "We made better time on the Grapevine than we thought."

The interruption caused Emma's cheeks to burn. But

her work ethic kicked in when the woman suggested they could come back later. Other, more immediate concerns banished all thoughts of a showdown with her husband.

That night, dinner consisted of Alexis Nathan's specialties mixed with two of Emma's side dishes. The result was Eastern dining that impressed the newcomers, celebrating their tenth wedding anniversary.

The couple, bookshop owners Elsa and John, seemed dazzled to be in the company of such a sought-after poet and acted indebted to Bennett for popping open a bottle of champagne and toasting them. From her high chair, Madelynn raised her sippy cup and blew kisses to everyone. Meanwhile, feeling like she didn't belong, Emma hung in the background, content to seethe.

"My wife writes for a magazine," Bennett said as if to draw her into the conversation. "She doesn't write as much as she did before the baby, but you might have heard of the publication. Might even carry it in your bookstore—*Iron Butterfly*?"

Elsa's eyes widened. "You're not the Emma Kuan?"

"I am." Emma did her best to act cordial. "Browning's my married name."

"I am such a fan. It's like you've lived the articles you write, but of course you haven't, I know."

Emma almost gave her usual response but stopped, realizing Rachel's warning voice was no longer whispering in her head. The knowledge freed her somehow. Plus, she was perturbed enough to tell the truth for once.

"Most of what I write is from personal experience." She was unable to hold her raw emotion in check. "My sister was mentally ill, and it killed her."

Elsa winced. "I'm sorry. I didn't know."

"Neither did I, until this morning when I found a letter from her to me," Emma plowed on. She'd explode if she didn't get her grievances off her chest.

"You should have told us," John said. "We could have gotten a hotel."

"No, I want to talk about it, you know? So if other people see the signs in their loved ones, they can do something about it."

"Maybe you could go public," Elsa said.

Emma shrugged in resignation. "I don't have any speaking ability."

"How do you know?" Bennett asked, surprising her with his interest.

Even Alexis Nathan joined in. "It is never too late to acquire a skill, especially when one is as passionate as you."

Madelynn put her hands above her empty plate and did a little happy dance in her high chair, indicating she wanted to get down. Emma felt glad for the distraction. Getting the baby ready for bed gave her time to think things through.

Rachel would never be part of any more ordinary routines, like caring for her baby. Had she ever been? Was her early childhood what had caused her wiring to unravel, making her always sad?

Well, Emma couldn't fix things. Any hope of that was over. Her sister was gone. And she wasn't coming back. No amount of sorrow or rage would change the past. But perhaps Emma could alter the fate of others struggling with depression by sharing Rachel's story.

Where to begin?

Slowly, the answer came, soft yet sure. It was there

in the memories of the past months—of Emma's friends painting walls with her here in The Nightingale, of them taking over to find her a wedding gown, and of them banding together the day Jack was born.

She felt, especially in this moment, lucky to have the sisterhood.

Early Sunday, she phoned them, and by ten, they'd joined forces at the teahouse where Rachel had left Bennett. The place wasn't open yet to customers. The ladies sat around a table where photographs of nineteenth-century poets hung on the walls. An Oriental garden, as seen through the floor-to-ceiling window, appealed to Emma's sense of beauty.

To begin, Audrey brought out special utensils and offered the mouth-watering pastries Liam had made for them. She prepared a tea called Russian Caravan—an aromatic blend with a sweet, malty, and smoky taste.

"This ceremony's truly an art form," Emma said, impressed. "Thank you all for meeting with me. And thank Liam for watching Jack."

Audrey sat down with them at the table. "Liam and I owe you a lifetime of tea ceremonies. We can't begin to express our gratitude."

Lucinda's eyebrows drew together. "Em, we're all worried sick about Madelynn."

"It's a scary time," Emma said. "I just wish I didn't feel like I'm being torn in two."

"What do you mean, sweetie?" Madison asked.

Emma held her teacup, warming both hands. "I know now why all of you were so unhappy and fed up with my sister." She told them about what had taken place in the bar, told them, too, about the letter she'd found, and even went so far as to read it to them.

"This does shed a different light," Audrey said afterward, patting the moisture from her eyes with her napkin. "It's too bad none of us knew."

Lucinda leaned forward. "It sucks big time," she admitted. "What can we do to help you through this?"

"It's no longer enough to write about anonymous families," Emma said. "To let people know about the pitfalls of depression, I have to learn how to speak well about what I know. It's rough now with Madelynn being ill. But if I don't at least begin to work toward a goal, I'm afraid my emotions will eat me alive. If I could tell my story in my own way—well, in an effective manner—that's where all of you come in."

Lucinda slid a notebook from her purse and drew a group of circles. "What time frame are you shooting for? What core elements do you want your audience to take away? Do you aim to start with small groups of women or go for a larger, more diverse crowd?"

Emma appreciated Lucinda's input, and she answered the best she could. As a journalist, she'd used the practice of clustering ideas, but the procedure proved easier with the ladies involved to provide feedback.

Madison paced. "If you can prepare a speech, I can get a cameraman to videotape you. That way, we can gauge your voice, the content, and body language—find out what needs improving."

"That would be fantastic," Emma said, truly thankful.

"If you need some quiet," Audrey put in, "the teahouse is always open to you."

Emma had no comeback. She just wrapped her arms around the ladies who were eager to help her transfer her pain, if at all possible, into something positive.

Chapter 27

"We've got to shut down The Nightingale until Madelynn's fully recovered," Bennett said after Elsa and John had left.

He didn't know what kind of repercussions his statement would have, but as if on cue, his daughter laid her head on his shoulder and closed her eyes.

Emma stroked Madelynn's forehead. "Pooh Bear," she said in a gentle voice and to Bennett added, "I'll make the calls."

While she went to work in the office, he put his daughter down for a nap. He patted her back. Finally, she closed her eyes, and he pulled up a chair to watch over her through the crib slats. As an infant, she'd made little sucking noises as she drifted off. She still did to this day, no matter how faint. But when her breath stuttered, his heart stilled.

Rosie raised her head and regarded him with what had to be concern, and he was about to act when Madelynn inhaled sharply and fell into a restful slumber.

"Hey," Emma whispered from the doorway sometime later.

"I'm coming." He left Rosie in charge. "How did it go with the guests?"

"They were all sympathetic and cooperative. I got them all rescheduled without anyone acting too bothered. Only one sourpuss threatened to stick his head in the oven."

"That's good—wait, what?"

She playfully snapped her thumb and index finger against the back of his neck. "I just wanted to see if you were listening."

"That's mean," he said with a grin, chasing her downstairs and around the room like he had when they'd been carefree and deliriously happy in their sugar shack.

Gracefully, she jumped on the couch and slapped the cushion. "Come sit with me."

Arousal surged through him, but he sat close enough that only their knees touched. As much as he wanted to stray into their bedroom with her, he realized they had to use what little time they had to discuss what they could and could not change. "I can help you become a first-rate orator. My dad taught me everything I know."

She laughed. "And you sound just like him."

"Is that a bad thing?" He hadn't meant to raise his voice.

"Not for you, but for me… Oh, I don't know how to say this. I'll just come out with it if you don't mind. No offense intended."

"Please do."

"It bothers me when I hear politicians' wives sounding exactly like their husbands—same expressions, intonations, and body language. I want to be myself, not a carbon copy of you or anyone else."

"I get it." Under other circumstances, he would have agreed and even found her comment humorous. Today, though, he felt left out and resentful.

He had read Rachel's letter. He'd like to say that he completely forgave her for everything. But the truth was, although he empathized with her constant battle with depression and felt shocked when he learned her reasons for leaving him, he couldn't forgive her for Madelynn's prenatal neglect. She probably wouldn't have had any health problems if Rachel had taken care of herself. No excuses.

Except...

The fact remained if she hadn't died, Madelynn might not have gotten the intervention needed for her survival. No, he didn't condone suicide, but in a way, Rachel's act seemed a sacrifice of sorts, and for that, he would remain forever grateful. If only she could have reached out, but she'd been in hiding because she hadn't wanted to tarnish his fucking name.

He wished things in The Nightingale were back to how they had been before everything went wrong. If only it were possible to immerse himself in the simple pleasure of being at home, of making love to his wife. His chest ached with his need for normalcy.

That feeling lasted seconds before he heard Madelynn cry out from the nursery. He flew upstairs in a state of panic. He turned on the light and picked her up from her crib. She felt slightly warm to the touch, which could be explained away by her just awakening from sleep. But weren't those shadows under her eyes? There must be a reason.

"There, there, little one, Daddy's here." He felt Emma's presence behind him.

"Is she okay?"

"I think whatever the doctors are giving her isn't helping."

She started to reach for the baby. "Bennett, you don't have to worry about that. I'll take care of her. I'll call the—"

"Do you think I can do anything else when my daughter's hurting?"

"Everything's going to be all right, so don't concern yourself over—"

"Seriously?" He rocked Madelynn in his arms, struggling to keep his voice low. "If your sister hadn't met me, she wouldn't have stopped taking her meds, and she wouldn't have spiraled out of control. She wouldn't have gone away if I hadn't been about to run for office. If it weren't for me, she'd still be alive, and we wouldn't be here with a sick baby."

"We wouldn't be here with *any* baby."

Her statement jolted him with the truth. "*We* wouldn't be here at all," he admitted.

As he'd known before and just had it reinforced, Madelynn's existence had brought them together. She was what had absorbed them in the routine that made up life as they knew it—the sweetness and joy. Now her illness threatened all he held dear. But more than anything else, Bennett needed to keep his daughter safe.

"Let's move her into our bedroom." His chin sank into Madelynn's curls as he looked at his wife. "That way, we can see her every move."

"Not a bad idea, but where will she sleep?"

"In our bed, of course."

Thus began a vigil in which both watched over the baby without getting much sleep. Madelynn seemed to rest easier being near them, which satisfied him. They would break her of this habit the child-rearing books warned against when she got better.

The next several days were hard. Bennett didn't go anywhere. Oh, Rosie and he went on a lot of walks along the beach, Madelynn in tow. He sent Emma across town to work on her project with her friends. After all, he didn't want her to think he was holding her back.

This new normal had him questioning all his former beliefs. His perfect life had gone sour. Most of it was his fault. He wouldn't blame Emma if she decided to pack up and leave him. He had caused so many problems by just being alive.

Although guilt weighed heavily on him, he called his father each night, then June and the rest. Hearing their voices made him better able to cope. He let the TV drone in the background when he wasn't talking to his family or friends—anything to keep from being alone with himself since his thoughts forced him into a tailspin.

He wondered, constantly, about what Emma was thinking. He wondered how they could live in the same house and suddenly be strangers. As the days passed, numerous times he longed to touch her—to hold her. He remembered when she'd first brought up the idea of marriage, saying if they got sick of one another, then it was over. Split bedsheets, she'd called it. Was that where they were headed? He didn't know.

To be frank, Emma would fare well without him. On the deepest level, his presence didn't matter. She didn't need him. From day one, she'd challenged him with her independence. That's what he loved about her, yet it was what drove him wacky.

That said, he'd seen Emma at her most vulnerable. That first day when they shared an umbrella in the rain, she'd looked up at him with her magnificent eyes, charmed him silly, and ended up going home with him. The night when she'd gotten trapped in the ghetto, and he'd come to her rescue—and again when she fell from his sailboat. He struggled to imagine how it had felt, their kissing in the rain, and longed to feel that way again.

So when she showed up that morning in the kitchen with one of her famous lists, he snatched it from her and said, "I'll do the shopping today."

"You? But you never leave the house anymore."

"My going will give you time alone with Madelynn."

Her jaw dropped open. "If you'd like."

He walked out, his eyes aching in the sun's bright light. He realized this wasn't him getting his wife back. Sadly, this was more like granting her joint custody.

****

Emma had never known the true meaning of terror until Madelynn woke from her nap, gasping, her skin as pale as the white sheets under her, lips blue. Emma retrieved her monitoring equipment from the nightstand and cried out for Bennett. Then she recalled that he had gone to the market.

Alexis Nathan rushed into the bedroom. "What is it, Emma?"

"Madelynn's heartbeat is fast, blood pressure's high, and her oxygen levels are dangerously low."

"Call 911."

She did so, then got ahold of Bennett. Help arrived within twelve minutes. When she stepped inside the ambulance, the noises were deafening—the hiss of pressurized air, the cardiac monitor bleeping, and an EMT asking questions that Emma somehow answered.

Yes, the doctors had been confident the hole would close by itself, but it hadn't done so. Yes, the baby was scheduled for surgery on June 15th, but the prescriptions to build up her resistance weren't working, and her health had worsened.

Madelynn's eyes were closed, the color still drained from her face, but the oxygen flowing through a nasal cannula appeared to aid her breathing.

Twenty minutes later, Emma stood by while a paramedic and a nurse worked to evaluate Madelynn. The scene moved like a bad dream, the baby taking oxygen into her lungs, the quiet voice of the nurse saying something Emma couldn't hear over the squeaky wheel on the cart an orderly had pushed into the room.

She needed her husband.

Bennett entered minutes later, looking like he'd run all the way. His jacket hung off his shoulders, and his hair had fallen into his eyes. Him seeing his daughter and becoming teary-eyed at the sight of the monitors and tubes made Emma's chest feel bound with tight elastic.

She gave him a tender nudge. "I'm glad you're here."

He glanced up at her as if surprised. "I came as fast as I could."

The nurse added, "Madelynn's in good hands."

Emma wondered if there was such a thing when, in her experience, the people she'd loved the most died. She longed to admit this to Bennett, to hear his voice losing its restraint, to be like it used to be—so compassionate it sounded spiritual. She needed that.

Out of the corner of her eye, she noticed their cardiologist arriving and talking to the night crew. He performed an assessment and then addressed Emma and Bennett. He told them what to expect in the next several hours.

By three a.m., Madelynn lay on a surgical bed in the prep room. Even though Emma managed to smile while reading to her, she felt raw inside, like she hadn't done enough. If she had, they wouldn't be here.

One of the nurses had begun to escort the parents from the room when Bennett said, "If my daughter wakes and sees we aren't there, she'll be afraid. Is there some way we can be near her during her surgery?"

That was asking for the moon, and Emma had guessed the nurse's response but couldn't help hoping her husband might have enough clout to hold sway.

"Mr. Browning, you'll have to go and let us do our job," she said amicably, allowing no special privileges.

Bennett accepted her verdict grudgingly, and he and Emma left down the corridor, their arms touching.

"She'll be fine," he said with forced optimism.

"I know." She knew no such thing.

"She has to be."

"You're right." She wanted it more than she had anything else in her life.

"Nothing else would be acceptable—you know?"

"Yeah, I do." And she couldn't think past that.

They spent the hours that followed in the waiting room. An urge had poured through Emma like hot oil. She needed her husband back, confiding in her like before. She needed to tell him she loved him. Holy crap, had she just come up with the L word?

Yes, and she had to let him know right now.

But he was keeping some of their friends up to date by phone. Then he was making small talk with Charles and June. Rai, Eddie, and Liam joined them around six.

By seven a.m., the TV had started pumping news flashes showing the two candidates who had won the primaries. Emma had forgotten all about the senate race. She thought about their days leading up to this point— their exchange of ideas, values, hopes, and dreams.

Sometimes, they'd argued. Sometimes, they'd planned for the future. Did Bennett ever regret getting out of the election?

As if reading her mind, he said, "The smartest thing I ever did was to quit that race."

Then he shut off his phone and buried his head in his hands. She couldn't take any more of their self-imposed standoff and rubbed his back, knowing he wouldn't react to her or anyone else trying to comfort him when his daughter's life hung in the balance. If only the surgeon would reappear with good news, then they would both be able to breathe again.

Within the next hour, while Bennett and Emma still waited anxiously for an update, Charles Browning gave an account of Madelynn's condition on social media and asked people to pray for her.

The urgency of his plea drove home how dire the situation had become. Hadn't mattered how many times they inquired. The response was pretty much the same.

"These surgeries can take a long time, but we should know soon."

When soon turned into another hour, Emma feared something had gone very wrong.

****

Bennett's stomach dropped with the sensation of falling down a black hole he couldn't escape. To stop it, he saw Madelynn at the ocean, saw himself lifting her over his head and running with her on his shoulders along the seashore. He heard her giggle, the *tee-he-hee*. Her first steps, the flowery dress she'd worn at the wedding, where her tiny feet wobbled but miraculously supported her down the aisle.

A crowd had gathered in the waiting room, and he

realized that he and Emma weren't the only ones waiting for news about a loved one. He focused on the others and listened. A child's father had suffered a heart attack. A mother's son was in a car accident. An older man's wife had fallen down their stairs. The hospital wasn't just there for him. A world of people existed who were waiting. Knowing this felt good. He wasn't alone. He never had been.

He found himself reaching out and taking Emma's hand in his own. "I'm here."

Her eyes shone with moisture. "Thank you."

She rested her head on his shoulder, and for the first time in a long while, he felt he could come through anything with her at his side.

And in the next moment, their surgeon, still in his scrubs, entered—his cap covering all but a few loose strands of dark hair. "Madelynn did great," he said with a grin. "The surgery took longer than anticipated, but it went well."

Everyone cheered, including those still awaiting news. Bennett felt the exhilaration like a hum that seemed to overflow and take in the entire universe. No man was an island—or person.

No person was an island.

"Your daughter's in recovery," the doctor added. "Allow us time to stabilize her before you see her in intensive care."

"How long?" Bennett asked.

"Give us an hour."

He made a few quick phone calls to let people know about Madelynn. Wouldn't matter if a hurricane were hurtling up the coast from Mexico. Order, peace, and all that was sunny skies had spread around him, stilling all the previous storms.

Bennett whispered in his wife's ear, "I'm going to track down a chapel."

"A chapel?" she said as if she'd never heard the word before.

"Almost every hospital has one. I plan to spend some time being thankful."

"I'll go with you."

They were all alone in a nondenominational chapel with a stained-glass window emitting a soft light and pews that felt cool against his back—welcoming after the last turbulent hours. Emma sat beside him, and that made everything perfect.

They bowed their heads, and he didn't know if Emma, so independent and private, spoke to God, Buddha, or Mother Earth. Didn't matter when family, friends, and even people who had never met Madelynn had joined in prayers. The strength of this comforted him. And he felt more grateful than ever for having his little girl in his life. And for Emma.

When he first met the woman who'd become his wife, he'd believed all he wanted was a partner—someone who would stand by him. No matter what. Now he realized he wanted more. What had drawn them together, and had from the start, were their differences. She had taught him what mattered to women today—what mattered most to her, and it had become what mattered to him.

These thoughts made him reach beyond all his former boundaries and take the initiative to admit something he'd never had before. "I love you, Emma." He took her face in his hands. "And I'll thank God every day for the gift of having you in my life."

"That's good, buddy, because I'm not going anywhere."

He kissed her lightly at first, then deepened it to hard and demanding.

She moaned a little and pulled back, looking at him with starry eyes. "I believed I'd never meet a man I could love, and then I met you." With a warm smile, she touched his cheek. "And we both know how that turned out."

"You love me?"

"I do, more than you'll ever know."

"Ah, Mrs. Browning, I'm right there with you." This rising emotion, the stimulating, heart-pounding joy of it, allowed him to add brightly, "Are you ready to go see our daughter?"

"I thought you'd never ask."

A word about the author...

Melody lives in Sacramento (the City of Trees). She writes Women's Fiction with romantic elements. She's partial to poetry, sun, rain, strong coffee, and her writing room surrounded by books. Besides California, she and her late husband lived part-time in a condo in Oregon overlooking the Pacific. That gave her a love for beach towns, whale-watching, and sunsets—all the things that inspire the Love is a Beach series. The writing process fascinates her, the alchemy of layering and developing characters, the tinkering with language. There's so much to treasure in the world: family, friends, and those random, everyday moments that make life grand. She hopes to give her readers all of that.

~*~

Find Melody online at:
https://www.melodydeblois.com/
https://twitter.com/Melody_DeBlois
https://www.facebook.com/melodydebloisbooks/
https://www.instagram.com/melody.deblois/
https://www.pinterest.com/deblois0181